Reality TV
Bites

Also by Shane Bolks

The Good, the Bad, and the Ugly Men I've Dated

Reality TV Bites

Shane Bolks

AVON TRADE

An Imprint of HarperCollins*Publishers*
www.harpercollins.com

REALITY TV BITES. Copyright © 2006 by Shane Bolks. All rights reserved. Printed in the United States of America. No part of this book may be used or reproduced in any manner whatsoever without written permission except in the case of brief quotations embodied in critical articles and reviews. For information address HarperCollins Publishers, 10 East 53rd Street, New York, NY 10022.

HarperCollins books may be purchased for educational, business, or sales promotional use. For information please write: Special Markets Department, HarperCollins Publishers, 10 East 53rd Street, New York, NY 10022.

FIRST EDITION

Designed by Sarah Gubkin

Printed on acid-free paper

Library of Congress Cataloging-in-Publication Data
Bolks, Shane.
    Reality TV bites / Shane Bolks.—1st ed.
       p. cm.
ISBN-13: 978-0-06-077311-3 (pbk. : acid-free paper)
ISBN-10: 0-06-077311-1 (pbk. : acid-free paper)
1. Women interior decorators—Fiction. 2. Chicago (Ill.)—Fiction. 3. Reality television programs—Fiction. I. Title.

PS3602.O6544R43 2006
813'.6—dc22
                                                                2005055875

06 07 08 09 10 WBC 10 9 8 7 6 5 4 3 2 1

For Mathew, my Dave.
No one will ever believe I wrote this before meeting you.

Acknowledgments

Eternal gratitude, love, and thanks to Courtney Burkholder and Christina Hergenrader, for telling it like it is.

Erika Tsang, for making me look like a winner without making me feel like a loser.

Evan Fogelman, for always treating me like a superstar. You're *my* superstar!

Between the Devil and the Deep Blue Sea

I've heard it said that in order to find her prince, a girl has to kiss a lot of frogs.

Start calling me Wart Lips.

When I was a little girl I'd dress up in my pink leotard, ballet slippers, and tulle skirt, paint my nails Pretty Princess Pink, and set my rhinestone tiara high on my red pigtails. Then I'd line up my subjects—Malibu Barbie, My Little Pony, Strawberry Shortcake, the Cabbage Patch Kids, the Monchhichis, and a stuffed white kitty—and play princess.

The object of the game was simple. I ordered everyone around. If any of my vassals disobeyed—Strawberry Shortcake in particular had a stubborn streak—I'd threaten to banish her to Ick Land, i.e., the hallway where my older brother Grayson waited to pounce on her and pull off her head.

If my subjects were good and obeyed me, then they earned the privilege of sitting with me on my pink-canopied daybed and watching through the bedroom window for the noble prince's arrival.

I'm still watching.

Come to think of it, not much has changed in the twenty-something years that have passed. I still get dressed up, I still paint my nails, and I still have to deal with those stubborn Strawberry Shortcake types.

Only on days like today, I wonder why I even bother with the someday-my-prince-will-come routine.

I'm wearing a cream silk blouse and black wide-leg trousers, à la Katharine Hepburn in the early 1940s. I'm not into vintage footwear—sixty-year-old foot odor is not appealing—so I've got on three-inch black satin slides by Anne Klein, and I'm sporting a matching bag. My nails are painted OPI's Chicago Champagne Toast, a nod to the city where I live, and my red hair is a perfectly straight, shiny cascade down my back (I checked earlier in my bathroom mirror).

I look like a princess—a princess surrounded by a bunch of screaming, red-faced buffoons, a dozen sweaty guys in jerseys and shorts that are too big, and a toad I was hoping would turn out to be my prince.

Translation for those of you not living in Fairy Tale Land like me: It's the last game of the Bulls basketball season, I'm at the United Center, seated directly behind the players and next to Dave Tivoli, aka the toad.

A howl goes up from the crowd and the toad jolts me as he jumps out of his seat. "Go! Go! No, no, no! Damn!"

The referee makes some motions, and a deep bass voice booms, "Foul on Chicago number three, Tyson Chandler. Rockets number fifty-five Dikembe Mutombo to the free-throw line."

"That wasn't a foul. Come on!" Dave and half the auditorium scream. I stand and peer over the players' heads. Not that I care what's happening. I just need to stretch my legs. Dave's arm goes around my waist, and I glance at him. His eyes are still on the game, but his touch sends a tiny shiver through me anyway.

Pressed against me, Dave's body is tense and focused. I wonder how all that power would feel concentrated solely on me. Under me . . .

"No." Dave slaps his free hand to his forehead and I look back at the court. The Rockets player is still at the free-throw line.

"Dave?" I say quietly near his ear.

"Hmm?" He doesn't look at me, then suddenly he yells, "Yes! Yes! He missed. One more to go. Miss! Miss!" There's a split second of silence, and even I have to look. The ball sails toward the basket in a perfect arc—and falls just short.

The crowd roars, and Dave pulls me hard against him and kisses me. It's not a long kiss, or even a particularly passionate one, but something about Dave always sends my senses spinning.

By the time I reel said senses in, we're sitting again, and I say, "What was that all about?"

"We're still ahead. Mutombo's got to be hating that he missed those free throws. He played for Chicago before we traded him to Houston."

"Hmm. Fascinating." I had meant what was the kiss about, of course.

"No way!" Dave jumps up again to watch the game, and I sit back and sigh.

I have no idea how I got here. I mean, I know how I got here—in Dave's Land Rover—but I don't know how it's come to this. How I—Allison Lynn Holloway—have come to be sitting in a sports stadium with a toad.

I look over at him: tall, football player build, spiky blond hair, nice butt . . . Okay, he's a hot toad. I'll give him that. I met Dave a few weeks ago. My best friend is dating his best friend, so we ended up hanging around together, then moved to hanging around on our own.

Dave isn't my type. At all. Not even his looks. Dave's all casual and rugged-looking. I like some refinement in a man. And Dave's a guy's guy—"Hey, man, how's it hanging?"— and all that macho bullshit. An advertising exec with Dougall Marketing, Dave lives in an apartment in Wrigley-ville. My type owns a Porsche, a penthouse, and his own company.

Dave and I had been out five or six times when he called last week to ask me out again. I was having trouble getting a handle on Dave at that point. He seemed to like me, but he wasn't taking any of my cues to move things to the next level.

It isn't so much that I'm dying to sleep with Dave, though I'm not opposed to the idea, but I don't want to jump into bed if that's all it is. I've been there before, bought the requi-site "I Had Sex and All I Got Is This Lousy T-shirt," and I'd rather use my frequent dating miles elsewhere, thank you.

It didn't take a genius to see that Dave would need a lot of work. And while it's true that *Chicago Home & Garden* called me "an inventive interior designer with a flair for the under-stated," inventive as I am, I just don't have the patience to make over a man after remodeling rooms all day. So when Dave called again I gave him the let's-just-be-friends speech. Or was it the it's-not-you-it's-me speech?

I don't know. Dave's a jock; I don't have to be inventive. The point is, I thought that was the end of him.

Until a few days ago, when he decided to impose his too-yang environment on my happily balanced yin.

Coincidentally, we happened to be lunching at the same restaurant. He was sitting with some fellow ad execs, and I was presenting my new feng shui ideas to a longtime client. Between the appetizer and the entrée, the waiter brought me a Melon—vodka, midori, pineapple, and lime juice.

Okay, so Dave's no fool. He knows I love Melons. And he knows Le Colonial is the only place that makes them right. He probably also knows that in the past I've dragged my best friend, Rory, across town to Le Colonial solely because I craved a Melon. Le Colonial is on the low end of expensive, but Rory is always saying things like we'd get a better deal from Jabba the Hutt, which I think means we're getting ripped off.

I don't care. The Melon is worth it.

But it hadn't occurred to me—well, not seriously occurred to me—to order a Melon that day. I've been to business lunches where the clients drank me under the table, but I doubted Mrs. Bilker-Morgan drank anything stronger than herbal tea. Edith M. Bilker-Morgan is Old Money, having been part of Chicago society since the earth under State Street cooled. But more important than the fact that she's a founding member of the Chicago elite, she's also on intimate terms with my parents. In Edith M. Bilker-Morgan's presence, I don't even allow myself to entertain thoughts of Shirley Temples.

But when the waiter set the Melon in front of me and said it was compliments of the gentleman, then inclined his head toward Dave's table, I was too surprised to object. I'd seen the toad when I walked in, and he'd seen me. I thought we were ignoring each other.

There's no question he knew I was with a client—a

stodgy, sober-looking client—and he'd sent the drink any-way. Then—and this is the most aggravating part—when I looked over, he winked.

Winked!

Like we had some private joke between us or something.

Did he not understand the let's-just-be-friends-it's-not-you-it's-me speech? Was I going to have to give him the lecture again? If so, I decided to add a section detailing why an ugly Regis Philbin silver tie and matching shiny shirt should never be worn outside of Halloween.

Mrs. Bilker-Morgan's voice stopped me. "Well, Miss Holloway, are you going to drink it or am I?"

"I was thinking I should send it back."

She huffed. "Allison Lynn Holloway, I'm going to call Mitsy this very afternoon and tell her she failed miserably in her attempts to raise you. In my day, we called a boy like that a real catch. If you don't want him, I do."

I stared at Edith M. Bilker-Morgan, then burst out laughing. She may be almost eighty, but she cuts to the point quick and pretty as a pair of pinking shears. Then Dave came over, introduced himself, and somehow, face-to-face, talked me into going out with him again. I didn't even realize I'd agreed until he left and Mrs. Bilker-Morgan asked if he was my steady.

Please.

Not only was he so not my steady, I thought we'd broken up.

But life isn't that easy with Dave. To get what he wants, he can be unbelievably manipulative. Exhibit A: the afore-mentioned Melon Incident.

And of course Exhibit A led to this evening and the Bulls game. Dave said we were going to do something really exciting—at which point I was thinking private jet to New

York and mind-blowing sex in the bedroom at 10,000 feet. So when Dave picked me up and told me we were going to the Bulls game, I wondered if, were I to commit assault, a shoe could be considered a deadly weapon. See, Mrs. Bilker-Morgan wouldn't think Dave was so great if she'd known basketball was his idea of a date.

Yeah, it's partly my fault. The jet thing is way out of Dave's price range, and he might not have presumed basketball was exciting to me if I hadn't pretended I liked it the last few times we were out. I didn't lie or anything. Dave knows I was a cheerleader, and I sort of let him assume that meant I liked sports.

The crowd at the game settles down, and Dave sits and smiles at me. I return the favor by shooting him the withering glare I copied from my mother, Mitsy, who, in her heyday, could wither a man at fifty feet.

Dave grins and shakes his head. "I'm not ignoring you." He takes my hand, and I forget what I was about to say.

Exhibit B: If Dave can't use alcohol or little old ladies to manipulate a girl, he gets physical.

I struggle to remember why I was angry, and then a voice startles me with a loud time-out announcement.

Oh, yeah.

I'm surrounded by sweaty equivalents of the Jolly Green Giant, and the toad beside me doesn't seem to realize this is not the fab fete he made it out to be. "Is the exciting thing we're doing this?" I gesture to the court.

He winks at me. *Again.*

"Look, Dave, sports are fun"—I have to suppress a shudder when I say this—"but not exactly exciting."

"What are you talking about? This is probably the best game of the season."

"Dave." I wait until I have his full attention. "I know I'm

using some two-syllable words here, so focus really hard. Sporting events are not, no matter who is playing, exciting."

"But if the Bulls win this game, they go to the play-offs, *and*"—he gestures to the seats—"we've got the best seats in the house."

Though I'm sure the effect of my expensive eyebrow wax is lost on him, I raise one of my perfectly arched brows. "If I am not mistaken, while you may consider basketball a way of life, the majority of the civilized world still considers it a *sport,* and therefore it falls under the not exciting category."

Okay, let me just point out here that I say this in my most scathing tone. And let me further point out that the big, dumb toad isn't affected in the least.

He keeps smiling, leans over, and says, "So, Red, what are you trying to imply here?"

I stiffen. "Do *not* call me that. My name is *Allison*."

"Maybe to the civilized world, but to a barbarian like me, you're Red." He strokes my hair, letting the sleek auburn sheet spill over his hand, then lifts my fingers and kisses them . . . What were we talking about?

Argh! The physical thing is the biggest problem with Dave. Whenever he touches me, a shiver runs all the way from my toes to the roots of my hair. Seriously, my *hair* tingles. No other guy has *ever* made the roots of my hair tingle. And that makes Dave very dangerous. I either have to make him over or get rid of him.

Neither idea seems tenable at this point. I've been sitting here all night contemplating my dilemma, and I've still got nothing. I gaze disinterestedly at the game. The score is pretty close. Rockets: 81. Bulls: 79.

The ref blows a whistle and play begins again. Othella Harrington takes the ball down the court, skillfully evading the Rockets defense. I scoot to the edge of the bench and crane my neck to see over the Goliaths in front of us.

Harrington nears the basket and turns to throw the ball, just as Yao Ming from the Rockets rushes by and collides with Harrington, knocking him over. Yao takes possession of the ball.

"What the hell!" I jump up and watch as Yao Ming dribbles the ball down to the Rockets side of the court and slam-dunks it. The Rockets side goes wild.

"Foul!" I yell. "That was a foul."

Beside me, Dave yells, "I can't believe this."

In front of us Benny, the cute Bulls mascot, jumps up and down in frustration as play continues and the Rockets' treachery goes unpunished. Then, to add insult to injury, Clutch, the Rockets mascot, bounds over to Benny the Bull and points and laughs.

The Rockets bear has to be the stupidest mascot of any NBA team. He's gray with a big white muzzle and a goofy grin, and he's dressed in a red-and-white jumper and big red shoes. Benny the Bull hangs his head.

"No, Benny," I call. "Stand up to him."

"Hey, Red—" Dave begins.

Clutch wags his big red butt in poor Benny's face, and that's it. I slip off one of my deadly heeled Anne Klein slides and throw it as hard as I can at Clutch, hitting him square in the ass. He jumps, turns, and the crowd around me goes wild. Really wild.

Before I know what's happening, there's a shower of cups, plastic forks, wads of paper, and a big foam finger raining down on Clutch.

The Bulls players part, and Clutch rushes forward screaming obscenities. Wow. I didn't know mascots knew words like that. Then he bends down, reaching under the players' bench, and lifts a huge red-and-white cooler. He holds it over his head, pretending he's going to drench us. By now the scene is being broadcast on the arena's big screens, and the Rockets fans are cheering Clutch on.

All of a sudden, Benny pantomimes coming to our rescue, but as he rushes forward he trips over one of his big hoofs, stumbles, and knocks into Clutch.

"Oh, shit," Dave and I mumble as the contents of the cooler gush over our heads. People near us scramble to escape the wave of bright blue Gatorade surging from the cooler, and through the waterfall, I catch a glimpse of Dave and me on the big screens dominating the arena.

For a moment, the crowd hushes, then hell really breaks loose. Dave and I stand there stunned. My first thought is to reevaluate my aversion to the color orange. It might be worth the horror of wearing an orange prison jumpsuit for five to ten if it means the satisfaction of killing or seriously maiming Clutch.

One of the guys behind me, who's dripping with blue Gatorade, jumps over the chair next to Dave and lunges for Clutch. The two go down in a tangle of gray fur and human limbs. Another spectator follows suit, then Benny the Bull joins the fray, butting Clutch with his horns.

The crowd surges forward. I cover my head to protect it from the onslaught, but Dave grabs my arm roughly and pulls me up. "Let's go!"

I stumble after him, rushing against the tide of humans rising to join the melee. I cry out when my one remaining heel gets caught on the edge of a stair. Dave looks back at me, glowering. In one swift motion, he bends down, frees my foot, and slips the shoe off, then pulls me by the wrist.

Finally, we break out into the corridors of the United Center. The place is practically empty, as most people are watching the fight, so Dave and I take a moment to lean against the wall and catch our breaths.

I glance at my soggy clothes and wonder if Gatorade stains silk. Then I look at Dave. His spiky blond hair is flat against his face and rivulets of azure meander down his cheeks to drip onto his blue-splotched T-shirt.

"You look like that blue guy from *Sesame Street.* Grover," I say. "But worse." I smile at his dark look.

"Want to know how you look?" He swipes a drop from the tip of my nose.

"Don't push it, Grover."

"Fine." He gestures to a TV screen broadcasting the fight, which is still going on. "Got anything to say for yourself?"

"What? Like that's my fault?"

"You threw the first shoe."

"Yeah, and if I'd been thinking straight I'd have thrown one of yours." I watch Clutch crawl out from the heap of Bulls fans piled on top of him. He's still got that annoying grin. "Anne Klein is way too good for that foul-mouthed bastard."

Dave gapes at me, then laughs. Really laughs. He throws his head back and laughs until even I start smiling. Finally he manages, "Come on, Red. If you promise not to piss off any more mascots, I'll buy you a new pair of shoes."

Forty-five minutes later, we're sticky but dry, and standing on the hardwood floors in the foyer of my town house. I'm wearing red flip-flops with fake flowers from Target and cradling a mammoth Diet Coke. Dave's holding two White Castle bags. "One thing about you, Red. You're never boring."

I sip my Diet Coke. "I'd invite you up"—I gesture to the stairs leading to the living room, kitchen, and the . . . bedroom—"but you'll get blue all over my white furniture."

He raises a brow. "Like you got Gatorade all over my leather interior?"

I nod and sip my drink again. Dave watches me, his eyes focused on the way my lips wrap around the straw. I wish I didn't like Dave so much. I wish every time I was with him, I didn't want him to ever go home. "We might be able to work out a deal," I say and set the cup on the floor.

"I'm listening."

I step close to Dave and kiss his jaw. His arm comes around my waist as though it were a habit. "You can come up, but you have to take off your clothes first."

His hand tightens, and when I lean in to give him a playful kiss on the lips, he pulls me harder against him. I back away before we end up on the floor in my foyer, my hands tugging his shirt out of his jeans and deftly flicking the button loose in the process.

Dave catches my wrist. "Not a good idea."

I smile. "Scared?"

"Of you? Hell, yes. You eat guys like me for breakfast."

I lift his hand to my lips and kiss his palm, then his wrist. "Not breakfast. But I haven't had dinner tonight."

I move close to him again, but this time he backs away. "I'm going to pass."

I smile. "Right."

"Look, Red, I really like you, but—"

I stare at him, unable to believe what I'm hearing. Is Dave *rejecting* me? After all I've been through tonight, this is really too much. I point a finger at him. "Don't you dare fucking say it's not you, it's me. I already used that one on you."

"That wasn't what—"

"You know what?" I cut him off. I feel like I'm being drenched with ice-cold Gatorade all over again, and this time

I'm fighting back. "It's been fun, but you're dripping blue on my expensive tile."

"Fine. I'll go. Here." He presses one of the White Castle bags into my hands. "So you won't be hungry." And then he turns, opens my front door, and walks out.

For five minutes or more, I stand in the foyer, speechless. This has never happened to me. To my knowledge, this has never happened to *any* woman. Straight men simply do not walk out on willing women. Is Dave gay? Or could he just not—I gulp air and drop the White Castle bag—does he not want me?

I sit on the tiled floor—sticky, gross, and wearing Target flip-flops—and stare at the door Dave walked through. It's not until patches of rose peek through the slim window shears on either side of the door that I crawl to my knees, then my feet, and trudge upstairs to shower.

A week later, I've moved on. Dave? Dave who? A *Real World* marathon and a healthy dose of *Queer Eye* have erased Dave from my thoughts completely.

Hello, my name is Allison, and I watch reality TV.

A lot.

Hey, it's good entertainment. I know the shows aren't as authentic as they claim, but nothing in the world is real anymore. It's all about how we perceive reality.

In fact, that's one of the main facets of my job—extensive manipulation of the public's perception of reality. I work at Interiors by M, the most prestigious interior design firm in Chicago. I'm an associate designer, and I specialize in color and furnishings. Most of the junior designers' worktables are on the spacious floor of the firm, but the three associate designers and Miranda, the M in Interiors by M, have our own offices with large glass windows. In my office, three walls look out onto the floor, and one overlooks the city. Interiors by M is on the seventeenth floor, so I have a good view of the skyscrapers.

"Come on, Google, hurry up," I say, glancing at the screen, then back at the skyscrapers. I don't always talk to my iMac, but I've got a meeting in five minutes, and I've been trying to get a definition for repoussé for the last fifteen. Miranda, my boss, refuses to pay for a high-speed Internet connection, so the search is taking forever.

I spin around, hit Play on the stereo, and grab the *Sourcebook of Decorating, Designing, and Detailing* from the bookshelf behind me. Swing music plays quietly, and I glance through the glass walls of my office into the reception area where Miranda is dictating something to Natalie, her assistant.

I check the computer again, then begin flipping through the book, trying first the index, then the table of contents for a listing. The music to "It Don't Mean a Thing" comes on and I start to sing along. "It screws up your day if you ain't got repoussé."

The phone rings and I roll my eyes. Is there anyone who doesn't want something from me this morning? It's not even morning anymore, I realize as I check the computer's progress and notice the clock in the screen's right corner reads 1:13. I now have two minutes before the meeting.

I swivel my chair toward the phone, press the blinking light with a long, manicured nail, painted in OPI's demure Taupe-less Showgirls, and purr, "Allison Holloway."

"Allie, it's me. You can turn off the Kathleen Turner for a sec."

"Rory, I *am* Kathleen Turner."

"Yeah, and I'm Princess Leia. Look, I need a favor, okay?"

I flip another page in the sourcebook. "I'm listening." Out in the reception area, Miranda is welcoming several men— presumably our new clients—while Natalie rushes to make coffee and answer the phone. "But make it fast. I'm late for a meeting, and I still have no clue what repoussé is."

"It's metalwork that's hammered on the back side."

"How do you know that?"

"I know everything. Okay, so now that I've helped you, you help me. I need you to go out with me and Hunter and some of his friends tomorrow night. I can't be the only girl again. I've already been exposed to dangerously high levels of testosterone."

I finally find repoussé in the sourcebook and study the pictures. Rory was right, except, "You forgot to mention the embossing and outlining in repoussé, and the answer is no way."

"Allison, please. Dave will be there . . ."

"Then definitely no. How many times do I have to tell you I hate his guts and hope he gets run over by a Mack truck?"

"I thought you wanted him to burn in hell for all eternity."

"Hey, I can be flexible."

"I'm not saying you're not, but you keep saying you hate him and won't tell me why. You guys only went out like half a dozen times. What happened?"

"What happened is that tomorrow night is a play-off game," I say, completely avoiding her question, "and I don't want to spend any of the ten or so short hours I escape Miranda the Maniac with a bunch of beer-swilling, basketball-chugging sports junkies." Not to mention, *Survivor All-Stars Meet the Big Brother All-Stars* is on.

I glance into the reception area again, and Miranda gestures to me. I swivel so my back is to the glass window between us.

"And what are you going to do in those ten short hours?" Rory asks. "Sit home and paint your nails?"

"Maybe." I look at my nails, but the manicure is already perfect. No maintenance required.

"Wouldn't that time be better spent in a fun, relaxed atmosphere where you have at least a sixty-four percent chance of meeting an eligible guy?"

Have I mentioned that Rory is an accountant?

"Well, I might just have to take my little thirty—" Okay, sixty-four from a hundred is . . . wait, sixty-four plus six, minus—"

"Thirty-six percent," Rory offers.

"Whatever. I'll just have to take my chances."

Rory sighs. "Okay, Allie, I didn't want to have to do this, but if you insist on behaving like an astromech droid, you leave me no choice."

Rory's an accountant and a *Star Wars* nerd.

The intercom on my desk beeps. "Allison, can you come out here? I need you in the next meeting," Miranda trills.

"Rory, I have to go."

"Two words, droid brain: Cody Maxwell."

I grit my teeth. "Rory, that was eleventh grade. You can't guilt-trip me with that. The statute of limitations has run out."

"Really? Because I thought a lie lived forever," she says, somehow managing to sound like innocence incarnate.

"It wasn't a lie."

"Then what do you call impersonating your mother on the phone to convince Cody you were too sick to go to the Winter Dance with him?"

"I *was* sick."

"Sick with lust for Kyle Reitmeier. That was the night you two—"

"Fine. I'll go to the goddamn sports bar, but I won't like it."

"I understand."

"Allison? Allison!" Miranda screams through on the intercom.

I ignore it. "And if that jerk says one word to me, I'm out of there."

"I'll give Dave fair warning."

"Fine."

"Fine."

"Allison! I need you in the conference room now!"

Fricking maniac. "No need to warn Dave, Rory. Miranda's screaming has now rendered me both insane and deaf. Hey, do you think that qualifies for workers' comp?"

"Bye, Allison."

There's No Business Like Show Business

On the way to the meeting, I stop in the ladies' room for a quick touch-up. Natalie's in there, probably hiding from Miranda.

Natalie is pretty in a librarian sort of way. She's got long brown hair and a small face, and she's so thin sometimes I wonder if she's got tapeworm. When I walk in, she smiles weakly. "Hey, Ms. Holloway."

"Hi, Natalie. Surviving?"

"Yeah." She turns the cold water on, removes her glasses, and splashes her face. I set my makeup bag on the shelf above the sink beside her and extract my essentials. I run a brush through my hair, retouch my lipstick, and blot the shine from my nose, then I step back and give myself a quick appraisal.

In the mirror, I notice Natalie watching me. "You're so

pretty, Ms. Holloway. Have you ever thought about being a model?"

"No, but thanks. My brother is a model. Grayson Holloway? He was in those bottled water ads a few years ago."

Natalie's large brown eyes widen behind her glasses. "Really? That was your brother?"

"Cute, huh? He's still single."

Natalie blushes and looks down.

"Want an intro?" I'm totally serious, too. Gray would stay out of trouble more if he were dating a girl like Natalie.

"Did you see that episode of *America's Next Top Model* last night?" Natalie asks.

"Oh, my God, yes!" I glance at the door quickly to be sure no one will interrupt the ritual reality show rehash Natalie and I have once a day. I don't mind if Natalie knows I'm a reality show junkie, but I wouldn't want it to become public knowledge. "Can you believe Kristen L. didn't get kicked off? I hate her. She is so mean to Kristen K."

Natalie nods furiously. "But neither of them are as pretty as Kristen R. She should be the next top model. Ms. Holloway, *you* should be the next top model. You should audition!"

I smile. "It would be pretty cool to be on a show like that, but not *America's Next Top Model.* I'd want to be in charge, you know? Like Simon on *American Idol* or the woman on *The Bachelorette.* I'd be a good bachelorette."

"Yeah." Natalie nods. "Maybe you'll get a chance to be on TV before you expect."

I frown. "Unless the producers of *The Apprentice* are coming here, I don't think that's likely."

Natalie shrugs and looks at the floor. "You never know," she murmurs.

"I better go before Miranda has an aneurism. It's almost one-thirty."

"Okay. Talk to you later, Ms. Holloway."

I walk out, shaking my head. Natalie is so sweet. She's like twenty-two—a bit young for my older brother—but the poor girl worships me. I'm not used to that. Most women don't like me until they know me.

And men? Most men like me even *before* they know me.

I think that's a combination of several factors. I pause. Through the windows of the conference room, I can see that the meeting has started, but now I'm thirsty, so I beeline for the break room and a bottle of water.

I pass a kid from mailroom, and when I turn into the break room, he's still watching me. See, guys—Dave notwithstanding—like me. Why? I'm a size two and my bra size is 32C. And no, I haven't had plastic surgery, and I don't kill myself at the gym. Sorry. If size ten, 36A were in vogue, I'd be the one out of luck.

Why else? I come from money—lots of money. My parents are very, very rich. Imagine Chicago society as the Sears Tower. Okay, now look way up. No, *way* up. See those tiny dots waving at you, all stiff and condescending, from the 103rd floor? Meet my parents, Mitsy and Donald Holloway. I'm their youngest, Allison.

But I've had my share of pain and disappointment in life. My family, though rich, is far from perfect. My father was one of those absentee dads who worked so late he never made it to my dance recitals or choir concerts. My mother is on The Committee. I don't even bother specifying which one anymore because she's on so many. Sometimes when I was little I'd wish I had cancer so that my mom would pay as much attention to me as she did to raising funds for kids who were terminally ill.

And then there's my brother. There are good things about older brothers and bad. The good thing is that their cute friends are always around. The bad thing is that their cute friends are always around.

The first time I thought I was in love it was with one of Gray's cute friends. I was fourteen; the guy was eighteen or nineteen. Bottom line: He used me for sex and discarded me. I will never forget that feeling of powerlessness and rejection. I still get flashbacks.

And I remember the last time I thought I was in love. Bryce is not a friend of my brother's, but there was still that same feeling of vulnerability when he broke it off two months ago. He said I didn't have time for him, and he found someone else. End of story.

Except he was the first guy in a long time I thought I might really like, and he didn't care enough to forgive a few late nights at the office. We were decorating Oprah's studio, for fuck's sake. I'd thought he was The One, and then he dumped me for Another One. I can't stand feeling all weak and useless like that. No more.

So I've pretty much decided I won't ever fall in love. And really, when I sit and analyze my feelings, it turns out that I've never been in love anyway. Why should that change?

I reach the conference room door and pause, hand on the doorknob. I don't get it, this obsession with love. Why all the hype? Why all the sonnets and Michael Bolton ballads? In my mind, relationships are mini–power struggles. If a guy knows you love him, you give up your power. And if you let a guy get too close to the real you, that's when you open yourself up to the serious pain and heartache. So I'm glad I didn't open myself up to Dave. It would have made his rejec—what happened—harder to take. Besides, Dave is so not the man of my dreams.

Typically my dates are a little more sophisticated than burgers and Gatorade. For instance, a year or so ago, when I was dating the son of a prominent politician, we jetted to Paris unexpectedly to dine on *le tiramisu de pommes au pain d'épices avec glace vanille* at Maison Blanche. Another time one of Gray's model friends got me into a film premiere, where I sat next to Orlando Bloom.

Even as a kid, I was—well, spoiled. For my sixteenth birthday, I not only got a Mustang convertible, but Mitsy took me shopping in Milan. A lot of girls get clothes for their birthdays. I went to Fashion Week in the most stylish city in Europe for an entire new wardrobe.

Not that I'm above basketball games or anything. Like I said, I was a cheerleader from sixth grade until my senior year at Lincoln High. I've had more than my fill of sports and jocks. But I'm not a cheerleader anymore, and *entre nous,* there's nothing stylish or sophisticated about basketball.

Now, if my best friend Rory heard this she'd say I was kidding myself. She believes love is the greatest thing since Luke Skywalker. She can't remember a time when she wasn't in love, and she's always loved (yawn) *the same guy.* Crazy, huh? She wouldn't believe that I've never really, truly been in love.

At least not with a man. I once saw a pair of Jimmy Choos that made my heart go pitter-pat, but other than those . . . oh! and the Hermès Kelly bag my dad gave me for my thirtieth birthday. It's gorgeous—red Ardennes leather with goatskin interior and an adorable lock, key, and cloch-ette. The perfect shoes, the perfect bag. If that isn't love, I don't know what is.

So I have money, great clothes, and good friends. I also have a great job, which isn't going to be so great now that I'm late for this meeting. Miranda is probably really pissed. See, life isn't all sports cars and mansions.

I slip into the conference room, doing my best to ignore Miranda's glare, and slide confidently into a seat beside Josh, my partner in design. I twine my OPI Taupe-less Showgirls fingers together, steeple two fingers under my chin, and survey the room. Miranda is seated across from me, Josh next to me, and three or four Japanese businessmen occupy the chairs at the head of the gleaming glass table. Behind me, someone takes a seat, but I don't peer around to get a look. A small Japanese man is speaking when I glide in, and once I'm seated, he continues.

In Japanese.

He talks, waves his arms, points out the window, then at the artwork on the walls, then gestures to his companions. I don't know what he's saying, but it must be pretty involved. Finally he opens the black leather notebook in front of him— nice, wonder if it's Coach?—and reads, flips the page, and keeps reading. When he's done, Miranda, Natalie, and Josh turn to the young Japanese man seated next to the speaker. Hmm—cute, not too shabby in Hugo Boss.

The guy wearing Hugo Boss nods at his employer, nods at us, and says, "Mr. Kinjo say he is most honored to work with you."

We wait. I mean, Kinjo talked for like five minutes; that can't be it. But the translator makes another bow and defers to Mr. Kinjo.

Kinjo starts to talk again, and I give Josh a sidelong glance. He rolls his eyes heavenward, and it's not too hard to read his mind: *I need a drink*. A moment later, he scribbles on the pad of paper he's pretending to take notes on—but on which he is actually drawing raunchy pictures—tears it off, and slides it in front of me. Mindful that I am supposed to be entranced by our speaker, I pretend to ignore the paper, then

I unsteeple my hands and, still keeping my eyes focused on Mr. Kinjo, unfold the note.

> Nice of you to finally show up, beotch.
> Are those shoes Prada?

Still pretending to be vastly interested in Kinjo's monologue, I extract a pen from my appointment book and jot an answer.

> Jealous? How about we scratch each other's eyes out over martinis?

I pretend to stretch, shift, and slide the note back to Josh. A moment later he drops his pen, pretends to bend over and pick it up, and drops his reply in my lap.

> Rehab or Lacquer Lounge?

Kinjo is *still* talking. What can he possibly be saying? And why is Miranda smiling like she understands? I scrawl LL and 6 on the note and pass it to Josh under the glass table. He reads it and, since everyone is paying rapt attention to Kinjo, blows me a kiss.

"Mr. Kinjo also say he expect this venture to be great success. And further he is honored to have support of Mr. Parma, who is here from Europe to oversee the project."

Everyone whips their attention to me, and I freeze, thinking I've been caught passing notes in class. And then I realize they're looking behind me, and I turn to see an extremely attractive man dressed in dark slacks and a stunning royal-blue linen shirt sans tie.

His eyes, as startlingly blue as his shirt, are on me. Kinjo starts another long monologue, of which I'm sure the translator will give us the abbreviated version, but I don't turn away from Parma.

What kind of name is that? It sounds familiar for some reason. I size him up: thick dark hair styled expertly to look as though he just woke up, heavy-lidded eyes, aristocratic nose, and a full mouth, set in that debauched European style. Not the pursed look of the British or the open sensuality of the Italians, more of the cynical, slightly amused look of the French. He's dressed in Armani, and his long limbs rest languorously in the chair. He appears perfectly at ease, and yet there's a sense of the patrician about him. A sort of benevolent condescension.

Now this guy is the definition of my dream man.

He watches me size him up, and while I take him in, his eyes skim over me, making no secret about the perusal. I'm wearing a thirties-style fawn-colored cigarette skirt and fitted jacket with a chocolate silk shell underneath. My legs are tanned and bare and my feet are strapped into three-inch open-toed Prada sandals, the exact color of the OPI Taupeless Showgirls polish on my fingers and toes.

Our eyes meet again, and to my amusement and chagrin, he deliberately glances at Josh, then me, takes a pen—no, a limited-edition Montblanc pen!—from his shirt pocket and jots something on the paper before him. That's a five-hundred-dollar writing instrument. He folds the note with slow, elegant movements, then places it on the table between me and Josh.

By this point, Miranda seems to have noticed that Kinjo is not the only person in the room, and she's watching me. But more important, *he*'s watching me. Parma.

I skate the note carelessly over the glass until it's before me but leave it on the table unopened. I attempt to appear completely engrossed in Kinjo's speech, but every few seconds, I run a fingernail over the note.

At that point the translator passes out thick documents, which look like contracts. I pick up the note, press it to my lips, and watch Parma's slow smile. A moment later, I notice everyone signing the documents, so I scrawl my signature and set the note on top.

Josh looks at the note, then me, and when I meet his gaze, he quirks a brow. Poor boy. This is why all of Josh's boyfriends leave him. He's too eager, too impulsive, too open. Of course, those are the exact qualities I love in him.

That and he knows good shoes.

Josh starts to squirm. To put him out of his misery, I slowly unfold the note. Two words:

I'll buy.

The words glide across the page in an elegant script that perfectly mirrors Parma's outward appearance. I haven't heard his voice, but I imagine he speaks formally, his accent soft and Gallic.

Josh reads the note over my shoulder and practically breaks into excited applause. I, on the other hand, pretend to ponder the issue. The delay is too much for Josh, and he finally snatches the note and writes:

BEWARE. We're not cheap.

Then he folds the paper and passes it over his shoulder to Parma. The Japanese guy beside Josh frowns, but Josh gives him a don't-even-think-about-messing-with-me-because-I'll-bitch-slap-you-without-a-second-thought look, and the guy turns back to the discussion. Meanwhile, Parma takes the note absently, opens it, and then nods at us, as though to say he's up for the challenge.

That's what he thinks.

Mr. Kinjo, wonder of wonders, finally stops talking, and the translator asks, "Then we are in agreement?"

"Perfectly," Miranda says. "Interiors by M will make *Kamikaze Makeover!* an absolute television sensation."

The anticipatory warmth pooling in my belly at the thought of a cocktail or two with Parma grows cold, and I shuffle the papers before me in confusion. "Excuse me, Miranda. Did you say television?" My heart is beating fast now. Is this what Natalie meant when she said I might be on TV sooner than I thought?

But maybe it's like the time we remodeled Oprah's studio. We'll be decorating the set for Kinjo's show.

Miranda shoots me an annoyed frown but answers in a sugary tone that fools no one. "Oh, Allison, I forgot that you came in late. This is Mr. Kinjo and his business associates, Mister—"

The translator comes to the rescue. "Hai." He bows, and not sure if I'm supposed to do the same, I bow back. He smiles, which either means I'm a stupid American trying too hard or that my bowing was the right thing.

Then he says, "I am Peter Yamamoto, this Mr. Watanabe." He gestures to a flashy guy with long straight hair and a garish red tie.

"He the director," Yamamoto says. "This is Mr. Fukui." The man to the right of Watanabe waves at me with four fingers. He's wearing a lavender shirt and matching tie.

"Mr. Fukui is top designer. And so is Mr. Takahashi." Takahashi is the frowning man sitting next to Josh.

"And this"—Miranda interrupts, pointing at Parma—"is

Nicolo Parma. He's a major investor from—where is it again, Nicolo?"

He smiles. "My family lives in Roskilde, but I travel so much, I consider myself a resident of the world."

"He can be a resident of my world any day," Josh whispers.

"Sorry," I whisper back. "I've got dibs."

"Nicolo," Miranda continues, "is the man who referred Mr. Kinjo to us."

Nicolo smiles at Miranda, and she blushes. Miranda is at least forty-five, thin as a rail, with platinum-blonde hair pulled tight into a jeweled clip. She wears power red almost every day and has a tendency to tap her sharp hellfire-red nails on the glass conference table. She's as hard as the three-karat rock on her finger. But when Nicolo smiles at her, she turns pink from her neck all the way to the dark roots of her blonde hair. Miranda, diamond-hard, cold as a meat locker, and, I often suspect, the spawn of Satan, is blushing. Now I have seen everything.

Since Miranda still hasn't answered my question—and that's not an accident, by the way—I say, "And what is it that Mr. Kinjo has contracted us for? Is he planning to buy property in Chicago?"

Oh, I hope so. Even though it would be great to design another television studio, I prefer residential work. Maybe Kinjo's going to buy a section of Gold Coast and build luxury town homes, and maybe he's hired Miranda—which really means the associate designers, me and Josh, and maybe Mia, but she just had a baby and has been working at home most of the time—to come up with a design for the interiors. Window treatments, color schemes, pewter knobs on the kitchen cabinets, pewter faucets and clear glass bowls in the sinks. And carpet—or would Persian rugs be better? Yes, but only if Kinjo uses hardwood floors. Oh, but then it would be such a shame to cover that gorgeous wood.

"No, Mr. Kinjo is not buying property," Miranda says, shattering my design concept. "Mr. Kinjo is an assistant to Ramosu Kobayashi, the owner of Dai Hoshi, Japan's largest media conglomerate. He's here to fill us in on the details for the new show."

I glance at Josh, but he appears almost as clueless as I am. Almost. His expression is grim—not a good sign.

"What new show?"

Miranda smiles, if you can call what a snake does smiling. "Allison, the one we discussed last week. Honestly, where is your head today?"

Right on my shoulders, where it always is. What is Miranda up to now? We never discussed a TV show. Miranda never even so much as mentioned Dai Hoshi or Kinjo or a European hottie. I would have remembered the hottie part.

"Oh, you know me, Miranda." And she does, which is why she didn't mention any of this until now. When it's too late.

"*Kamikaze Makeover!,* Allison, dear. You're going to be on the next number-one reality TV show."

I've Got a Crush on You

"Okay, but Josh, don't kamikazes kill themselves?" I say, lifting my half-full martini glass from the bar. "They crash their planes into aircraft carriers or something."

Josh rubs his bald black head, checking himself out in the mirror behind the bar. "I look good," he says.

"Yes, your head is very shiny."

"It's a fashion statement, sweetie. Black lacquer, like this place." And his shiny head does sort of remind me of the decor at the Lacquer Lounge. But the rest of him looks like Mekhi Phifer.

Great. I'm sitting on a bar stool next to a bald Mekhi Phifer, admiring himself in the mirror behind the lacquer bar.

"Josh, kamikazes?"

"Allison, World War Two is so over. This is the twenty-first century."

"Well, fiddle-dee-dee," I say in a pretty good Southern belle accent. "This corset squeezes all the air out of my head, and I simply cannot think. Why, I'm woozy at the very thought that a foreigner was in the same room as my very own self." I sip my vodka martini.

Josh glances behind him. It's a little after six, but Nicolo has yet to make an appearance. "Frankly, Scarlett, I don't think the man gives a damn."

I roll my eyes at the bad joke. "He wasn't coming to see you anyway."

"That's what you think," Josh says. "My gaydar went off the moment I saw him."

"You should take it in for a tune-up."

"We'll see. I haven't filled his spot on my team roster yet. I'm holding a place." He leans close and whispers. "In the starting lineup."

"Get ready to trade him to me, coach. But before we start negotiations, tell me about this show. Is it like *Trading Spaces? Queer Eye? Extreme Makeover?*"

"No, my reality show queen." Josh samples his Cosmo. "Think *Extreme Makeover* meets *The Iron Chef.*"

I bolt forward in horror. "There's cooking?"

"Not unless you feel adventurous," says a low male voice, tinged with an accent I don't recognize right away. A warm hand slides over my shoulder as Nicolo materializes out of the ambience.

"How adventurous are we talking?" I say, looking into his stunning blue eyes.

"That is up to you," he murmurs. He takes my hand and kisses all four fingers, slowly and deliberately. "Are you a—what is it you Americans say?—ah, daredevil. Are you a daredevil?"

I raise a brow and reply in my Kathleen Turner voice, "I've been known to play a little Truth or Dare."

"Hel-*loh*? I'm standing right here," Josh interrupts.

"Sorry, Josh." I squeeze his arm.

"Nicolo Parma," the hottie says, holding out a hand.

"Josh Bryant."

"Allison Holloway."

Nicolo takes my hand again, turns it palm up, and kisses my wrist. My pulse jumps, and I imagine I can see the vein in my wrist throb. Oh, this guy is too perfect.

"Enchanted, Miss Holloway. You smell divine."

"I am going to be ill," Josh mutters.

I'm going to faint. I swallow the rest of my martini, feeling its warmth mingle with the lingering heat of Nicolo's lips on my skin. The vodka is strong, and that's a good thing, especially now that my knees are weak.

"So, you are the American designers. I have studied your work. Impressive but conservative." His eyes remain locked with mine. Is that a challenge?

"This is the American Midwest. We give the client what he or she wants," I say. "We aim to please."

"I see." He smiles, slow and sexy, then signals to the bartender hovering within eavesdropping distance and she dashes in front of us.

"Brandy. And another vodka martini for Miss Holloway. Josh?"

"I'm fine."

"So you're from Roskilde?" I say. "Where is that?"

Nicolo smiles. "Denmark, though my family has Italian roots. And you?"

I hold up a lock of red hair. "Irish and English."

"Me, too," Josh says, straight-faced.

"This is what I love about America. Strange and interesting, the two of you together," Nicolo says, looking from Josh to me. "In America, we are all equal."

"Do you think so?" I say. As fantasies go, I've never met this guy's equal. Handsome, wealthy, sophisticated, and intelligent—where has he been all my life?

He smiles. "I admit, there are exceptional cases. Are you exceptional, Miss Holloway?"

"I'm sorry, that information's classified."

"I have a security clearance. Will that suffice?"

I shrug. "I suppose I can take a look at it in private."

Nicolo gives me a sultry smile and hands the bartender a fifty as she returns with the drinks. Wow. That's the fastest service I've ever gotten.

"So, Nicolo," Josh says, "speaking of the show . . ."

"We were not, actually."

Josh sneers. "Little hint there, Hamlet. Enough touchy-feely. Allison wants to know about the show. You're the investor, right?"

"I am one of several," Nicolo answers, somewhat evasively. "Kinjo is the creative force. But I am the executive producer, and it is I who suggested expansion. And where better to start than this United States, yes? You Americans love the home-decorating shows."

"I guess that's true," I say, ignoring Josh's snort, "but don't you think the market's oversaturated?"

"Ah." Nicolo holds up a finger and his eyes positively gleam. "Not if you have a flashy concept."

"And you think you have one."

"Kinjo has one, and I am munificent enough to benefit

from his hard work. I think Josh was saying something about *The Iron Chef.* The concept is similar, but we have the iron decorators."

I cross my legs and Nicolo follows the movement. I allow my skirt to ride up just a bit. "I've never seen this chef show. What's the premise?"

"You've never seen *The Iron Chef?*" Josh gasps. "I thought you'd seen every reality TV show."

I give him a tight smile. "Not the cooking ones."

Josh shakes his head. "Allison, sweetie, sometimes you are so clueless. Okay, so there are three Iron Chefs, and they're like the best chefs in the world. So all these top Japanese chefs want to compete against them, but they have to pick one iron chef." Josh sets his empty Cosmo glass down. "They compete in a fully stocked kitchen, but they have to use one particular ingredient in everything they cook. Like last time I saw it they were given abalone. Abalone—in dessert! Another time leeks or something. Fucking crazy."

"I don't even know what a leek is."

Josh waves a hand. "It's big. It's green. End of story. So they get this crazy ingredient, and they have like an hour to make a ten-course meal or something like that, and then the judges taste the food and usually the winner is the Iron Chef. But sometimes the competing chef beats him."

I look at Nicolo. His attention is still on my legs. Normally, that would be a good thing, but I'm getting into this whole show concept, and I want his complete attention. "Nicolo."

He raises his eyes, but he's in no hurry, apparently not in the least concerned that I might not appreciate his ogling me like I'm a chunk of meat. Gorgeous as he is, I don't— but that's not the point. "Please tell me that *Kamikaze Makeover!* isn't all about asking us to compete against some iron decorators by doing something creative with chartreuse polyester in an hour."

"That is exactly the idea, but you have more time than an hour."

"How much?" Josh asks darkly.

"Eight."

Josh's jaw drops. "Oh, you are trippin'. Even *Trading Spaces* gets two days! Look, we're professionals, not circus animals trained to do tricks. Why would I want to decorate a house in eight hours with some ugly-ass chartreuse polyester?"

"Ah, chartreuse polyester." Nicolo nods. "I will have to remember that. But polyester or not, you want to play because the prize, should you win, is one million dollars."

Josh squeals, and I gape at Nicolo. "One million for the firm?"

"One million each—you, Josh, and the lovely Miranda."

"Three million dollars?" Josh wheezes. "Is this a joke?"

"No joke. I am—as you say—the producer."

This is truly difficult to believe. I mean, it's so totally perfect—well, apart from the chartreuse polyester thing. I am going to be on a reality TV show. I am going to be filmed day in and day out. I'm going to be a celebrity. And all I have to do is be me. Well, not the real me—the fabulous me.

I would have done this for nothing, so a million dollars in addition is just the welting on my footstool. But Nicolo doesn't need to know that. In fact, the writers of the *Reality TV Addict's Guide to What's Real* cautioned aspiring reality TV stars never to trust producers. What if this whole thing is just a trick on me or Josh? Like that one show, *My Big Fat Obnoxious Fiancé.* I eye Nicolo—if that's really his name—suspiciously.

He merely smiles and offers to buy me another drink. I haven't eaten since this morning—my usual low-fat blueberry muffin and nonfat, peppermint mocha latte—so I decline. Then, somehow, Nicolo ends up offering to take us to dinner. Josh, smart boy, declines, so it's me and the producer—if that's really his job.

I have to admit it briefly occurs to me that going to dinner with Nicolo might be construed as a date. I've learned from long experience that dating guys I work with is a bad idea. But this is a producer. Everyone knows the normal rules don't apply when reality TV is involved. Nevertheless, best to tread cautiously.

"The Drake," Nicolo tells the driver when the black Lincoln Town Car pulls up to the curb outside Lacquer Lounge.

"Nice." I settle in, and Nicolo hands me a flute of champagne from a bottle that's been chilling in a bucket. I tug my skirt down and hide a smile with the glass when Nicolo frowns.

"You have been to the Drake before?"

"Several times. Is that where you're staying?"

"For now. The penthouse Kinjo acquired for me should be ready before the end of the week."

"Is it decorated? I know a great interior designer."

"So do I," he says and leans in for a soft kiss. Okay, this is a little fast for me, but European men are like that. And this guy is gorgeous. He's probably never been told no in his life. Well, there's a first time for everything.

The kiss is surprisingly gentle for a man who was all but devouring me with his eyes ten minutes ago. It's deliberate and seductive, and, oh dear . . .

Business plus personal equals bad, my besieged brain reminds me. I force myself to pull away, pushing my hair back and taking a large swallow of champagne to cover my unsteadiness. From the corner of my eye, I see Nicolo open his mouth to speak and then close it. That threw him off a bit. Word of advice: Always keep a man guessing.

"The kiss was not to your liking?" Nicolo's voice slides over me through the shadows of the car.

Direct. I like that. "Oh, it was very nice," I say. "More champagne?"

Nicolo takes my flute without question and refills it. He's not looking terribly pleased about it, though. If I were him, I wouldn't be, either. One minute he's an executive producer, the next a go-to man.

He hands me the champagne I have no intention of drinking, and I smile. "Thank you."

He leans in for another kiss, but as much as I'd like him to kiss me again, chaster thoughts prevail. I draw back and gesture out the window. "Have you been down to the lake yet?"

"No." He sits back, seemingly resigned. "Do you recommend it?"

"I do."

He sits straighter. "Perhaps you would play tour guide on Saturday. I am certain there is much of Chicago I have not seen." He reaches out and runs a finger lightly over the exposed skin between my knee and the hem of the skirt.

I draw in a slow, shaky breath. Obviously, I should stop him. This guy's got to be handled carefully (i.e., we go no further than that kiss I let slip by earlier). The course of action is clear and smart, and yet I don't stop him. He's already slid his hand deftly between my knees before I'm able to say, "Saturday isn't good for me."

His hand freezes, then inches farther up my thighs. "I'm confident you can fit me in."

I stifle a moan and dig my fingernails into the leather seats. Oh, my God. I am so tempted to allow this exploration to continue. But it's a bad, bad, *bad* idea.

Of course, it doesn't *feel* like a bad idea, but when you

take the work thing and the I-just-met-him thing plus the producer thing, that's a lot of things. And all bad.

I bite the inside of my cheek. As much as I want Nicolo's hands on me, I can't give in to my desire. Besides, I think as my cheek starts to hurt, isn't it a bit egotistical to assume that I'd be so willing to . . . accommodate him? Must wrest control back and keep it this time.

I slam my thighs shut and almost have to stifle a sob at the effort it takes me to resist. "Oh, I wouldn't think of canceling at this late date."

He scowls—yes, *scowls*—I don't think I've actually seen a man do that in real life. "Is there another day more convenient, then?"

I purse my lips, direct my gaze at the ceiling, and pretend to mentally run through my plans for the week. All the while, his hand is warm, solid—and trapped—between my legs. Not that he's trying to escape. Not that I want him to.

"Can't think of a day I'm free—oh, but actually tomorrow night is—oh, no, I'm watching the game with my friend Rory."

The car slows, and Nicolo bites out, "Drive around again." His eyes haven't left my face, and I finally turn my gaze toward him, loosening the pressure on his hand a fraction.

"What game?"

"Basketball. The Bulls are in the play-offs."

His lips tighten in a thin line, and I'm impressed with his restraint. There is only one sport the typical European man enjoys: soccer. Every other sport—baseball, football, golf—is substandard. Nicolo appears to be of this opinion, but instead of ranting about how ridiculous basketball is and how he'd rather have his testicles ripped off and mounted in a Plexiglas frame than watch a Bulls game, he says, "I will join you. Where?"

Now, if he had *asked* if he could join me, if he had offered to escort me or take me out before the game or after, I would have let this go. I might even have nixed the basketball game entirely, even though Rory would have killed me. But Nicolo did not *ask* if he could accompany me. The real me—as opposed to the composed, fabulous me sitting beside Nicolo—is kind of excited that this guy likes me so much, but what kind of girl would I be if I let him see through me so easily?

It's important not to expose one's vulnerabilities too early, if at all, so I say, "You know, I'm not certain where we'll be." I slide back in the seat, extricating my leg from his hand. "Let me give you my friend Rory's number. Call her tomorrow and ask if you're invited. She can tell you where we'll be." I pull a business card from my bag and look at him expectantly. I have a perfectly good pen in my bag, but I am going to wait for Nicolo to offer his Montblanc. Here's another hint: Always make the guy work for it because men are a strange species. They don't appreciate what they don't work for.

Nicolo frowns, then sighs because this wooing stuff is *such* hard work, and at last pulls the Montblanc from his jacket pocket.

"Thank you." I write Rory's name and work number on the back of the card and hand it to him. The car is rounding the corner, and I see the Drake's bellboys and porters up ahead. "Stop here, please."

"The hotel is a bit farther," Nicolo says.

"I know. But I'm not going to the Drake." I gather my purse and open the door when the car stops. "I'm not hungry anymore."

Nicolo leans across the backseat. "At least allow me to drive you home."

"No thanks. I can make it on my own." I close the door and walk away.

I grab a cab back to the office, but instead of getting in my car to drive home, I head back upstairs. Natalie's still there, and when I walk in she looks up, surprised.

"Natalie," I say breathlessly. "You're good at research, right?"

She nods, staring as I bend down to remove my Pradas. I'm all for fashion, but I've been wearing these heels for thirteen hours now, and that's enough of a homage to haute couture for a day.

"Good, come to my office. Quick!"

She jumps up and races after me. I flick on the lights in my office, boot up the computer, and slide into the chair behind the drawing board that constitutes my desk. "Grab that chair, Nat." I point to a cushy orange retro chair, and Natalie drags it closer. While the computer wakes up, I turn to look at her. "What do you know about Nicolo Parma? Something about his name sounds really familiar, and I can't figure out why."

"Maybe he's produced other reality TV shows," she says, pushing her glasses back on her sweaty nose.

"No, it's something else. Parma. Parma. Where have I heard that?"

"It's a part of Italy."

I turn to the computer and click on the Internet icon. "God, this computer is so slow."

"You should do a disk cleanup," Natalie says.

"What's that?"

"Here." She reaches past me and starts messing around with the settings. "Okay," she says finally. "That should help. It got rid of unnecessary stuff and freed up memory to make the computer faster."

"Great." Now when I open the Internet, I'm able to get Google almost right away. When the search box pops up, I type "parma" in. On the screen, Google displays entries.

I scroll through the choices—Parma, Ohio; Parma, New York; Parma, Michigan—ha! Parma, Italy. I click and after a pause, there's a list of hotels and pictures of old buildings. At the bottom of the page I find a link for history. I click on that and read the highlights to Natalie. "183 B.C. founded. Ruled by the Visconti, Sforza, the French. Pope Paul III established a Duchy. Joined kingdom of Italy in 1860."

I sit back to think, and Natalie leans forward. "When did the French rule Italy?"

"Napoléon probably. He took over after Louis the Sixteenth and Marie Antoinette got their heads chopped off. The Italians got rid of their king, too, in the forties. It was just a few years ago that they allowed the exiled royal family—Prince Victor Emmanuel, of the House of Savoy—back in." If there's one thing I know, it's royalty. Comes with the wanting to be a princess thing. I didn't like school much, but when I wanted to learn something—like, say, the lineage of the royal families of Europe—I had no trouble.

"The French tried monarchy one last time after Napoléon. They asked the Bourbons back but—" I clap a hand over my mouth and stare at Natalie.

"What?" she says, eyes wide.

I reach for the keyboard, but my hands are shaking now and I can't type. "Type 'Bourbon-Parma' in," I say.

Natalie reaches forward and starts typing.

"No, it's O-U-R and there's a hyphen."

Natalie hits search, and a site about the royal house of Bourbon comes up. With shaking fingers, I point to the link for the genealogy of the Bourbon-Parma branch.

Natalie clicks on it, and we scroll down, past all the princes and princesses—Robertos, Giuseppes, Marias, Antonias, Philippes—"Oh, my God! Stop."

Natalie jumps. "What? What?"

"There. That's him." My heart hammers, the room is too hot, and my head is spinning. "Oh, my God! I knew it." I can barely squeeze the words out.

Natalie squints at the small type and leans closer. "Prince Nicolò Thierry Ferdinand Ignazio Alfonso Roberto Paolo Tadero Giovanni Bourbon-Parma, born Roskilde 6 December 1970." She looks at me. "Wow. That's a lot of names."

"That's the guy who was here this afternoon. Mr. Parma."

"What?" Natalie steps back, stumbling against her chair.

"Parma is Prince Nicolo Bourbon-Parma. A real prince." I look at Natalie. "Get Josh on the phone."

"Yes, Ms. Holloway."

She races back to her desk and lifts her phone, simultaneously punching buttons on her keyboard to bring up the file with employee contact info. A moment later, she buzzes me. "Mr. Bryant on line two. He sounds mad."

"Thanks, Nat." Normally, the first person I'd call with something like this is Rory. But I'm too excited to explain, so I'll brave Josh's temper. I pick up. "Josh, you are not going to believe this." In the background I hear loud music and voices. Natalie must have gotten Josh on his cell.

"You're in bed with Don Juan. Happy, happy, joy, joy. You're taking me away from a gorgeous Cuban with a lisp. You *know* how I love a lisp."

Actually I didn't know that. "Josh, forget the Cuban. You are not going to believe what I found out. After I left Nicolo I came back to the office."

"You're at work? Sweetie, go home. Sex in the workplace is so last year."

"Josh, will you shut up and listen? I Googled Nicolo and you are not going to believe this." I pause for effect, then say, "He's a prince. It's right here. His whole family line. I mean, the family doesn't rule any countries or anything. They haven't since like 1860, but he's descended from royalty, and he still has the title! Do you know what this means?"

"No, but you're going to tell me."

"I went out with a real prince. If this works out, I could be a princess!"

Come On with the Come-On

Okay, actually, after further research, I realized I can't be a princess. Since the Bourbon-Parma family is no longer reigning, only the issue of princesses and princes of the line are titled. Unless a prince marries a girl who's a princess already, she doesn't carry the title of princess. Still, it's pretty much the closest to being a princess a girl could imagine.

Needless to say, I'm in raptures. A reality TV show and a prince. My life is perfect. Really perfect. Meeting my Prince Charming is all I've dreamed about since I first read *Cinderella*. Rory knows this, so as soon as I see her, I give her the 411 on the prince and the show.

"So the film crew didn't show up today," I tell her. "I think they'll be there Monday, but I'm getting a little nervous. I mean, Miranda can't or won't tell me anything and the translator abbreviates everything the iron designers say into three words or less."

A roar goes up and Rory and I glance at the big-screen TV on the patio in front of us. Not that I can see the game. There's a wall of men guarding the television. Rory and I are sitting on the wooden steps, arms drawn around our knees, dressed in shorts and T-shirts. Rory's drinking a beer, but I'm nursing a gin and tonic. Not my favorite, but the liquor here is crap. I don't really like gin, so drinking cheap gin can't ruin it for me.

"But you're going to be on TV," Rory says when the noise dies down. "And you might even win a million dollars." She tucks a strand of her straight light brown hair behind her ear. She cut it a few days ago so that it grazes her chin, and the style really flatters her small face.

"It will be fun to be on TV, but I'm afraid that all my mess-ups are going to be broadcast for the world to see."

"But you're not going to mess up," she says with perfect confidence. I marvel at her complete faith in me. One thing about Rory, she's loyal. "And you're going to be an unofficial princess!"

"I hardly know Nicolo. I think it's a little early to plan the wedding." I've already gotten the whole thing planned anyway.

Rory finishes her beer. How can she drink that stuff?

"I don't think it's too early. Every man you meet falls in love with you."

I roll my eyes. "I don't know where you get these ideas. Bryce didn't fall in love with me."

A groan erupts from the patio, and the mournful sound complements my feelings. Rory puts her arm around my shoulder. "Bryce was a nerf-herder. I thought we established that."

"*You* established that."

"Allison, it's time you took all thoughts of Bryce and blasted them into the far reaches of an asteroid field to be pulverized with all the other refuse. Then start thinking about how nice Princess Allison sounds."

"Don't tell me the rumor's true," Hunter says, taking a seat beside Rory. And, as if they're two parts of a whole, she melts effortlessly into him. "The whole way here, Rory wouldn't stop talking about the prince that called her at work and wanted to know if he could watch the game with us."

"Well, it's not every day that a prince calls me, okay? Like if a princess called you, you wouldn't be excited."

"A princess already does call me," Hunter says and kisses her cheek.

Gag, gag, gag. Hunter is just too good to be true. Don't get me wrong, I like him and everything. I've always liked him, and I've known him since elementary school. But when all the cheerleaders were gaga over his blue eyes, his dark hair, and his athlete's body, I wasn't interested. Hunter will always do the right thing. The expected thing. There are no surprises with Hunter, and I like surprises.

"So Rory tells me you're going to be on TV."

I nod wearily. "The show's called *Kamikaze Makeover!* It's supposed to be like *Iron Chef* but with decorators. It's Josh and me against the Japanese. They start preproduction tomorrow."

"Cool."

"It *looks* cool, but there's something weird going on. You know how these shows are. There's got to be something we don't know. And these Japanese guys. I think we need to get a new translator." I see a tall guy with unmistakable confidence stroll in, and my heart starts beating hard. Oh, my

God. It's Nicolo. I didn't actually think he'd show. But then the guy turns.

It's Dave. How could I possibly confuse Dave with Nicolo? Dave's hair is kind of an ash blond, thick and spiky, sort of like Brad Pitt's, while Nicolo is all dark and European. I suppose they're built about the same, but Dave walks around like a *Tyrannosaurus rex* and Nicolo moves like Fred Astaire.

"Why do you need a new translator?" Hunter asks.

Still watching Dave, praying he doesn't spot us, even though I know avoiding him all night is impossible, I say, "Because his answers are too short." I glance at Hunter. "Mr. Kinjo and the director, Watanabe, talk and talk and talk, and then the translator will say, 'Mr. Kinjo say hello.' What is that? How long does it take to say hello in Japanese?"

"Not long," Hunter answers. "Hey, Dave! Over here." He waves at Dave and I grind my teeth when Dave turns and flashes the three of us a smile. Why does he have to look so good? I really, really hate him.

He lopes over, his legs too long to emulate the refined aristocratic gait Nicolo's mastered. Where *is* Nicolo? Am I getting rejected again? If he doesn't show, prince or not, he's getting a royal send-off.

"So, what's the score?" Dave asks, after he and Hunter shake hands, slap shoulders, and make grunting noises.

"Bulls down by three last time I checked," Hunter answers.

"Yeah? Rory keeping you too busy to watch the game?" Dave jokes, then pulls Rory to her feet and into a bear hug. "Hey, space cadet. You look different."

Rory fingers her newly shorn locks. "I had my hair cut."

"Oh, yeah. It looks . . . shorter."

"Now that's a compliment for you, Rory," I say, rising to stand with everyone else. It would be better if I ignored

Dave, but not nearly as satisfying as making snarky comments. "A girl pays two hundred dollars for a cut and highlights and all a guy can say is, 'It looks shorter.'"

Dave rubs his chin and studies me with those golden eyes. Have I mentioned Dave's eyes? They're like something you'd see on a lion—deep, enigmatic, and compelling. It's so not fair.

"Hey, Red. Good to see you're glad to see me, as usual."

Argh! Why can't I ever be cool and aloof with Dave? Why does he always cut straight through my bullshit?

"Guys." Hunter's tone is full of warning. "Don't start."

Dave shrugs. "It's okay. I think I know what the problem is."

"You were born?" I counter with a smile, but inside my heart stutters. I cannot let him have the chance to tell everyone he rejected me.

"No." Dave chucks my cheek lightly with his hand. "You're just jealous because I gave Rory a compliment and not you."

There's a shout from the patio, and Rory says, "Hey, let's go watch the game."

Dave and I ignore her.

"Me jealous? What reality are you living in?" But it sounds as defensive as I feel.

And Dave just smiles indulgently, then says, "Don't worry, Red, I've got a compliment for you, too."

I cock my head. "Oh, good. This I have to hear."

He winks at me, and I want to scratch his eyes out. "You look good in shorts and a T-shirt," he says, giving me the once-over as if I were a used car he's thinking of buying. "No blue Gatorade this time and less prissy than usual."

My jaw drops. "Prissy? Prissy!"

"Allison . . ." Rory begins, but before I can tell her to stay out of it, before I can smack Dave, before I can do anything, Dave grabs me up and hugs me, pressing my face into his chest so that no one can hear me.

See why I hate him? See? God, but he smells good. Argh! "I hate you," I mumble, and then I feel his lips brush my ear.

"No, you don't. You're just scared."

I stop struggling. Now how does he know that?

"You must be Rory." A male voice with a familiar European accent penetrates the cage of Dave's arms, the sound muted by the rapid beating of his heart. Hmm. Maybe he's not so unflappable after all.

"Allison?"

Dave releases me, and I whirl around and look straight into the stunning blue eyes of Prince Nicolo Thierry Ferdinand something-something Bourbon-Parma. "Nicolo. You made it."

He takes my arm, draws me expertly away from Dave, and kisses my hand. Suddenly I feel like I'm once again in control, no longer transparent with my feelings and emotions on display. "I could not stay away," Nicolo says.

My cheeks warm. "I'm glad. Nicolo, these are my friends. I think you spoke to Rory on the phone." I gesture to Rory, who's standing beside Hunter, staring at the prince like he's— well, like he's a prince.

"Hi," she says.

Nicolo takes her hand and kisses it. "Enchanted."

Hunter sticks his own hand out, right under Nicolo's nose. "Hunter Chase. I'm Rory's boyfriend."

Nicolo shakes his hand, their grips hard enough to turn their hands white. "Lucky man."

Men. Everything is a competition. Nicolo looks at Dave, then me. "So, those are my friends," I say, ignoring Dave. But the jerk refuses to be ignored. He shakes hands with Nicolo and says, "Hi, I'm Dave."

"Nice to meet you."

I watch Dave and Nicolo shake, trying to discern how hard they're squeezing. But it looks like a normal handshake, and I don't know how to feel about that. Hunter was jealous simply because Nicolo told Rory he was enchanted. But Dave, who's taken me out and kissed me (and rejected me), doesn't appear jealous in the least. And Nicolo, who's here because it was the only opportunity I gave him to see me outside of work, isn't exactly green with envy after he walks in and sees me in Dave's arms. Okay, have I completely lost my touch?

"Want a beer, Nicolo?" Dave asks.

"Sure. A Hasen Bräu would be good."

"What the hell's that?" Dave asks.

Nicolo frowns. "Then a Kölsch."

"I think your foreign beer choices are limited to Heineken or Corona," Hunter offers.

Nicolo glances at me, as if I can shed some light on the beer question, and I hold up my glass. "The gin and tonic isn't too bad. If you don't like gin."

"Ah, nothing then."

"Sure?" I ask. "Dave's buying."

Nicolo laughs, a deep sound that gives me goose bumps. "Money is not the issue. Unfortunately I cannot stay long."

"Why not? Nicolo"—I pull him into a corner with the neglected dartboards—"you're not going to leave me here with these—*sports fans,* are you?"

"I am left with no other choice. Work." He brings his hand up, and at first I think he's going to touch my cheek. Instead, he caresses a lock of my hair, lifting it to the light when he reaches the ends. "Like golden fire," he murmurs. "I am sorry to go, especially as I will miss you more than you will me." He leans close and brushes his lips over mine.

I forget to breathe for a moment as Nicolo's hand meanders down my back, finally settling on my waist.

"I don't know about that," I say when he pulls back. "Nicolo, I know who you are." I glance at the floor, wondering if he'll be unhappy that I've found out his true identity. Maybe it was part of the reality show, and now I've gone and ruined it. When I glance up, Nicolo's got one brow raised.

"Who I am?"

"You're a"—I glance around and lower my voice—"a prince."

He grins and leans close. "It is not a secret."

Yeah, right. That's what the writers of the *Reality TV Addict's Guide to What's Real* said he'd say. "Then why didn't you say so before? Why'd you have Yamamoto introduce you as Mr. Parma?"

He tucks a tangle of hair behind my ear. "Because that is who I am. 'Prince' is merely a courtesy title. My family is not poor, but we live and work like everyone else."

"Oh." When he says it that way, it's not quite as exciting. "So, are you leaving on royal business?"

"No. Regular business. I think there has not been royal business for over a hundred years. But if it were royal business, be assured I would take you with me. We princes are good at rescuing damsels in distress."

There's a groan from the patio and a chorus of "goddamnits" and "oh, hells."

"Hopefully, my distress won't last much longer. I think I talked Rory into leaving early with me to watch *The Iron Chef* since she's got seven thousand channels."

"What a good student. Homework on a Thursday."

"Do I get an A?"

"Is an A good?"

"Very good.

"Then I give you three." And he leans down to kiss me again. Very nice. I kiss him back, surprised that kissing a prince isn't as different as I thought it would be. Strike one for the fantasy.

We stand there talking for another ten minutes or more, hands clasped and Nicolo's thumb rubbing my palm in slow circles. Before he leaves, he kisses me once more and says, "I know you said you were busy, but I have been invited to a cocktail party tomorrow evening and have no date. If you find that your schedule changes . . ." He waves a hand.

This guy is good. He's figured out that a head-on assault isn't going to work with me. Now he's trying indifference.

"Of course, inviting you out on such short notice is absolutely inexcusable—"

"Not to mention, we're working together. I generally avoid dating men I work with," I add.

"—but I thought you might be interested in meeting my cousin Prince Sixte Louis Charles Vincenz Christian."

Another prince? Oh, dear. "He's here from Denmark, too?"

"No, no. He lives in Florida. Palm Beach."

"Oh." There's royalty living in Palm Beach, and I never even knew it. How . . . unromantic. I should say no, but Nicolo is more than good. Not only has he apologized about the short notice, he throws more royalty into the deal. "Well, how could I miss the chance to meet—?"

"Sixte."

"Right. But it's not a date. It's a professional outing."

He inclines his head. Smiling, I give him my address and cell number, and he promises his driver will arrive by nine. Then he kisses my hand, all the way to the fingertips, and says something that sounds like silk feels.

"Was that Italian?"

"Sì."

"What did it mean?"

"Until tomorrow."

And then he's gone.

"He didn't even drink his beer." Dave walks up and leans on the wall beside me, invading my corner with his broad shoulders and annoying height. I'm five-eight, so he must be at least six feet.

"I guess you'll have to drink it," I say, scanning the patio for Rory.

"I don't want a Heineken. You drink it." He hands the beer mug to me, but I wave it away.

"Can't. I'm leaving. Where's Rory?"

He points to a picnic table, and I spot Rory and Hunter sitting together. They're completely oblivious to everything around them, locked deep in conversation. Sometimes I wonder what the two of them have to talk about. I mean, she's a *Star Wars* sci-fi junkie and he's an ex-jock marketing exec. And somehow they're still perfect for each other.

"What are they talking about?"

Dave shrugs. "You know them. It could be anything from intergalactic warfare to organic pet food."

"Pet food?"

"Hunter wants to get a dog, but Rory doesn't want him to feed it dead animals."

I smile. "Yeah, she gave me the same lecture when I got Booboo Kitty."

Dave shakes his head and drinks the Heineken anyway. "I still can't believe you named your cat . . . what you did."

"Why? I'd end up calling her that anyway. Besides, she looks like a Booboo Kitty."

"She looks like a mutant feather pillow," he says not quite softly enough.

"Good thing she'll never have to see you again. I wish I was so lucky," I mutter.

I head over to Rory and Hunter. I have to skirt around thirty or so slack-jawed guys, awed by the Laker Girls' half-time show. Sometimes I miss learning those routines with the other girls. It can be such a rush when you get it right.

"Rory, it's nine-fifteen. Are you ready?"

"Aw, you have to go already? It's only halftime," Hunter says.

"*The Iron Chef* won't wait," Rory says and stands. "Besides, now you can watch the Laker Girls instead of pretending to listen to the genealogical breakdown of Luke Skywalker's family tree."

Hunter puts a hand on his chest as if wounded. "But I *am* interested in Luke Skywalker's family tree. All those crazy Skywalkers."

"Bye, Hunter," I say and pull on Rory's arm until she detaches her lips from his.

"Did you drive?" I ask as we leave the bar and breathe sports-free air for the first time in several hours.

"No, Hunter did."

"Okay, we'll take my car."

Rory skids to a stop. "Allison, if we take your car you have to promise not to drive like you're trying to beat the *Millennium Falcon* at the Kessel Run."

"Oh-kaay." We round the corner, and I deactivate the alarm on my BMW Z4 parked on the street. Of course Hunter and Dave would choose a place without valet.

"Allison, that means don't speed."

"Rory, I never speed." I climb into the car, and Rory reluctantly follows. "It just *feels* faster when I have the top down. You know, physics and all that." I start the engine, press the button to lower the top, and we're off.

"Allison!" Rory screams over the wind and my Benny Goodman CD. "I took physics, and I'm not buying it. Creator! Watch out for the pedestrians!"

Ten minutes later, pretty good time to get all the way to Old Town where Rory lives, I say, "Rory, we're here. You can open your eyes."

"I am never driving with you again."

"You always say that." I pull into the empty parking spot next to her car, and follow her into the apartment building singing "Flat Foot Floogee." By the time we get to her apartment, Rory's singing, too. She never stays angry for long.

We burst into her apartment, and I flop on the couch while Rory heads for the kitchen. She reemerges with a bottle of wine and a pint of Double Fudge Brownie. Now we're talking. Why would anyone want to sit at hard wooden picnic tables, drink warm beer, and watch sweaty grown men run around chasing a ball? This is much better.

Rory hands me a spoon and flips the TV on, surfing until she finds the right channel. *The Iron Chef* starts in five minutes, so our timing is perfect.

Rory's still humming the song, then she says, "What's a floogee? For that matter, what's a floy, floy or a flou, flou?"

"What's wrong? You don't collar this jive?" I say, digging into the pint. "That's just frisking the whiskers."

Rory stares at me. "Where did you learn to talk like that?"

"Grandma Holloway. She'd put on her best drape, truck on down to the gin mills in the Land o' Darkness, and alligator with the hepcats at the Cotton Club. You've heard of Cab Calloway, right? She collared him, Duke Ellington, Cole Porter—all the gates and their killer-dillers."

"It's almost like speaking Klingon."

"If you say so. Shh. The show's starting."

We watch *The Iron Chef,* me staring in total incredulity and Rory laughing her ass off.

"This is the stupidest show I've ever seen," I say during a commercial break. "Who is that guy in all the ruffles and gloves? And why is he biting that pepper like he's some kind of animal?"

"I don't know," Rory says around a mouthful of ice cream, "but it's funny. I like the woman. She's always excited about the desserts."

"She's insane." I scoop out the last of the ice cream. "How could anyone get excited about a dessert with mushrooms? That's not dessert. Oh, my God. If this is what *Kamikaze Makeover!*'s like, I'm doomed."

There's a loud pounding, and Rory and I jump. "Who is that?"

Rory rolls her eyes. "Probably Hunter. We didn't see each other much this week." She hands me her ice cream spoon and heads for the door, now vibrating. "Cut it out! I'm coming, you Mynok!"

"Why don't you just move in together already and get it over with?" I say, settling back on the couch. Hunter is going to have to wait until I see whether the Iron Chef or the challenger wins tonight. Poor guys. They both seem really nice.

"We brought bourbon!" a not-so-nice voice bellows. "French, since we know you like them."

I close my eyes and put my arm over my face. Dave. What the hell is *he* doing here?

"Are you drunk?" Rory asks Hunter when he stumbles in.

"Not really," he slurs. "Not as drunk as Dan."

"Who's Dan?" Rory says, helping the wobbly Hunter to the chair across from where I'm sitting on the couch.

"Him. *Dan.*"

"Dave?" Rory says.

"That's what I said."

Dave plops down next to me. Right next to me. Rory's couch is huge, and Dave has to sit practically on top of me. He holds out a half-empty bottle of bourbon. "I'm not drunk." And he's probably not. He doesn't look or sound drunk. Hunter's such a lightweight. Even in high school he was a goner if he drank anything stronger than beer.

"Want some? It's like twenty bucks a bottle. French, so I think even Prince Bourbon-Parma would approve."

I grit my teeth. "His name is Nicolo, and he's not French. He's from Roskilde."

Dave uncaps the bourbon and drinks it straight. Yuck. "Where the hell is Roskilde?"

"Fuck if I know," Hunter says, and holds out his hand. Dave, idiot that he is, hands Hunter the bottle. Rory snatches it up.

"I'm going to get you water and an aspirin or you're going to have a hangover tomorrow."

Hunter smiles at her. "Thanks."

She ruffles his hair and looks at me and Dave. "Want anything?"

"A gun?"

Rory ignores me and says, "I'll get you a glass of water, too, Dave." She disappears into the kitchen.

"After all the trouble I went through getting you a sip of Gatorade the other night, how come you don't offer to get me a glass of water?" Dave asks me.

"Because I don't like you." I grab the arm of the couch and attempt to pull myself out of Dave's trap. He doesn't try to stop me, just runs a finger down my back, following the line of my spine all the way to the waistband of my low-rise jean shorts. I freeze.

"You don't really hate me, do you?" he asks, but his voice is low so Hunter doesn't hear.

I glance at him over my shoulder, a sarcastic remark all ready to go, but his golden eyes look so sincere that I falter. "You weren't even jealous, were you?" I whisper.

Shit! Why did I say that? I wasn't planning to say that.

Dave doesn't answer right away. He looks like he's thinking about it, then sort of shrugs and says, "Should I be?"

"What does that mean?" I hiss with a glance at Hunter.

"Means what I said."

"I was kissing him."

His face darkens. "Yeah, I saw that," he mutters.

"So, you don't care?"

Shut up, Allison. Shut up. You *don't care.*

"I don't like it, but you're going to do what you want."

I glance toward the kitchen to see if Rory's heard the argument, then turn back to Dave. "That's right. I'll do what I want."

I heave myself up, ready to flounce away, when Dave murmurs, "I will, too."

I round on him. "You will, what? You're going to *cheat* on me?"

"Can I cheat? Are we together?"

Goddamnit! Why does he always do this to me? I get all confused and turned around when I talk to him. "You know what I mean!" I finally shout.

Hunter cringes. "You're not going to throw anything, are you?"

I ignore him. On the couch, Dave spreads his arms over the back and levels his gaze on me. "Maybe I am drunk, because I'm not following you."

"Forget it. Why are you even here? You don't like me."

"Why do you say that?" Dave rests an ankle on his knee,

appearing even more relaxed than ever. Meanwhile, I'm as tight as an arrangement by Count Basie.

"You know why." I turn away from him, intending to join Rory in the kitchen, but she's standing frozen in the doorway, watching the battle.

"Is all this because I wouldn't sleep with you?"

My jaw drops, and if I were a cartoon, the top of my head would come off and steam would shoot out. Rory's hands fly to her mouth to stifle a gasp and Hunter's lips form an O.

I round on Dave. "Please. I wouldn't sleep with you if—"

"I was the last man on earth. Yeah, I've heard that one before."

"Then you should know this one, too. Fuck you." I stomp down Rory's hallway toward the bathroom. I'm perilously close to tears, but no one needs to know that if I can get the door closed before I start crying. I'm almost there when Dave's hand snatches my wrist and he pulls me into Rory's bedroom and shuts the door.

"What are you doing? Get out of the way." I try to push past him to open the door, but he takes my shoulders and backs me against the wall. Despite the fact that I hate him, I'm breathing hard and the look in his eyes is making me very, very warm.

We stare at each other, then he says, "So you think because I wouldn't sleep with you that means I don't like you?"

"I never said that." I try to think of some biting remark, but a traitorous tear slips free instead.

Dave catches it with a finger. "Are you crying?"

"No." I sniffle, and three more tears make their getaway. Dave shakes his head. He must have sisters because he's not freaked out by tears like most guys are.

"Red, have you ever considered that maybe I didn't sleep with you *because* I like you?"

"My name is Allison."

"Allison," he murmurs and traces a finger along my cheek.

"That doesn't make any sense. If you liked me—"

"I would have fucked you?" His voice is hard, but his touch is gentle when he runs his hand through my hair to cup the back of my head. "If that was all I wanted from you, I would have taken it. On our first date."

I snort. "Please."

He raises an eyebrow, and I shut up. After all, I'm standing here, shoved up against the wall, his arms around me, and his leg parting my thighs. Now isn't the best time to argue the point. "So what *do* you want?" I ask, then shiver at the way his eyes darken to goldenrod.

"I don't know yet."

I shake my head. "Then just forget the whole thing."

"I don't think so."

Jerk. Who is he to tell me when this—nonrelationship relationship—is over? But before I can correct yet another of his misguided assumptions, he pulls me to him and kisses me. Not his usual playful kiss. Not even a nice kiss. This is not the kind of kiss men give women in movies—at least not the kind I watch. This is hot and rough and so electric I feel like I stuck my finger in the light socket.

And then Dave begins to pull back, and I can't let him. I *should* let him, but this kiss is too amazing. So I grab his shirt and pull him closer, and his hands are all over me—in my hair, on my face, cupping my breasts, fitting me to his body. Finally we break apart. I'm panting and Dave's not exactly unruffled. He leans his head over my shoulder, resting on the wall behind me. His hands are snug on my waist and his breath tickles my ear.

"Still think I don't want you?" he murmurs, his voice like velvet next to my ear.

"I don't know."

"Still crying?"

I stiffen. I hate that he saw that. "No."

He moves to nuzzle my ear, whispers, "Still hate me?"

"Yes," I moan. He kisses my neck then my jawbone, his mouth like a slow-acting drug.

"Sure?"

"I never want to see you again," I say, trying to catch his mouth with mine.

He manages to evade my lips, then kisses me softly on the forehead. Not what I had in mind, and before I even open my eyes, the toad steps back, opens the door, and says, "If you change your mind, you know how to find me."

Life Goes to a Party

It's the first day of filming, and I take deep breaths in the elevator to calm myself. When I get off on the seventeenth floor, the camera crew will be there, ready to film my every moment. I smooth my navy Carolina Herrera wrap dress. I thought about wearing something flashier—my wool Schiaparelli military brisk suit—but then I decided I didn't want to look like I was trying too hard.

When the elevator door opens, I consider going back down. I hadn't expected things to look quite so crazy. There are three guys toting huge black cameras and followed by guys holding furry gray mops on the end of sticks. The staff is trying to look busy, and at the same time, talking really loudly to be heard by the furry mics. Miranda is in her office. It looks like she's posing for publicity photos, and Josh is standing next to Natalie's desk while a woman holds up what looks like a little tape recorder and points to it. Josh is the one who prevents my escape.

"Sweetie, you're here! Finally!"

Finally? It's quarter to nine. I'm early.

At Josh's words half a dozen people turn to look at me. A moment later, they descend, and I'm wired and propelled into my office for my own publicity photos and an interview. You know how on *The Real World* the cast gets pulled aside to explain their personal take on something? Or on *Queer Eye* how the friends and family of the straight guy make comments throughout? That's what this footage is for.

They hook me up to a wireless body lav mic, and since I don't have a pocket or waistband, a woman attaches the transmitter to the back of my bra. I look like a hunchback, and I have to lean forward when I sit. While they're hooking all of this up a guy who reminds me of Ron Howard reviews the rules for me.

"Okay, Allison, just want to remind you that everything you do or see today and in the weeks ahead falls under the confidentiality agreement. Don't talk to your friends, your family, and especially not to the media about anything. You got that?"

"Sure," I say. Like anyone's going to care about a show pitting interior designers against one another.

I've been sitting and talking for what feels like hours when I spot Nicolo through my office window. He's standing in the middle of the office talking with Miranda, and I wonder how long he's been here. One of the producers has a book of questions—I swear, it's like two hundred pages—and they just go on and on. The lights are hot, my back is starting to hurt from leaning forward, and Natalie's been giving me frantic looks for the past forty-five minutes. My phone hasn't rung once, which means she's holding my calls. I've gotten no work done this morning, and it's past eleven.

The *Reality TV Addict's Guide to What's Real* says that producers often try to wear you down, so they can get footage of you all harried and bitchy. I'm resolved to stay as cool as Antarctica. And yet still friendly and approachable.

Nicolo looks up, sees me, and smiles. His blue eyes crinkle when he does that, and it looks really sexy. Miranda gives me an annoyed frown. What's up with that? She's married. I think.

"So would you call interior design a hobby then, Allison?"

"Huh?" I look back at the Ron Howard producer interviewing me. "Oh, um. No. It's my job, not a hobby."

He waves a hand. "But you don't need the money. Your parents are quite well off."

"I don't want to talk about my family," I say. Then, at his raised eyebrows, I add, "My parents are rich, but it's not my money. In any case, I like interior design. I'd do it even if I didn't have to." I just wouldn't work for Miranda. Speak of the devil, Miranda catches my eye, taps her watch.

"Is that all?" I say. "I really have to do some work."

The producers try to throw a few more questions at me, but I swivel toward my computer and pretend to ignore them. I always thought it would be fun to have people asking me all sorts of questions about myself but believe it or not, after half an hour I was sort of sick of me.

I glance over my shoulder, and the film crew is still there, still filming. "Just go about your usual routine," the Ron Howard producer says. "We want some footage of you working."

Okay. I turn back to my computer and try to look busy. Normally, the first thing I do is play a game of solitaire, then read my hotmail, then play another game, then read my horoscope. Obviously, that's out. I decide to check my work e-mail, and when I open it, the camera guys zoom in. The first thing I see is a message from Miranda with the subject line all in caps: STOP TALKING ABOUT YOURSELF AND GET TO WORK.

I scramble to close the screen before the camera gets a shot of that. Okay, I'll check my voice mail. As I pick up the phone, the producer says, "Can you put it on speaker, so we can hear, too?"

I'm not thrilled with the idea, but I guess it's part of the show. I press the button for my voice mail, and a computer-ized voice says, "You have sixteen new messages."

"Shit," I mutter. Then I glance at the camera. "I mean, su-per." I smile—or at least try to.

"First message. Nine twenty-one A.M.," the computerized voice says.

"Ms. Holloway, this is Edith M. Bilker-Morgan. You were to call me at nine sharp to discuss my choice of side table for the study. I do not like the photo of the yellowish white one you sent. You called it"—there's the sound of paper rusting—"distressed. I am *most* distressed. Please call me back. If it's not too inconvenient."

"Ouch," the cameraman says, and I keep on smiling.

"Second message. Nine twenty-seven A.M."

"Ms. Holloway, this is Sherrie from Dr. Orion's office. I'm calling to confirm your appointment for a pelvic exam and Pap—"

"Next message!" I say, hitting the forward button.

"Nine forty-two A.M."

"Hi, darlin'. It's Daddy. I know it's still a week away, but are you coming to the lake for Memorial Day? You know how your mother gets when—"

"You know what?" I hit the button to disconnect. "Maybe I'll check messages later."

The intercom beeps, and I almost jump. "Allison?" Miranda's tone is short and sharp.

I clear my throat and smile at the camera again. "Yes, Miranda?"

"Quit playing around and get out here. Mr. Watanabe has arrived, and we need you in the meeting."

"Thanks, Miranda. I—" But I hear a *click,* and she's gone.

"Excuse me." I head for the conference room, and the camera crew follows. On the way, I pass Nicolo. He's leaning against the desk of a petite blonde junior designer we hired about a month ago and flirting with her. Note to self: Fire Britney. Or is she Katie?

I give him a smile, and his eyes follow me. I glance back, but the camera crew is still following, and wouldn't they just love to get a shot of me flirting with Nicolo?

About halfway through the meeting with Watanabe and the rest of the Japanese contingent, which Nicolo never does bother to join, I motion to Miranda to speak privately. We won't miss anything anyway as the meeting is being conducted in Japanese and Yamamoto is translating about a tenth of it.

In fact, for the past twenty minutes, Josh and I have been playing tic-tac-toe. Miranda meets me just outside the door, and I cover my mic with my hand. I don't know if that will mute my voice or not, but I can't get it off by myself.

"Miranda," I say as soon as she closes the door. "Do I have to be in on this meeting? I need to get the details and schedules together for the Wernberg project. We were supposed to have a team meeting on that at one."

Miranda glances at the conference room, keeping her mic covered, too. "That's not going to happen today, Allison. We'll do it Monday."

"That's a big contract, and I still haven't seen the budget.

I've got Josh's numbers on the lighting and some preliminary numbers for the furnishings, but I haven't talked to Lila or Dylan about the flooring or the interior finishes. And who's checking on the codes?"

"I need you in there, Allison. Give what you have to Dylan and tell him to be ready to present a complete budget Monday."

I frown. "Dylan's only been here a year."

"And it's time he proved himself. Your budgets are always off anyway."

I gape. "One multiplication mistake and—"

"It was a five-thousand-dollar multiplication mistake. Now go talk to Dylan, then get your butt back in there." Miranda goes back to the conference room, and I head across the room to Dylan's workspace. He's got his Luxo lamp over his drawing board, and he's erasing something from canary-colored tracing paper.

I cover my mic. "Dylan?"

"Yeah?" He doesn't look up.

"Miranda and I need a favor."

Now he looks up. He's got brown eyes and long dark lashes. Very cute, except that he's about twenty-two and engaged.

"We need you to get the budget together for the Wernberg project. I'll have Natalie give you everything I have so far, but it's not much. We'll need the numbers by Monday."

He swallows. "Okay. You know, I haven't really done a budget before."

Damn Miranda. This is so unfair. Normally I would help the guy out, but I have to get back to the stupid meeting. "Just do your best. I'm sorry. I'd help, but—"

Dylan glances at the conference room. "TV calls. Don't worry. I'll take care of it."

"Thanks, Dylan."

"Anything I can help with?"

I turn to see Nicolo standing behind me. He's wearing a charcoal suit with a red power tie and his eyes are sapphire blue. "Thanks, but I think we've got it under control." The way I say it, I almost believe it myself.

"I am looking forward to our date tonight."

I glance around. No camera crews watching. "Me, too. But it's a professional outing." I tap his tie with my fingernail, painted OPI's Wanted . . . Red or Alive, then run my finger down the length of the crimson silk. Nicolo smiles.

"Until tonight." And he walks away. I grind my teeth. I'm not liking the constraints this TV thing is placing on me. I have no time to work, no time to flirt . . . I wonder if this is how Carson feels on *Queer Eye*? Well, if Carson can do it, so can I. We all have to make sacrifices.

"Okay, sweetie, I'm here now." Josh kisses my cheek. "It's all good." Josh steps into my apartment dressed in black leather. A short attractive guy peeks around Josh.

"Jello. I'm Carlos from Cuba." Carlos is dressed in sandals, slim Guess jeans, leather belt, and a wife beater with an open button-down shirt over it. His clothes are pressed and the pants hug his ass, but his look is intense, and the five-o'clock shadow belies the usual baby face I'm used to on gay Latino guys.

"Allison from Chicago."

"Ooh, jou look gorgeous." He waves a hand, indicating I should spin for him. I do, stepping back so he can see the complete effect. The dress is black with a fitted bodice that extends all the way down my hips. Then it fans into a full skirt. My arms and shoulders are bare except for two silk straps that snake behind my neck and cross over my bare back.

"Vintage?" Josh asks.

"Hmm-mm. The thirties. Ever heard of Jeanne Lanvin? This is from her mermaid line." I motion Josh and Carlos to follow me upstairs and into the kitchen. I have a great kitchen. It's got white marble countertops, white walls, pewter drawer pulls, and a stainless steel fridge. It stays white because I never cook.

Josh and Carlos sit on bar stools, while I lean against the counter.

"So, what am I here for?" Josh asks. "You look scrumptious."

"Are you sure? I could wear the Paquin or the Schiaparelli." I raise my hand to my lips, then quickly lower it before I gnaw off my OPI Russian to a Party nail polish.

"No, no," Carlos chimes in. "Jou look perfect. But jou no look like jou want to go, does she, papi?"

Josh shakes his head. "What's the story, sweetie?

"Bad night last night. I had another run-in with the toad."

"That's the Davester," Josh whispers to Carlos.

"Nicolo showed up and Dave was there and—"

Josh gasps and clutches Carlos's hand. "You had a threesome!" he hisses.

"No, I"—but suddenly I'm thinking about Dave on one side and Nicolo on the other, and I wonder what it would take to make that happen—"you know, I've never understood how threesomes work. Is it everybody with everybody? Because—yuck. Anyway, last night Dave was at Rory's after the game, and we started arguing. I said some stuff, and I swear I don't know where it came from." I put my hands over my eyes, careful not to touch my face and my makeup. "The next thing I know, we're in Rory's bedroom making out, and I'm telling him how mad I am because—you know."

I don't want to say the part about how Dave rejected me in front of Carlos.

"You were *kissing* him?" Josh looks horrified.

"I know I keep saying I hate his guts, and I do. But when I get around him . . ."

"You can't resist." Josh nods. "No need to explain. I have the same problem with Justin Timberlake."

"You know Justin Timberlake?"

"No, sweetie. I hate Justin Timberlake, but whenever I see or hear Justin Timberlake, I can't resist him. You should see my closet. I have piles of magazines with Justin Timberlake pictures. I'm like a celebrity stalker or something."

"Jou scare me," Carlos says to Josh, shaking his head. "And jou"—he points to me—"jou got it bad. Jou got to forget about the toad."

"Exactly," Josh adds, "you've got the princetopolis on the line now. He needs your full attention."

"I help jou," Carlos offers. "Jou have any chickens around?"

"No." I don't even want to know why he's asking, but I'm suddenly glad Booboo Kitty is sleeping under my bed.

"Too bad," Carlos says. "But when I get home I make a potion for jou and give it to papi." He gestures to Josh. "That strong magic. Jou take that, jou forget the toad. Also, jou go get laid. That works, too."

Well, I don't know if I'm going to get laid, but if Nicolo sees me in this dress and doesn't try to get me into bed, I'll seriously question what team he's playing on.

Nicolo calls a few minutes later to say he's on his way, and I've just pushed Josh and Carlos out the door when the bell rings again.

I glide back down the stairs, open the door, and raise my brows. "Nicolo. You look better than tiramisu." Way better.

Maybe I should suggest we stay in? I reach out and finger the tux's material. "Armani?"

"Good evening." Nicolo smiles and takes my hand, opening it and kissing the palm.

"Come in," I say. "I just need to grab my bag."

But he doesn't release my hand. "You are exquisite. The gown is vintage, yes?"

I give him a nod of approval. I love guys who know fashion. I love vintage, and my collection can't be fully appreciated if a man doesn't know a little about fashion. But not too much. "Know the designer?" I ask and hold my breath.

"Valentino?"

"No." I relax. "Lanvin. Her mermaid line."

"I have not heard of her." Nicolo follows me inside. "But I like her very much." He takes my hand and pulls me to him. "I like the way she looks on you." He leans down and kisses me, his hand skating up my bare back, leaving a trail of warm tingles. He's handsome, knows fashion, and leaves me trembling. Any second the alarm clock is going to go off, and I'll wake up and realize this is just a dream. A delicious dream, but a dream.

When the kiss ends, he murmurs in my ear, "I like your hair up." His hand spreads out over my bare back, warm and solid. "But it looks better down."

I frown.

He nods expectantly. What, am I supposed to take it down now? I didn't spend twenty minutes pinning it up to take it down now. It's sweet that he likes my hair, but not that sweet.

You know, I've always thought my green eyes were my best feature, especially if I wear green or blue, but most men like my hair. I'm thirty-two, so I probably should have cut it by now, but I can't quite bring myself to do it.

If I were a princess, I probably wouldn't be able to change it without a royal decree.

"Ready to go?" I say breezily, starting up the stairs. He follows, pausing in the living room while I grab my clutch from the kitchen table.

I switch off the kitchen light and say, "Bye, kitty!" to the empty room.

"You have a roommate?" Nicolo asks when I walk back into the living room.

"Cat. White like everything else."

Nicolo is studying my living room, his dazzling blue eyes taking in every detail. This would drive Rory crazy. She can't stand being scrutinized because she's so afraid she'll be found wanting. Every time I come over she tells me she's sorry her apartment is so dirty, when it's obvious she just vacuumed.

I love for people to see my house. If it's a little dusty, that doesn't faze me. But the cleaning service was here yesterday, so the house is polished and sparkly.

"White is a risky choice," Nicolo says after a long silence.

"I don't mind risk."

"No? Better and better," he says, eyes skimming over me as though I were the room now. "But so much white." He gestures to the room. "You had to exercise care in choosing the tones."

"I stuck mostly with ivory. I reupholstered the couch and chair in a heavy ivory tapestry and then used the remainder to make the window valances. The material for the curtains was harder to find. It looks sheer and lets a lot of light in, but you can't see through them from the outside."

Nicolo nods. "Yes, you need light to make such a pristine room work. And the cherry"—he motions to the armoire where I hide the TV and DVD player—"the white brings out the rich tones in the wood."

I smile. "I love cherry, and nothing looks better with cherry than ivory. It's a classic."

"I see you are a classic woman. Vintage dress, elegant decor, timeless beauty." He smiles and my pulse jumps at the warmth in his eyes.

"That's just the icing on the cake." I haven't had this much fun flirting in a long, long time. Especially when I really shouldn't be. Maybe *because* I shouldn't be.

He takes my arm and we walk downstairs toward the door. "Then I shall have to lick the icing away as quickly as possible. I want to taste the cake."

"I think that can be arranged."

A little while later, we pull up to the Four Seasons on East Delaware Place, and I smile with anticipation. The Four Seasons is elegant, understated, and European in style.

"Good evening, Mr. Parma. Ms. Holloway," the doorman says as Nicolo and I walk into the lobby with its Italian marble, crystal chandeliers, and curving, intricately carved wooden stairway.

"Hello, Jordan. Good to see you again."

I wink at Nicolo. A week in Chicago and the doorman already knows him. I gaze at the chandeliers before moving forward. I love chandeliers, especially at night when the lights twinkle like a million diamond-cut stars. One of these days I'm going to have a house expansive enough for a chandelier. I glance at Nicolo to see if he's thinking about houses with chandeliers.

The hotel manager spots us and hurries over. "Mr. Parma. You are here for the Bourbon-Parma affair?"

Nicolo inclines his head. "Yes, Jean, merci."

Bourbon-Parma affair? Just how much royalty is in Chicago at the moment?

"Right this way." He shows us to a private elevator and instructs the porter to take us to the pool level. I arch a brow at Nicolo, but he gives nothing away.

As we step off the elevator, I hear the strains of music and the clink of silver and china. I can't remember seeing this floor of the Four Seasons before, so it's a pleasant surprise when we enter. Classic in style, the room is dominated by the rectangular pool. Surrounding the glass-blue water are Roman columns and, above them, a mammoth domed glass ceiling. A wide expanse of windows along one side showcases a view of downtown Chicago. Tables with delicacies are scattered about the room, and a few unobtrusive waiters are dispensing champagne and wine.

I take a glass from a passing waiter, and Nicolo does likewise. "Nice," I say. "I thought you were staying at the Drake."

He nods. "I am. Sixte and his wife, Valencia, are here at the Four Seasons."

"Allison, dear! How good to see you." I turn to see Jellie Abernathy sliding toward me. We were friends in high school, but I've recently bowed out of bridesmaid duty at her upcoming wedding, so her warm welcome is a bit surprising. Jellie air-kisses both my cheeks, missing by a mile, then stands back and smiles at Nicolo.

"Jellie, this is Nicolo Parma. Nicolo, Angelica Abernathy. We went to school together."

Nicolo kisses her hand. "Enchanted."

"Oh, Allison, I feel like I haven't seen you in forever. You've met my fiancé, Marshall, right?" She indicates a short, handsome man standing behind her. We exchange more greetings and small talk until we're joined by another couple and it starts all over again.

Now I remember why I rarely go to these things anymore. I'm bored in less than an hour. No one actually says anything of any consequence. I love talking about fashion. I can hold my own in discussions of finance and politics. I can even manage a few noteworthy comments on art and theater. But the inevitable start of the name-dropping exhausts my patience. I smoothly extricate myself from the group and make a circuit of the room, stopping to talk to real estate moguls, government bigwigs, and old friends.

I'm talking crown moldings with the mayor's wife when one of the waiters approaches and hands me a note.

"Excuse me," I say and step away. The note's from Nicolo, asking me to meet him and his cousin in the presidential suite.

On the way back to the elevator bank, I glance at the pool and imagine the reaction were I to jump in. Of course, I'd peel off my dress first. One does not jump in a pool wearing a Lanvin. I wonder if peeling the dress off or jumping in the water would make more of a splash.

I take the elevator to the forty-sixth floor and step into luxury. The Four Seasons spares no expense on their best rooms. I knock on the door and a servant in a tux admits me into a small marble foyer dominated by a live flower arrangement on a gilt table. He opens a door on my left, and I enter a small hallway with more flowers and muted light. To my right is a powder room done in pink marble and ahead is the living room.

The decor up here is also European—dark handcrafted wood, tasteful upholstery, plush carpeting. The view from the huge windows is a panorama of Lake Michigan, framed by heavy royal-blue drapes with gold fringe. Nicolo turns from one of the windows, the indigo of the sky and azure of the lake in stark contrast behind him. "Allison, come in. Meet my cousin Sixte."

I step into the living room, and smile at the assembled party. There's a mahogany dining table to the left with eight plush chairs. The ivory pillar candles have almost burned down. Directly before me are several club chairs and two couches in delicate ivory and blue chintz.

Nicolo indicates a man reclining on one couch. This must be Sixte, though he looks almost nothing like Nicolo. He's older, dark with an orangey tan, and he's got a pencil-thin mustache. Beside him is a waif-thin woman in a peach A-line dress from Narciso Rodriguez's spring line. Four or five other men, all lounging carelessly, cigarettes drooping from their mouths or fingers, look up as I enter. "This is Allison Holloway," Nicolo says. "She is the best interior designer in Chicago."

I smile and approach Sixte. "A pleasure to meet you. Nicolo's told me so much about you."

He glances at Nicolo, then back at me, but doesn't rise or even sit up. I'm expecting an air kiss—a handshake at least—so I'm a little taken aback by the cool welcome.

"Please sit down, Allison," his wife says with no trace of a European accent. "We were just discussing Philippe de Villiers' presentation of Les Sables d'Olonne. Three women are racing this year. Do you sail?"

I take a moment to shift gears. Les Sables d'Olonne. Nonstop yacht race around the world. "I used to. My parents have a house on Lake Geneva."

Sixte and his wife frown. "Switzerland?" Nicolo asks.

I shake my head. "Wisconsin."

I get several blank looks, but before I can explain how

upper-crust Lake Geneva is—how it's the "Newport of the West"—the topic moves to car racing.

This is interesting. I've never been the unfashionable one before. I know almost nothing about car racing, so I sit on the edge of a cushy chair and listen until everyone's discussing plans for Fashion Week in New York.

"I loathe New York," Sixte says, drawing another cigarette from his gold case. "I loathe fashion."

"We must make an appearance, no matter how tedious," his wife, Valencia, says.

"All those clothes and girl after girl, all flat-chested," another man who I think Nicolo called Maxmillian whines.

The group is silent for a moment as everyone but me drags on their European cigarettes.

"Oh, Allison," Valencia says after a moment. "Would you like a glass of wine?"

"Thanks."

"Red or white?"

"Red." I glance back at Nicolo, resting on the arm of the chair, leaning casually across the back. He gives me a bored look. Being royalty isn't quite as fun as I'd fantasized. I'm missing *The Amazing Race* for this?

A shriek sounds from across the room where Valencia is standing at the dining table. "What's wrong?" Sixte asks.

"We're out of the Dom. de la Romanee."

Sixte actually sits up at this. "Call down and order more."

Nicolo rises. "I will do it."

Valencia shakes her head. "The hotel won't have it. We're in *Chicago*. The best they'll have is a 2000 Château Mouton Rothschild."

"We could try for the 1986 Rothschild," Maxmillian suggests.

"Oh, what's the use?" Valencia flops down on the couch beside Sixte.

"I could drink white," I say, but no one acknowledges me.

"This is all so tedious," Sixte says.

I agree.

When we arrive back at my house, Nicolo doesn't try to wrangle an invitation to come inside. He sighs and kisses my cheek. All that ennui can really tire a guy out.

I've Got the World on a String

After a weekend of frantic reality-star wardrobe shopping, life looks less tedious and I'm looking TV-ready. Jeweled cuff from Emanuel Ungaro, leather ankle boots from Tod's, jeans from Michael Kors, a new bag from Bottega Veneta, and a top from Luca Luca. I went to Louis Vuitton, too, but I didn't buy anything. I just like to say Vuitton. If only Trinny and Susannah from *What Not to Wear* could get a look at me.

I walk into work early Monday, before the camera crews have arrived, wearing my new Michael Kors jeans, black stiletto boots, a sheer black top, and OPI's Would You Like a Lick-tenstein on my nails.

"Roo-woo! Call the fire department because you're scorching!" Josh pops his head out of his office and watches me walk by. "Miranda isn't going to like it. Stealing the limelight from her like this. And you're wearing jeans on a Monday."

"She can suck it up. These jeans are Michael Kors."

"It's not only the jeans, sweetie." Josh slips into my office right before I can close the door in his face. "I don't know if you noticed, but that shirt is sheer, it's showing a lot of cleavage, and if we move these little ruffles here—"

I swat his hand away.

"—we're going to see more than is technically legal."

"It's not that sheer, Josh." I sit down in my chair, prop my feet on the desk, and lean my head back. "This is going to be a long day."

"Tired from a hot date with His Majesty?"

"No." Josh walks behind me and starts massaging my neck. "Mmm, thanks. I have so much to get done today, and the cameras are going to get in the way."

Josh chuckles, and I glance up at him. "I never thought I'd hear you complaining about cameras." His hands massage my temples, but he's careful not to mess up my hair, which I'm wearing long, wavy, and supermodel sexy today.

"It's hard being a celebrity."

"I know, sweetie." He gives my shoulders a last squeeze. "And you look the part today."

I sit forward. "It's not too much?"

"If I was straight, I'd be all over you."

"Promises, promises. Speaking of which"—I pick up a file from under a stack of magazines—"where's the furniture mock-up for the Wernberg project?"

"I'm working on it."

"Josh!"

He holds up a hand. "Carlos and I had a fight and I indulged in a little pity party all weekend. I'll finish it this morning, then take you out to lunch to make up for being late."

I frown. "I guess."

"Oh, good! Where are we going? Le Colonial? I'll buy you a Melon."

"No." I don't want to think about Le Colonial or Melons. "How about—"

"Ms. Holloway, Mr. Bryant," Natalie says on the intercom. "The cameras are here. Mr. Watanabe needs you to come out and get—ah, miced."

I look through the glass window into the reception area. Nicolo is standing in the lobby, wearing a black suit, white shirt, no tie. He looks really hot, and he's staring at me.

"Here we go, sweetie," Josh says, pulling me up. "Let's show the princelet who's got the royal flush."

We're filming the first show Wednesday, and the preproduction conference is interminable. By the time I've called back the clients I missed Friday, it's after two and Miranda's assembling everyone for a meeting on the Wernberg project.

This is the first really big project I've planned and coordinated, so I'm actually on time for the meeting for once. I'm so on time that when I walk in, Nicolo's the only one there, sitting in the same chair where I first saw him. "Hey, why are you in here?" I ask.

"I thought it might be interesting to see you at work."

I frown, noting he's chosen an area out of camera range. "Are they filming this?"

He nods.

"Did Miranda okay that? I'm not so sure Wernberg wants our meetings about them made public." I'm not so sure I do.

"We have complete access. Miranda signed the contract." At my worried look, he motions me toward him. "Stop your worry. It will be used for filler only. Now then, come here and let me see what you are wearing."

I smile and saunter closer. When I stop in front of Nicolo,

he reaches up and runs a hand over my midriff, pale beneath the sheer black material. His hand climbs slowly upward, under the ruffles covering my breasts. A flash of heat courses through me, but I keep my expression sexy and casual.

When Nicolo looks into my face, I reach forward and slide my hand in the V of his white shirt, flicking another button, so the shirt is open to midchest.

"Oh, dear. It's a tête-à-tête," Josh says from behind us. I step back and give Josh a dark look. "Sweetie, save that look for Miranda. Here come the cameras."

Nicolo smiles and mouths "Later."

As Miranda, trailed by the cameras, walks in, I take a seat next to Josh. The meeting goes pretty well at first. Everyone likes my color choices and Josh's lighting design. The furniture mock-up Josh worked on all morning looks spectacular—one of his best.

"Okay," I say. "Everything appears to be on schedule." I flip through a couple pages of my notes. I try to ignore the cameras, Nicolo, too, but I've felt his eyes on me throughout. I wonder how much later "later" is.

"We haven't discussed the budget," Miranda points out, preening for the cameras.

I glance at Dylan. He and I haven't had time to go over what he's prepared, and I'm not going to hear it first on camera. "Miranda, why don't we save that for later?" I glance at the cameras so she won't mistake my meaning. But she's not watching me; she's smiling at one of the cameras, her head held high to keep her neck from looking wrinkled.

"Now is fine, Allison."

I look at Josh, and he says, "Can we take a moment to talk about Aguirre and Bailey. I spoke with them this—"

"Whatever you think is fine for them, Josh. Now, tell me about the budget we're presenting to Wernberg, Dylan."

Dylan passes copies to everyone and stands to run through the numbers he's worked up. Five minutes in, I stop him. This is a mess—Dylan's forgotten to calculate fees for inspection, he didn't include the cost for installation of the floor covering, and the consultation fee he's listed is based on last year's rates. If Wernberg saw this, they'd fire us before we even had a chance to present our scheme.

"Dylan, that's great."

He glances up at my interruption.

"Why don't you and I go over a few things in my office, and we'll finalize everything tomorrow."

Lila, a junior designer we hired about three months ago, who is still trying to impress everyone, says, "Where's the info on the SBCCI codes? Where are the Load Factor Tables?" She flips through the sheaf of papers. "We'd better get on that or we'll be late and end up having to cut corners like we did at Harpo Studios."

I inhale sharply, and the room goes silent. Harpo is owned by Oprah Winfrey, and Interiors by M just redecorated her studio. It was a major coup, a major pain in the ass, and very nearly drove Josh and me into rehab. "Lila," I say in the tense silence, "we didn't cut corners at Harpo. We were late getting the paperwork in, but I wouldn't say we cut corners."

Lila looks up at me, then seems to notice the cameras. She pales visibly. "Oh, right. I was just kidding."

"If all the kidding is over," Miranda says with ice in her voice, "let's get back to work." She rises and strolls out of the conference room. Thankfully, the cameras follow.

Dylan looks over at me. "I'm sorry, Allison. I told you I'd never done one of these before."

I shake my head. "It's okay, but I don't want to go over things with all the cameras around. Can you stay late tonight and we'll work on it?"

He nods. "Sure."

"I'll stay, too," Josh volunteers. "Carlos is still being huffy, so I've got nothing better to do."

We get the budget and the inspection papers worked out, but not until after ten. Tomorrow Josh and I plan to spend most of the day getting everything ready for the taping Wednesday, so I've put Dylan and Lila in charge of the Wernberg details.

I know I should feel excited that the first *Kamikaze Make-over!* is only two days away, but at this point, I couldn't care less. I'm exhausted from trying to balance the cameras, the interviews, the prep work for the show, and my other clients.

Who knew being a reality TV star was so tough?

Earlier this evening, when I finally admitted I was impossibly behind, I gave in and called Mia, home on maternity leave, and begged her to take two clients, then I asked a junior designer I've worked with before to take another. I kept people like Mrs. Bilker-Morgan, but playing musical clients isn't a good strategy. The more you play, the greater the chance that when the music stops, you'll be the one left without a chair.

Miranda says that the attention garnered by the TV show will make up for any slight a client feels, and that I'll be in even higher demand after the show airs, but I've kept more clients than I can really handle as a precautionary measure, and I'm starting to fall behind on my self-imposed deadlines.

Josh and I are the last ones to leave the office that evening, and we walk out together. "You should just sleep with His Highnesty and get him out of your system," Josh says. "All that sexual tension between you is making me edgy."

"I'm working too hard to even think about sex right now, Josh."

The elevator in the hall outside Interiors by M opens, and Josh hits the button for the parking garage. "Sweetie, you know what you're really doing, don't you⸮"

"Filling the chasm of my nonexistent sex life with work⸮"

"Oh, please. It hasn't been that long."

The elevator plunges downward with a whirr.

"Yeah, that's easy for you to say when you've got Carlos from Cuba."

Josh sighs. "I told you, we're having a tiff. Besides, I haven't decided about Carlos yet. He's bi, and I don't know if I want to date a guy who likes girls."

"Well, I don't know if I want to date a guy who has obnoxious friends."

"Yes, you do."

The elevator door opens, and we step into the parking garage. It smells like heat, oil, and exhaust.

"You just want to make the princeling work for it."

"I don't give a fudge what he does." I'm working on not cursing so I don't mess up in front of the cameras, and *fudge* is my new favorite word. "I'm going to watch my reality shows on TiVo, then sleep. If I'm lucky I won't dream about LSC Codes, occupancy classifications, and reverse stenciling." My heels click on the concrete, the sound echoing through the barren garage.

Josh waits, knowing I can't leave it at that. He's right.

"In a few weeks this fudging kamikaze show will be over," I say, "and if Nicolo's still interested, I'll think about it."

"Please. He's your fantasy man. You've dreamed about this guy."

"Yeah, and I have to wonder if he's real."

"Is anyone⸮" Josh says. Then, "What have we here⸮"

Josh slows, and I follow his gaze. Nicolo is standing beside my BMW, looking cool in casualwear: black slacks, black silk shirt, leather jacket thrown over his shoulder.

"I'm calling later, and I want details," Josh says, then turns abruptly and heads across the garage to his turquoise Jeep.

For a long moment I don't move, trying to figure how I'm going to handle this. Then Nicolo spreads his arms, gives me a disarming smile, and the next thing I know I'm walking toward him. I stop close enough to smell his cologne. It must be made with pheromones because I can't think of anything but pushing him up against the car and devouring that sexy mouth. "I'm too tired to go out," I say, surprised that my words trickle through the constriction in my throat.

"Then we should stay in," Nicolo says softly, his voice and tenor matching my mood, almost as though he can read my mind. "I will entertain you." He leans closer. "With my mouth, my hands, my body . . ."

Okay, this is really corny. I swear, if a friend told me a guy said this to her, I would laugh my ass off. But we're inches apart, his voice is low and seductive, his body's hot, and I deserve a little fun after the day I've had.

So instead of laughing at his cheesiness, instead of repeating my professional relationship mantra, I put my hand on the back of his neck, pull him to me, and kiss him hard. I don't know how long we stand behind my car, our tongues entwined, our bodies wrapped around each other, but when his hand slides under my top and touches skin, I pull away.

He frowns and sighs with frustration. I know exactly how he feels. The last thing I want to do is stop. I want him, and the role of good girl is a size too small.

But just because I've capitulated internally doesn't mean I'll let him see how I really feel.

"Allison, I will take you home, yes?"

I shake my head, not my body's first choice for a response, and my libido retaliates by certifying my brain clinically insane. But my suffering feels deserved. It wouldn't be right if Nicolo were the only one sexually frustrated.

"My car's right here." A voice that must be mine, but as it's not screaming, "Take me now," I'm not quite ready to claim ownership, then says, "We have a long day tomorrow."

"My driver will come back for your car, and the taping I will move to Thursday."

"No." Goddamnit! Yes. I meant yes!

His hands fist at his side and he glances away. He *really* doesn't like being told no. And that reassures my mind—if not my body—that I'm taking the right tack with him. There are a lot of good reasons not to get involved. He needs to give me a really solid one to change my mind this soon.

When he looks back, his face is impassive. "Then perhaps you would be interested in accompanying me to an event Friday evening."

"I don't think so—"

He puts a finger lightly over my lips. My body slumps with relief. Thank God something has finally made me shut up.

"A new designer, Ciara St. Loren, shows her fall collection at a private venue Friday evening. You have heard of her, yes?"

"Perhaps," I say evenly, but my heart has started pounding harder than it was a moment ago when he . . . well, it's pounding hard.

Ciara St. Loren was *the* new designer in Milan last year. The fashion gods called her spring collection both spectacular and innovative. This fashion disciple called it ridiculously expensive. Even I hesitated to spend that much on clothes, so

Mitsy bought me one of Ciara's outfits for my birthday. It must have cost my parents over a thousand dollars, but it looks so good on me, it's worth the price.

"My invitation allows me to bring a guest. Would you consider accompanying me?"

I should say no. All the reasons against getting involved rear their ugly heads, and the more time we spend together, the more involved we become.

I'm also thinking it might not be a good move to be seen together again so soon or so publicly. As it stands, only about five people really care what I do, but be seen repeatedly with a prince and pretty soon reporters are digging through my trash, there are topless photos of me in the tabloids, and my mom is buying a wedding dress to match the royal jewels.

Nicolo and I should just go back to my apartment, have wild sex until we've gotten each other out of our systems, and then go our own ways—his to rule a country and mine to decorate people's bathrooms. But as reasons to go, Ciara St. Loren is pretty damn persuasive.

"Friday?" I say. "I think I can reschedule a few things and join you."

"Good." He smiles, and I can tell he's genuinely pleased.

Not as pleased as I am, but not too many guys could stand up against Ciara St. Loren. I frown. No doubt he figured I'd jump at the chance to see her new line, and when I accepted, he got exactly what he wanted.

"I will see you Friday. But about tonight"—he leans in and kisses me again—"I have business tomorrow and will be away until Friday afternoon."

I glance up at him. "You won't be at the taping Wednesday?"

"Regretfully, no. But I am here tonight." He kisses my jaw, then my neck, and his hands slide under my shirt to hover, warm and solid, at the small of my back. "Let me take you home."

His hands slide around to my belly, and I almost gasp at the sensation. I'm aching for his fingers to stray higher. My bra clasps in the front, and it would be an easy matter for him to snap it open . . .

I pull away. "Good night, Nicolo."

He scowls, looking like a little boy who's had his chocolate chip cookie taken away. He reaches out and catches my hand before this Chips Ahoy! makes her escape.

"What do you want?" he says as though this is some kind of negotiation. "You want me, Allison, and I want you. I do not like to wait."

"Too bad." I can't hold back a laugh. I mean, did this guy ever grow out of the terrible twos? "Look, Cookie Monster, I'm not some petty official you can pressure, or one of your staff, forced to scamper whenever you say 'boo.' I'm going home. Alone."

His eyes darken with what looks like anger, but an experienced eye like mine sees arousal. The thrill of the chase and all that. Men. They're all the same.

Finally, Nicolo manages a smile, though it doesn't quite reach his eyes, and releases my hand. "I do not understand you American women."

Wednesday morning I'm lying on my couch, listening to the *Today* show and sporting cool, wet green tea bags on my eyes. I didn't get in from work until after midnight, and now my eyes are all puffy. Great. I'm going to be on national TV, and I look like I've got balloon implants above my cheeks.

My cell rings, and I answer without moving. "No, Josh, you don't look fat in whatever outfit you have on now."

"This is Rory."

"Oh. You don't look fat, either."

"Thanks. I was calling to wish you good luck on the show today. And I want to take you out for a gossip session and a drink. If you're too tired tonight, how about Friday?"

"Can't Friday. I have a da—professional outing."

"The prince?"

"No comment."

"Ooh, you're good. If I were a reporter, I'd back off."

"That's why you're not a reporter." I lift one tea bag and peer at the clock. "Rory, I have to go."

"Okay, how about Saturday?"

"Yeah, that would work—wait, no." I sit and flip a page on my planner, lying open on the coffee table beside me. "I promised Grayson I'd volunteer at this basketball camp for inner-city kids with him Saturday. He doesn't have his license back, so he needs a ride, and I haven't seen him in weeks. I'm not sure when we'll be done, but I'll let you know."

"You're volunteering? *You?*"

I frown. "Of course. I'm all for philanthropy."

"Gray guilted you into it?"

I sigh. "Yep."

"Thought so. Well, break a leg today."

"Thanks, Rory."

Okay, I thought when someone told you to break a leg that was supposed to be good luck. I'm going to have to do a little etymological research here because from the moment I get to work, nothing is right.

Well, it might be right, but it's not the way I want it—and that's really the only thing that matters. No wonder Nicolo isn't here for the taping. If he were, I'd tear him to shreds. We all would.

First problem: The van with the film crew, Josh, Miranda,

and me stops in Englewood. For those of you not familiar with the Chicago landscape, this is a great, big, ugly crater, i.e., a very, very *bad* area.

"Wait a minute," I say to the guy who's driving. He usually holds the furry mic. "Why are we stopping? I think I saw a body on the corner back there."

"Everybody out," he says, opening his door, but Josh, Miranda, and I don't move. The van with Watanabe and the Ron Howard producer pulls up across the street. I glance at the house in front of us. It looks like something out of the war zone in Iraq. I don't know how it's even still standing. It's a one-story shotgun house with a small porch and was probably white at one time or another, but now it's dingy gray. Well, the part of it not covered with graffiti is dingy gray.

I glance at the house next door and realize why the house is covered with graffiti. About six guys in baggy jeans that desperately need belts are kicking back on the porch of the little blue house. They're watching us with interest and drinking bottles of beer, even though it's barely ten in the morning. They're all wearing blue and white hats or bandannas, and when one of them catches me looking, he flashes me a hand sign.

Josh says, "Is that a school for the deaf? I don't know sign language."

I roll my eyes. "No, Josh, it's a gang. We're in gangland."

"Duck and cover!" Josh screams and dives to the floor.

I glare at Miranda, then notice that the cameras are filming our reaction. "Turn off the fucking camera."

The cameraman frowns at me. Thank God for the *Reality TV Addict's Guide to What's Real.* The writers pointed out that network reality shows can't use footage with profanity.

Watanabe gets out of the van behind us and hurries to our door. He says something in Japanese and points to the house.

He obviously wants us to get out, but I'm not moving. I stare at Miranda, waiting for her to tell Watanabe we're not doing it. Instead, she slips out of the van. I grab her arm. "What are you doing? I'm not going in there!"

"It's perfectly safe."

I shoot another glance at the gangsters next door. "Are you blind?"

"Allison, no one's going to commit any crimes with the cameras around. Come on. We're making a lot of money on this deal." She starts up the walk.

When I don't follow, Watanabe yells at me again. What is this? *Fear Factor?* I take a deep breath. I don't care what they offer me in there—I'm not eating maggots. I pat Josh on the shoulder.

"Let's go, Josh."

"You go," he mumbles, head still between his knees. "I'll cover you."

I finally manage to get Josh out, and we hurry through the Englewood war zone, diving into the shelter of the bunker (aka the house).

The family is still home, and I smile at them as I enter, my eyes flitting about. There's an elderly black lady with a cane and white hair, dressed in her best: a white blouse, demure black skirt, and sensible shoes. I feel like a tramp next to her, though I'm wearing khaki capris and a white T-shirt, nothing remotely objectionable.

Beside the grandma is a little girl with two braids, secured at the ends with red barrettes in the shape of bows. She's adorable in black Mary Janes, a pink skirt, and a white shirt that says "Princess." Her dark eyes are wide as she takes Josh and me in. She's holding the hand of an even younger little boy. He's wearing blue overalls. Their clothes are old and worn, but clean and pressed.

The camera guys are setting up to tape footage to use for before-and-after reactions. I'm already miced, but I wait for the crew to finish hooking the family up before I go over. While I wait, I can't take my eyes off the little girl. Who would have thought a child in this war zone would dream of being a princess? Who would have believed I'd have something in common with her?

"Hi." I reach for the grandmother's hand, and we shake. She's so little, and her hand feels like it's made of bird bones. "I'm Allison Holloway. Nice to meet you."

She nods. "I'm Eulalia Jackson, and this is Lena and Duke."

I smile. "Like Lena Horne and Duke Ellington?"

The tiny woman's eyes light up. "That's right. They're my daughter's kids, and she named them some Zulu names, but I can't remember them. She's in prison, so I call them Lena and Duke. Much better, don't you think?"

"Much." I look at the little girl. "How old are you?"

She holds up five fingers, then, reluctantly raises her other hand and lifts one more.

"Six?"

She nods.

"What about Duke?"

She holds up four fingers.

"Four? Wow. You guys are pretty grown-up."

"Excuse me, Miss Holloway. We need to get some footage of them alone," one of the production assistants says, and I scoot out of the way. An hour later, Mrs. Jackson has shown us around the small, neat house, and then the family's taken off to God knows where for the eight hours we've been given to do the kamikaze makeover. A carpenter and painter have arrived, and we're ready to start. Josh and Miranda are making notes and pulling out tape measures and yardsticks when Mr. Watanabe, the director, gives us our decorating staple.

A dozen vibrators. In various colors. Batteries included.

"What the fudge is this¿" I ask when Yamamoto hands me the box.

"Sweetie, if you don't know—"

"Shut up, Josh. I know *what* it is. *Why* is he giving it to me¿"

I look to Yamamoto, our little translator, and he turns to Watanabe, who says something in Japanese, smiles, and walks away.

"Uh-oh," Josh moans.

"Where's he going¿ What did he say¿"

"He say that the Japanese group have same challenge. You must use sex toy in every room. He say, be creative."

I look at Josh and then Miranda, who's come to examine the box o'vibrators. I hold them out to her. "Did you know about this¿"

"About what¿" She smiles innocently. Aha! Miranda *never* smiles.

"Miranda, I'm not doing this. This is not decorating. Did you meet that woman and her grandkids¿ They don't want vibrators in their house."

"They agreed to the contract or we wouldn't be here," Miranda says.

"I don't give a fudge. I'm not going to make that nice woman's house look trashy. My parents are going to watch this show. My grandma. I am not decorating with vibrators."

Miranda lowers her voice. "Then don't make it look trashy. Look at it as a challenge."

I glance at Josh. He appears undecided, but I'm firmly unconvinced.

"Fine," Miranda says, "then go back to the office. But you

might as well clean your desk out while you're there because Dai Hoshi is going to sue us for breach of contract, and when I'm done paying the legal bills, I won't have enough for your salary."

Fudge it! Why did I sign that goddamn contract without reading it? I feel like I've made a deal with the devil. Josh gives me a wobbly smile. "I think we're screwed."

I hold up a safari-print vibrator. "Well, we've got the right equipment."

Despite my reservations, I get to work. No one can say that I'm not a team player, and to my surprise, things go really well for the first hour or so. Josh and I are used to working together, and even Miranda can be tolerable when she wants to be.

First, Miranda outlines what she'd like to do to the house. The walls are white, so she wants to paint them and add touches of color to the living room with different fabrics and materials. We've brought a varied supply with us, so this shouldn't be a problem. A pillow here, a slipcover there, a throw rug over there.

Then Josh suggests we build some shelves. The Jacksons have a lot of books, but they're all in piles on the floor. I suggest we stagger the length of the shelves and offset them with artwork, and Miranda orders me to find some family pictures and frame them, using materials in the van.

There are only two photos in the living room, so I head to the bedrooms to find more. One of the cameras follows me, of course.

In the main bedroom, I find a photo album on the dresser and flip through it, looking for pictures to frame. I start at the back with pictures of Lena and Duke at Christmas and work my way to the front, where there are lots of black-and-white photos of women in forties-style dresses and men in hats leaning on shiny cars. Bingo.

But I don't jump up and get started. Instead, I look at the pictures for a long time. The buildings behind the men and women could best be described as ramshackle. The roads are dusty, the people's clothing threadbare and patched, and still the faces are smiling and full of happiness.

How could these people be so happy when they had so little? I think about my shopping excursion last weekend. I spent more than a thousand dollars, easy. Why does it take so much to make me happy?

Carefully, I take out the pictures, then head to the van to get supplies for frames. The carpenter is already out there, working on the bookshelf, so I use some of his materials. I decide to keep the frames simple, so I choose black wood and basic matting.

As I work, I can feel the eyes of the gang members on me, but the camera is on me, too, so I don't worry too much. About half an hour later, I look up to wipe sweat from my forehead and see the painter walking by.

Oh, my God.

His overalls are splattered with paint. Pink paint.

With a sense of impending doom, I look at the house and see it's half gray, half Frolicking Fuchsia. "Miranda!" I call. "You might want to come out here."

When she does, her reaction is about what I expected. "What is this?" she screeches, pointing to the house.

Josh follows and is immediately attacked.

"Josh, I thought you were bringing Tranquil Fern. Why is the painter wearing Frolicking Fuchsia?"

Josh looks at the house, runs to the van, and pulls out paint can after paint can. He moans. Miranda and I huddle

around, and I get a sinking feeling in my gut. In all the hur-
rying and mayhem of preparations yesterday, Josh must
have accidentally pulled fuchsia from the storage closet at
work.

"Do we have time to go back and get the green?" I ask.

Miranda shakes her head, then turns to the painter. "This
is all wrong. We'll have to mute the colors. Find me some
white, and I'll mix it to a pale pink." She stays at the van
with him while Josh and I head inside the house to work on
the shelf area.

The paint episode is put behind us, but by the time Miranda has it sorted out, time is getting short. We're all split
up, working faster now, and I'm in the back hanging curtains
in one of the bedrooms. I've just about got the draping right
when a face appears on the other side of the window. I'm so
wrapped up in what I'm doing that the face startles me, and
I jump back and squeal. The entire crew comes running.

The kid on the other side smiles, raises his spray can, and
keeps working.

"Hey!" I yell. I can't believe the audacity of this kid.
"Hey!" I storm through the house, out the front door, and
come face-to-face with the gang member. Besides my usual
accompaniment of cameras, I have an audience of other
gangsters, watching from the porch next door.

They're still drinking. One of them stands and says,
"How do you like our decorating?"

I follow his outstretched hand and see the gang initials on
the side of the neon-pink house. The kid holding the spray
paint can laughs, howling until I grab the collar of his T-shirt.
I don't usually manhandle adolescents, but I'm tired, dirty,
and running out of time on this project.

"Look, kid, what do you think you're doing? We're trying

to make this house look nice. You're vandalizing it. Maybe I need to call the cops."

He shakes my hand off and brushes his shirt back into place. "You go ahead, bitch. I'm only doing what those guys paid me for." He points to the front of the house, where Yamamoto and Watanabe are watching us.

I should have known. What is reality TV without conflict? I glare at the kid. "Fine. You earned your money. Now get out of here. You can wreck your neighborhood when we leave."

He snorts. "Right. Like you care. You act like you're doing this for us, but all you want is the money."

I find the painter and beg him to go back there and fix the damage, and in the meantime, I go back inside and join Josh in a heap on the floor.

Miranda is collapsed delicately in one of the reupholstered chairs. The six hours we've been here feel like a hundred and six, and we're sweaty, smelly, and covered with paint, caulk, sealant, and adhesive.

The house doesn't look as unfinished as I'd feared. It's been mostly painted, wallpapered, rearranged, recovered, uncovered, and, yes, accessorized with nine vibrators. We've made them into lamp stands, door handles, artwork, and book stands. I stare at them and hope Mrs. Jackson can forgive me. We still need to add some finishing touches—lighting, new materials, new sheets and comforters—but I think we'll finish in time.

On the floor beside me, Josh turns his head toward mine. "We'd better win."

"No million dollars is worth this." I put an arm over my forehead. "My parents are going to disown me."

"Better them than me," Miranda says. "Now that we've

made it through one show, the others should be a piece of cake."

Josh and I groan in tandem. "Ugly-ass houses, fine. Sex toys, fine," Josh says. "But I draw the line at anything truly tasteless."

I look around the bedecked and be-vibrated neon-pink house. "Josh, we crossed that line a long, long time ago."

7

I Won't Dance

Friday morning Miranda, Josh, and I assemble for *Kamikaze Makeover!'s* second taping. With only one day between shows, we're all pretty frazzled, caught between trying to keep up with work at the office and preshow prep work.

But we three had a little powwow last night, while we were packing supplies for today's show—no Frolicking Fuchsia faux pas this time—and we're ready for whatever the producers throw at us.

First of all, in preparation for another trek into the ghetto, we've all worn our grungiest clothes. TV cameras or not, this time we're not going to enter gangland dressed like moving targets. In our stained jeans, faded eighties concert T-shirts, and unwashed hair—except Josh, who's bald—we look like we've been living in the *Kamikaze Makeover!* van rather than just traveling in it.

But as soon as we've been on the road for about ten minutes, our sunny, take-no-prisoners mood grows overcast. We're not heading for Englewood. We're not heading for south Chicago at all. We're driving north on Lakeshore Drive, toward the North Shore and the heart of Chicago high society.

When we finally pull to a stop in front of a cottage that looks like it's straight from the pages of *Chicago Home & Garden,* I think we're all feeling even more anxious to turn around than we did in Englewood. The camera teams and production managers clamber out, and finally Miranda bestirs herself and says, "Well, at least we know we won't be using sex toys to decorate here."

"Yeah, but what *will* we be using? Do either of you know who lives here?" I ask.

The cottage is huge and looks to be a product of the early 1900s. From the attention to the setting and the landscaping, I'm betting it was designed by Jens Jensen, famous architect and conservationist.

Miranda shakes her head, but Josh nods slowly. "It's one of the Chippenhall residences. I did some work on it before I joined Interiors by M."

I close my eyes. "Not Lucinda Chippenhall."

Josh nods.

"Oh, man. I can't do this. Lucinda Chippenhall is on every charitable board and committee my mother's on. They're rivals. You know, who can get the most donations or the best bigwig to chair an event, even whose kids get into the best schools or marry the richest."

"Guess you lost that one," Miranda sneers. There are times when I really wish Miranda weren't my boss. Then I'd tell her where to stick her snide comments.

"The point is, Miranda, this woman searches for ways to make my family look bad. With me on the team, we can't win this one."

"Wrong," Miranda says, pointing a long red nail at me. "The homeowner doesn't vote. The team of professional judges does."

"I thought it was a call-in thing," Josh says. "Like *American Idol.*"

"No," she answers. "There are three world-renowned designers, and they judge."

There's a loud knock on the window, and we all jump. Yamamoto is outside, looking anxious and ticked-off. "Let's go," he mouths.

I take a deep breath and climb out. After I'm miced, we're shown into the gorgeous house by a woman in a maid uniform. We walk on Persian rugs worth thousands of dollars and catch glimpses of art worth even more, and then when we reach the living room, we stand in various locations for lighting tests and good camera angles.

"Josh," I whisper while one of the grips shines a portable light in my face. "What the hell are we doing here?"

He looks around the exquisite room with its simple, elegant decor: crystal Mikasa vases, antique lamps, lots of space and pale colors. Light spills into the room from the French doors at the back, and it glints off the crystal and makes the polished baby grand piano gleam.

"Penance," he answers finally. "I think this is hell."

I hear a *tap-tap*ping and look up to see a woman in a pink Chanel suit and tiny pink heels bearing down on us.

"No, that's hell," I say, then paste on a beauty queen smile.

"Oh, my," Lucinda Chippenhall of the pink Chanel says, looking around the crowded living room of her home. There are wires and cables piled high and thick as pythons snaking everywhere. About a dozen grips, production assistants, and technicians are standing around, some working, most chatting on cell phones, and then, in the center, are Josh, Miranda, and me: the three hobos.

"Allison Holloway?" Mrs. Chippenhall says, narrowing her eyes at me. "Is that you?"

The noise and talking around us quiet, and the cameras swing around to capture the moment.

"Hi, Mrs. Chippenhall. Isn't this crazy?" I give an innocent shrug.

"Hmm. You look . . . different. I thought you were prettier last time I saw you. How is your mother? She really should stop with the Botox."

I bite my tongue. As if Lucinda Chippenhall hasn't had her own share of work. God, if this section makes the show, my mother will kill me.

"Are you sure you're capable of this kind of work?" Lucinda Chippenhall asks.

Translation: I don't want some amateur like you touching my million-dollar house.

"Oh, absolutely," I answer. "You're in good hands. This is Miranda, the M in Interiors by M."

"I see. Still, I'll feel better if I'm here to supervise." She plants her feet and crosses her skinny arms over her tiny chest.

"Is that allowed?" I whisper to Josh, pulling at my faded, torn Smiths T-shirt from 1988.

"Are you going to tell her to leave?"

Hell, no. And the Japanese aren't going to tell her to leave, either. She might do something interesting they can capture with the cameras. Watanabe comes over and hands us a box. It's surprisingly light today.

Yamamoto then begins to explain our task. "The lady only give us permission to work in the living room. You have eight hours to transform it, and you must use all of these."

He tips the box and about thirty empty Campbell's soup cans pour out.

"Soup cans?" Josh says, keeping his voice low so that Mrs. Chippenhall—peering over a camera at us—doesn't hear. "We're not decorating with soup cans in Lucinda Chippenhall's home."

Yamamoto shrugs. "Then you lose."

"But why soup cans?" Miranda asks.

"American art. Andy Warhol used them. You will, too." He touches his watch, indicating that the clock is ticking.

Looking around the Chippenhall living room, it's hard to imagine thirty soup cans in here.

"This is never going to work," Josh mumbles, smiling for the cameras. "If there was some clutter, that'd be one thing, but this room—"

I know what he means. Everything already has a place, and the feng shui is perfect. Why would we mess with perfection? Of course, the Jackson house didn't need a pile of vibrators scattered throughout, either. A little paint, some curtains, and it would have been cozy as could be. I don't get this show. Most makeover shows take someone or something that needs fixing and make a transformation. This show takes places that are just fine and tries to mess them up. How did I get to be a part of this?

"Okay!" Miranda says, clapping her hands and securing the attention of the cameras. "Here's what we'll do. Josh, you and I will work on a new layout for the furniture. I want to open that space up"—she points to a corner that could be better utilized—"and distribute the furniture better. I'm also thinking brighter colors. Josh, mix me up a few different shades of blue." The room is pale yellow now, but blue would liven it up a bit.

I watch Mrs. Chippenhall's reaction to this, and though her lips thin, she seems amenable.

"Later we'll change out some of the fabrics," Miranda continues. "Allison, you can work on that, but first I want you to do something with those." She points to the soup cans. "Make them look"—she twists her mouth—"elegant."

She and Josh tramp back out to the van, one of the cameras following, while I stare at the pile of soup cans and Mrs. Chippenhall stares at me.

"You're not seriously thinking of putting those"—Mrs. Chippenhall points accusingly at the soup cans—"in my sitting room."

"Um . . ." I look at Watanabe, but he's smiling and nodding, lapping this up. "I'm going to make them into a work of art," I say.

Mrs. Chippenhall's thin lips narrow to razor-sharp. "Are you an artist? I thought you were a decorator." The way she says *decorator* makes me feel like one of her domestics.

Because I am the kind of person who takes the high road—and because were I to open my mouth I would probably get myself fired—I don't say anything. Miranda said to make these soup cans elegant. Elegant? Even Monet wouldn't make these soup cans elegant.

But that gives me an idea. I grab my sketchbook and make a quick design.

"What are you doing?" Mrs. Chippenhall asks, peering over my shoulder. Feeling like I'm back in sixth grade taking a spelling exam, I cover my sketch with my arm. Lifting my wrist a bit, I scribble some notes for Miranda and Josh to look at later. Then I put the sketchbook facedown and get to work stripping the labels off the cans. I intercept

Miranda and Josh on their way back in with the light blue they've chosen for the room. I explain my idea, and it's a hit.

But that means I'm going to need to cut about twenty-five of the soup cans in half. No one said we had to use the whole soup can. So I grab the carpenter, and he gets out the power saw and starts slicing. We've got about four cans cut in half when the clouds that have loomed all morning open up and big fat drops of rain pelt us. Obviously we can't use a power saw out in the rain, so we decide to wait it out. It's no major hardship—gotta love hanging out with a man who can handle powerful machinery—but after an hour of pouring rain, I can't afford to wait any longer.

"We're going to have to bring the saw inside and cut the cans there," I tell the carpenter.

He shrugs. "It's your ass, not mine."

We don't even have the saw halfway in the door when Mrs. Chippenhall swoops down on us. "*What* are you people doing?"

I motion the carpenter to continue. "I'm sorry, Mrs. Chippenhall, but it's raining outside and we can't work with electric saws in the rain."

"Well, you can't bring that machine in here!" She motions to her objets d'art and her expensive rugs.

"We'll be careful," I say, dropping a dirty tarp over her rug, but she's not convinced. She hovers over us, wringing her hands and ordering her maid to stand by with a broom and dustpan.

Finally the carpenter finishes cutting my cans. It's taken way longer than I'd planned, but I gotta give the hottie a break. Every time he turned on the saw Mrs. Chippenhall covered her eyes and looked ready to swoon.

By the time all my cans are painted, Miranda and Josh

have the room cleared and taped, and I give them a hand with the painting. We all take turns stumbling over Mrs. Chippenhall, who is constantly in the way, and when she starts pointing out spots we missed, I have the urge to spatter that pink suit with blue polka dots.

Fortunately, Miranda—seeing murder in my eyes—releases me from painting to go back to my cans for the detail work. Martha Stewart, look out.

After about six hours, with only two to go, the industrial-size fans we brought in from the van have done their work, and the walls are dry enough for me to start mine. Normally I wouldn't touch the walls for at least twenty-four hours, but I don't have much choice today. So while Miranda and Josh move furniture and sew throw pillows, I get out the yellow carpenter's glue. I apply it to the edges of a can and hold it up to the wall, ready to position it.

Just as I'm about to press the glue to the wall, Mrs. Chippenhall yells, "No!"

She startles me, and I drop the can, gluing it to the floor instead. Josh runs over with turpentine and cleans up the mess while I glare at Mrs. Chippenhall. But when Josh hands me the can again, I don't even have a chance to apply glue before Mrs. Chippenhall tries to snatch it from me.

"Stop it!" I tell her. "We're running out of time."

"I don't care. I don't want soup cans on my walls!"

I look at Miranda, then Watanabe. Watanabe is smiling. The little prick is loving this. Miranda gives me a long look, then turns her back.

What was that city in Vietnam where the soldiers killed all those innocent civilians and the military head honchos tried to bury the story? My Lai? Miranda's turning a blind eye now, but when the footage comes out, we're going to get an interior-designing court-martial.

Josh and I exchange looks, and then I nod at Mrs. Chippenhall, and Josh sweeps her up and off her feet. I think he would have carried her à la Rhett carrying Scarlett O'Hara, but she starts squirming and he ends up throwing her over his shoulder.

"I got her!" he calls. "Get to work, Allison!"

I do. In a frenzy of activity, I attach my half soup cans to the walls in random places. The soup cans are blue to match the wall and then painted with little pink, yellow, and red flowers for accent. With the angry cries of the imprisoned Mrs. Chippenhall echoing from the next room, I paint more flowers and stems, seemingly rising out of the cans on the wall above each soup can.

I take the last five cans and fill them with dirt and flowers from Mrs. Chippenhall's garden. I try my soup can vases in half a dozen places, Miranda offering lots of suggestions, and just before Yamamoto's watch beeps, indicating that time has run out, I place the last one.

Josh frees Mrs. Chippenhall and she *tap-taps* back into the room behind him just as time runs out. She doesn't even look at the room, but she points at me. "I'm going to get you for this, Allison Holloway. And your mother, too!"

While the camera crew films the room for the after footage, I look around. I wouldn't say we've improved the room. Soup cans don't look elegant, no matter what I do, but we've taken the room from elegant metropolitan to French country. Again, I'm not so sure that's an improvement.

I want to feel a sense of accomplishment after all this work, but like the first show, it just isn't there. We came in, we subdued the natives, we made the room over using the required materials, but I don't feel like we made the room better.

I think Miranda and Josh have some of the same feelings because they're silent on the drive back to the office. Fed up with work, I skip the office and go straight home and plop on the couch. I don't feel like getting ready to go out, even if it is a Ciara St. Loren fashion show with Nicolo.

Instead, I flip on the TV and *While You Were Out* is on. For the first time in recent memory, I switch the channel. *Fear Factor* is on the next station, and I turn that, too. E! has the *True Hollywood Story* of reality TV stars, but I can't stomach that, either.

I mean, what are these people looking for¿ Fame¿ Money¿ Why are they messing with lives that are perfectly good already¿ Why am I¿

When Nicolo calls a while later, I tell him I'll meet him at the fashion show. He doesn't like it, but I'm trying to keep our relationship casual and friendly. I learned a long time ago not to get involved with guys I work with. There was a professor at Columbia College in Chicago who taught History of Architecture I. Now I don't know about you, but I think *history, architecture,* and *ew!* But when I walked into Professor Montford's room—Stéphane's room—I remember thinking, *ooh.*

Stéphane Montford was an Olivier Martinez clone, but sexier. Longish brown hair, dark, brooding eyes, straight nose, soft sensuous lips. God, the man knew what to do with those lips.

He and I had a little fling the first semester of my junior year. It was really hot, then really cold. Unfortunately, Stéphane also taught History of Architecture II. For a whole semester, we glared at each other three days a week. And the bastard gave me a D!

Well, architecture isn't my forte, so maybe I deserved the D, but it taught me a lesson. Nicolo and I still have to work together for a few weeks, so if things don't pan out, I could be in for a shitload of misery.

Since this is a fashion show, I dress to kill. I put on a short, short, short black skirt by MaxMara, high, high, high heels by Jimmy Choo, and a white and silver top by Armani.

It's no fun being around a bunch of models all night, but I put in the extra effort anyway. The show's at an upscale club downtown. I've been there before, but I arrive a few minutes late, toss the car-struck valet the keys to the Z4, and walk in.

The club is dark, and a runway has been set up in the center of the dance floor. Funky techno music plays, and people are starting to find seats on both sides of the runway and standing at the second-floor railings. I don't see Nicolo, so I go to the bar and order a mojito with a stalk of sugarcane for garnish. I take a sip and scan the club. Still no Nicolo. But there are lots of Chicago bigwigs, and I wave at a couple from my parents' country club.

Someone comes up behind me, and I smile, anticipating Nicolo's low murmur in my ear. Snap! The strap of my bra slaps against my back.

"Ouch!" I spin around and there's Grayson, grinning like he used to when I first started wearing bras and he, four years older at sixteen, snapped them at every opportunity.

"I hate to tell you this, but someone stole the bottom of your skirt."

I roll my eyes. Big brothers. "Ha-ha. Snap my bra again, and the next time you're not paying attention, I'll snap your underwear."

"I don't wear underwear."

"Yeck. TMI."

"Aw, you know you love me." He hugs me, then says, "Since we're giving out info, what are you doing here?"

"I'm the guest of a VIP," I say and toss my hair like I used to at thirteen. It still irritates him. "What are you doing here?"

He leans one elbow against the bar. "I'm in the fashion show."

"Oh." I probably should have figured that out, since Gray is a model. Gray is the most gorgeous man on the planet. Yes, I know he's my brother, and my opinion is slanted, but I'm being totally objective here. Gray is the best-looking man I know. He's also my favorite brother. He's my only brother, but that doesn't make him any less great. Especially considering he's the only person that keeps me sane around my parents.

Looking at him now, it's hard to believe he's the same scrawny kid who sported two rows of braces, had stringy brown hair, and wore the same jeans and T-shirt until my mother pried them away from his dirty body to wash. Now the braces are gone, and he's got straight whiter-than-white teeth. Of course, you'd never know it because he never smiles. I guess smiling isn't cool in modeldom. His stringy brown hair is still kind of long and stringy, but it's the look now, and these days it's blond.

He's wearing tight jeans and a loose shirt, open to reveal his six-pack abs. He's very proud of those. We work out together sometimes, and I've learned that Gray and I have different ideas about how long a workout should last. The first time we went to the gym together, I left after an hour to get a smoothie. He told me he was going to finish with his abs and then he'd be done. I bought the smoothie, drank the smoothie, and then went looking for him, and he was still crunching.

Grayson is fab, but there is one annoying thing about him—wherever we go, girls fall all over him. It has to be the abs. I'd like to be magnanimous and say that all the fawning twentysomethings don't faze him, but Gray is pretty much a player. He needs a girl like Natalie to settle him down.

Now he's giving me that intense model look, which always seems sort of out of place on his baby face. He's thirty-six, but he looks twenty-four. Disgusting, isn't it? You'd think by thirty-six his modeling career and womanizing days would be over. Nope. Gotta love those Holloway genes.

"You look good," he says after a minute. "I like your hair that way, but you should push it forward more." He reaches out, presumably to perfect my hairstyle, and tousles it violently instead. Brothers never change.

I grab his hand and reach for his head, but he says, "Whoa! Not the hair, baby."

"Jerk," I say, pushing my once carefully coiffed hair out of my eyes, and he laughs and gives me a hug. He's like six-three, so even in my FM Jimmy Choos, I feel like a little kid again.

"I see you have found another companion," an accented voice behind me says. Gray releases me, and I turn to Nicolo. His face is hard and his mouth a thin line.

"Nicolo, I was looking for you."

"In his chest?"

I raise a brow and glance at Gray to see if he thinks this is as funny as I do. He's not smiling. I turn back to Nicolo. "Are you jealous?"

He snorts. "Not at all. If you want to go home with this pretty boy, go ahead."

See how young Gray looks? "Well, considering the pretty boy is my brother, I don't think that's going to happen. Grayson, Nicolo. Nicolo, Grayson Holloway."

"Hey," Grayson says, inclining his head coolly. I frown. You'd think the guy could at least shake Nicolo's hand.

Nicolo doesn't attempt to shake Grayson's hand, either. "I am sorry. I misunderstood."

The lights flicker up and down, and Grayson releases me. I didn't even notice that he still had his arm around my shoulder.

"I gotta go change. See ya tomorrow, Allie." He kisses my cheek and looks at Nicolo like he might say something but turns and walks away instead.

I shake my head. "Sorry, he was raised by wolves. He hasn't quite got the hang of human interaction yet."

Nicolo waves a hand and offers his arm. "I am the same way with my younger sisters. He is older, yes?"

I nod, distracted as Nicolo leads me to two reserved seats on the side of the catwalk. I've never been a front-row girl at a fashion show before, and when the lights go down and the music starts up, I can hardly contain my excitement.

The first model struts out in a gorgeous flowy chocolate dress, and I lean forward to memorize every stitch. Nicolo says in my ear, "Your brother was really adopted?"

"No." I glance at him. "Just a joke." I turn away, watching the next model, dressed in gray wool slacks and a checked wool peacoat, unbuttoned enough that we can see she's not wearing a top underneath.

"He does not look like you."

I glance at Nicolo, reluctant to take my eyes from the runway. "It's dark in here. If you saw us in the light, you'd be able to tell."

"Hmm." Nicolo seems satisfied for the moment, so I focus back on the stage in time to see a model in a black chiffon dress turn off the runway. Damn.

A few minutes later, the first male model comes out, and I sit forward to watch for Gray. I've seen him model a hundred times. He's really good—a natural—but watching someone you know so well put on a show can be pretty hilarious. He looks so mean, his eyes ferocious and his mouth pouty. It cracks me up every time.

A minute later he strides out in a charcoal suit—jacket, slacks, and tie—no shirt. I stifle a giggle. He has to show off those abs.

"Why do you laugh?"

I shake my head. "He cracks me up when he models. His face—" I start laughing again.

The next time Gray comes out—this time wearing a shirt, but also wearing fifties-style glasses—I start laughing again.

"You will upset him," Nicolo says.

"No, with the lights, they can't see anything up there," I say.

"Really?" I feel his hand on my thigh, and look down to see his white fingers caress the expansive area of leg between my knee and the skirt's hem.

I glance at him, and he's watching the models intently, as though the last thing on his mind is the way his fingers are now sliding up my inner thigh.

"Nicolo. I said the models can't see, not the rest of the audience."

"They are watching the models." His hand slides higher, and I gasp. His mouth curves into a smile as the tips of his fingers graze the lace of my panties. He gives me a sideways look, then one finger slides the scrap of lace aside and touches flesh.

Oh, my God. If he moves another fraction of an inch, I'm going to come off my chair. Somehow I manage a strangled, "Stop."

"You know you want this."

What? His hand moves again, but I don't feel any pleasure. "No, I don't. Not here."

He looks at me, his expression curious. "Stop your teasing. You are no virgin." He smirks. "Far from it, from what I hear."

My mouth drops open, and I wiggle away from his hand, which he pulls back very reluctantly. "Are you calling me a slut?"

His eyes skim my shirt, skirt, then shoes, his answer clear on his face.

"Excuse me." Ice-cold rage coursing through me, I stand and stalk away. It feels like all eyes are on me as I walk past the other front-row girls and through the club. Behind me, the show goes on, and I give the club's door a vicious push. I hate to leave good fashion. I hand the valet my ticket as the door swings open behind me.

"I grow tired of chasing you. I do not like standing on street corners and arguing. It is common."

"I guess I'm just a common girl."

He spreads his arms. "What did I do now? Do not tell me you didn't like me touching you. You were wet."

I dart a glance at the two remaining valets. They are trying very hard to pretend they didn't hear that last part.

"Well, that comment's going to be in the paper tomorrow."

He dismisses the valets with a wave, then gives me a narrow look. "I embarrassed you inside?"

I shake my head. "It'll take more than you feeling me up to embarrass me."

"Then what is the problem?"

"You treated me like a whore!"

The valets aren't even pretending not to listen now, but as they're both frowning at Nicolo, I figure they're on my side.

"I gave you pleasure."

"Bullshit. You wanted to see how far you could go. I'm

not some royalty groupie, following you around and waiting for a handout. You think because you've got a title, you can do whatever you want. Guess what? I'm not impressed."

He doesn't respond, and I don't know if his silence is out of agreement or anger.

The valet pulls up with my car and holds the door for me.

"You know what, little Prince Nicolo? Why don't you go home and enjoy your *droit du seigneur* there, because this American isn't interested in stroking your ego." I climb in, punch the button, and the BMW's top goes down. "Or any other part of you."

The next day, Gray doesn't say anything about Nicolo on the drive to the basketball camp, and I'm glad.

"This is a pretty area," I say when we're out of the city.

"Yeah. At least the last moments of my life will be spent in—Jesus, watch out for that truck!"

I wave his whining away. "Loosen up. You're supposed to be a cool camp counselor today." Grayson just winces as I pass an eighteen-wheeler, narrowly avoiding colliding with another car as I skirt in front of the truck a second before the oncoming car passes us.

The camp is on Fox Lake in Ingleside, an area west of Chicago. As I drive into the Illinois interior, the traffic thins, the lanes narrow, and the trees thicken. We pass pine, maple, oak, linden, and butternut trees. The buildings and houses disappear, and we drive by cornfields and farmhouses.

The area reminds me of Lake Geneva, Wisconsin—about ninety minutes from Chicago—where my parents have a cottage. Gray and I call it a cottage because everyone else does, but I doubt most people would consider a mammoth structure with two stories, a formal dining room, five bedrooms, three and a half baths, a pool, a garden, and a boathouse a cottage. Of course, compared to the medieval-style castles and English manor houses down the street and across the lake, our house *is* a mere cottage.

The first year we stayed in Lake Geneva for the summer, I was six and Gray was ten. There aren't a lot of happy memories with my family. My mom can be really cold and my dad was sort of absent, busy with business. In later years, Gray was in trouble all the time or zoned on drugs, but that first summer in Lake Geneva was like a fairy tale.

It was the July Fourth holiday, and we had two things on our minds: fireworks and swimming. We spent hours in the water. I must have asked Gray to throw me off the end of the dock a hundred times, and he did it every time. At night we built a campfire, although my mother argued that we had a perfectly good fireplace inside, and sat on logs roasting marshmallows for s'mores. I burned or lost all mine in the flames, but Gray gave me his, and I ate s'mores until I was sick.

"Yeah, you stole all Mom and Dad's attention, and you stole my marshmallows, too," Grayson says when I mention that summer. My tires crunch as we turn off the main road onto a smaller gravel one that will take us back to the camp. Almost immediately, the sky above us is obliterated by the thick foliage of criss-crossed tree branches above us. I was reluctant at first, but now I'm glad I agreed to come. The day is gorgeous—sunny and mild—and maybe I'll be able to sneak away from the kids and lay out by the lake for an hour. I know, I know, UV exposure, but it's too pretty out to stay inside today.

"Please, you weren't innocent, Grayson. You only gave me the marshmallows so I wouldn't tell Mom and Dad you were kissing that chick from the house next door. What was her name?"

"Hell if I know. See up ahead? That's the parking—slow down. Jesus Christ!"

I slide into a parking space. "How are you getting to the lake tomorrow? Want me to pick you up in the morning?"

Gray sighs. "I don't know, Allie. I know we always get together for Memorial Day weekend, but I don't feel like having it out with Dad again this year. Maybe it would be better if I stayed home."

I stare at him. "And leave me all alone with *them*?"

He shrugs.

"Oh, come on. Who's going to dunk me in the pool? Who's going to sneak into my room in the middle of the night and scream, 'I'm a vampire!' and scare the crap out of me?"

"Mom?" His lips thin, which is the model version of a smile.

"Right."

We climb out of the car and head toward a cabin with a sign reading "REGISTRATION."

"I think the last time she went in your room unannounced, she was more surprised than you."

"Shut up."

"What was that guy's name? Tony? Travis?"

I give him a playful shove. "Go away."

And he does. He leaves me to my own volunteering. I glance around, taking in the stereotypical rustic-looking cabins, mess hall, volleyball and basketball courts. In one area, canoes are stacked in bunches. Beyond that is a trail I assume leads to the lake, which isn't visible from here.

The atmosphere of the camp reminds me of Covenant Harbor, the camp across from Maytag Point in Lake Geneva. I begged to be allowed to attend the summer when I was eight, and I lasted about two hours. The counselors wouldn't let me shower and blow-dry my hair right after swimming, and that was that. Hopefully, this experience will be better.

Four hours later, it's almost two, and I'm still stuck in Registration. I've learned that this is a Bible camp for the churches in this area during the week—Camp Risen Son—and used by the city of Chicago on the weekend for a program to benefit inner-city kids.

I've also learned how to extract a splinter from a dirty big toe, how to check for lice, and how much Bactine to apply to a cut.

Now I'm showing kids how to make hand puppets from brown paper lunch bags. It beats going through medical forms and waivers for three hours, like I had been, but it's a far cry from Gray's job, which is playing basketball outside with the kids we're supposed to be inspiring. So far all I've inspired is a headache. And I've been cooped up inside without AC all day.

Cindy, the perky twenty-three-year old camp counselor supervising activities, bounces in the door—literally, because her blonde hair is in pigtails—and says, "Hey kids! Time for a snack! Popsicles and snow cones in the cantina!"

I've noticed that every sentence she utters is exclamatory.

The kids drop their projects and stampede for the door, and Cindy! and I are left standing in the detritus of paper bags, crayons, yarn, and glue sticks.

"Oops!" she says. "I guess I should have asked them to clean up first! I'll round them up and we'll clean this in a jiffy!"

She bounces back outside, and I kneel down to start cleaning up the mess. I'm wearing frayed jean shorts and a tank top, my hair pulled into a long, straight ponytail. Even so, I'm hot and sweaty, and there's a SpongeBob SquarePants

sticker on my knee. "Fudge this," I say to no one in particular, peel the sticker off, and head outside.

The camp feels deserted, but when I look a few yards
away I see kids and volunteers spilling from the cantina.
Poor Grayson, he's got kids dangling from his arms and one
clinging to each leg.

I head the opposite way. I'm just a few yards into the
woods behind the registration cabin when I start to see
patches of Fox Lake through the foliage.

All I can think is: Very hot. Lake cool.

I break out of the woods and into a huge smile. The lake
is gorgeous—blue, calm, and at present forgotten. There's a
dock down the shore a bit, so I stride over there, shake off
my flip-flops, and stick a toe in the water. Heaven.

I pull my toe out and look over one shoulder, then the other.
I look across the lake, squinting in the sunlight. No one.

Fudge it. I'm going in. I shed my tank top and shimmy out
of my shorts, then hop into the water in my white cotton bra
and panties.

The water at the side of the dock only comes to my
belly, so I wrap my hair into a bun on top of my head, and
squat down until my shoulders are submerged. I linger for
a moment, enjoying the feel of the sun, the cool water,
the soft sand between my toes, and then I hear someone
laughing.

Fudge! I scoot under the dock and peer through the slats,
but I can only see the edge of the woodline in front of the
dock, and the laughter came from the right.

"No, you're sweaty from playing basketball all day!" a
familiar voice exclaims. Cindy!

Thank God. If it was one of the kids, I'd get arrested for
indecency with a child or something. I'm about to pop out
from under the dock when I hear the low rumble of a man's

voice. Cindy! and one of the male counselors? So I'm not the only one who's abandoned her duties.

I can still come out, but I decide to wait and see if they keep walking. I'd rather not jump out of the water wearing only my underwear if at all possible.

Cindy! giggles again, and I glance through the slats. She's at the end of the dock, her back to the lake and her boyfriend facing me. I can't see who he is, but his voice sounds familiar. Gray? No.

Then the guy puts his arm around Cindy!'s waist, spreading his hand over the small of her back. My own skin warms in response as he pulls her decisively, confidently against him and lowers his head to kiss her. My heart starts pounding— partly because I'm afraid they're going to have sex right here at the end of the dock and I'm going to be stuck in the lake while they go at it, and partly because Cindy!'s guy is hot. I don't know what he looks like, but simply watching the way he kissed her turns me on.

I peek through the slats again, but they're still kissing. His hand hasn't strayed under her shirt or moved to cup her ass yet, so maybe they'll stop soon. Cindy! laughs, and I edge out from under the dock to get a better view. (Oh, come on, like you wouldn't?) She reaches up to hug the guy, and he leans forward to return the embrace.

Dave.

8

Let's Face the Music and Dance

Oh, my God. What the fudge is Dave doing here? What the fudge is he doing kissing Cindy!¿

Fudge. Is Cindy! his girlfriend¿

"Wait, basketball," I mutter to myself. Dave likes basketball and he's a professional, so that's why he's here. But why is he kissing Cindy¿ Argh! Who cares if he's kissing Cindy¿

Okay, stop talking to yourself and think about how to get out of here. Rory's mom, Sunshine, is always saying that if you focus and direct your thoughts, you can change the world. She probably didn't mean change it by making Dave and Cindy! go away, but it's worth a try.

I duck back under the dock, close my eyes, and concentrate. Go away. Go back to camp. *Omm . . .*

God, I feel like an idiot. I open one eye and peer through

the slats. Cindy!'s heading back into the woods! Yes! Thank you, Sunshine.

No, no, no. Dave isn't leaving with her. He watches her walk away, then turns back to the lake and stands, hands on hips, staring at it.

It's water, Dave. Move on. *Ommm* . . .

But he doesn't move on, and suddenly I realize he's not staring at the lake, but at the dock. There's no way he sees me under here.

Fudging-A! My clothes are up there.

Dave frowns and steps onto the end of the dock.

Don't be curious, Dave. *Ommm.* Walk on. Walk on. *Omm.*

He starts down the dock. I swear, sometimes he does stuff just to piss me off. His footsteps echo above me, and I crouch back into the shadows. I'm going to have a word with Sunshine about all this energy-focusing crap.

Dave stops, bends down, and picks up my tank and shorts. "Armani? Who cuts up Armani jeans? Who leaves"—he pauses and peers through the slats—"is someone down there?"

"Go away."

He crouches down. "Allison?"

"No, it's not me—I mean, her." Damn.

"Are you naked under there?"

"No. Go away, Dave."

He looks at my clothes, then back at me. "What are you doing?"

Irritating man! Why does this stuff always happen with Dave? Why does he always see me at my worst? Why doesn't he ever see the glamorous Allison?

I duck out from under the dock, kneeling so my shoulders remain submerged in water. "Hand me my clothes. Stop grinning like that."

"Sorry." He holds my shorts and tank out, the clothes looking very small in his hand, but as I reach for them, he snatches them away.

"Dave!"

"You should have gone skinny-dipping." He eyes my bra strap. "If you get back in these clothes with wet underwear, you'll be uncomfortable the rest of the day."

He's right. I knew there was a reason people skinny-dipped. Well, another one.

"Here." He untucks his white T-shirt and pulls it over his head.

"What are you doing?" Not that I mind seeing his bare chest a foot from my face. I remember one time he told me that he played football at UCLA. He's got the perfect build for it.

"Use my shirt to dry off. You'll have to go commando, but it's better than wet underwear."

Hmm. That's actually a pretty good idea. His shirt will be wet when I give it back, but in the sun, it'll dry fast.

"Fine." I stand upright and put two hands on the deck to hoist myself up. Dave holds out a hand.

"Come on, I'll pull you out."

"Thanks." I wasn't looking forward to scrambling onto the deck in my underwear, which I think I mentioned was white cotton and in which I am now the star of my very own modified wet T-shirt contest.

Dave hauls me up, then hands me his shirt. He doesn't make a big deal of looking me over, but he doesn't look away, either. God, why couldn't he be a lecherous jerk? He'd be so much easier to hate.

"So, what are you doing here?" he asks as I slip his T-shirt over my head. It smells like things I'd associate with him—campfire smoke and pine. Masculine things. The shirt falls to mid-thigh.

"I'm volunteering. My brother's working here."

"Your brother? That's got to be Grayson."

"How'd you know?" I pick up my shorts and reach under the shirt to wriggle out of my panties.

He shrugs. "You two look a lot alike. Same"—he gestures vaguely—"oversupply of gorgeousness."

I glance at him sharply. Why did he say that?

"Want me to turn around?" His gaze lingers on the hem of the T-shirt. My hands are hidden beneath, but it doesn't take much to figure out they're on the waist of my panties.

"Why? My modesty's shot anyhow." I drop the underwear on the deck and step into the shorts.

"So you have modesty?"

I lift the shirt to button the shorts. "And you were being so nice."

I unsnap the bra, extract one arm then the other, and drop it to the ground. It lands on Dave's tennis shoes. Turning my back to him, I slip off his shirt and shake out my tank top.

"Do they have a class to teach girls how to get out of bras like that?" he says to my bare back. "So, you're a 32C."

I tug the tank on, then spin around and snatch my bra out of his hands. "Hey!" I scoop up my panties, fold them and the bra, and start for the shore. "Thanks. I really didn't want to be arrested for indecency with a child."

"Probably should have thought of that before you stripped down."

I glance over my shoulder. "Wow. Ya think?" I say and keep walking.

"Nice to see you, too. You're always sweetness and light."

"Save it for Cindy!"

At five o'clock, I'm starving, I'm bored, and I'm tired of all the hormone-infested boys staring at my braless chest. They're nipples, kids. Get over it.

Finally Grayson stomps into the registration cabin, where I'm now helping the nurse out with three kids who rolled around in poison ivy. "Hey, ready to head home?" Grayson asks.

I glare at him.

"That's a yes, I see. Hey, guys, what happened?"

"Poison ivy," the three eight-year-olds answer in unison. "It itches."

"Is Miss Allison making it feel better?" an unwelcome male voice says. I glance toward the door as Dave and Cindy! walk in.

"Tell her to kiss it. That usually helps." Dave winks at me, and Cindy! giggles.

I am barraged by pleas from the three boys for me to kiss their boo-boos. I persuade them to let me kiss their foreheads, as they didn't get the poison ivy there, and I kiss all three before they scamper to the parking lot to board the bus home.

"You know my sister?" Gray asks Dave, who's got his arm around Cindy! now.

"Yeah. I'm friends with Hunter and Rory."

Grayson frowns, and I say, "High school."

"Oh, yeah. Rory was cute, and that Hunter kid took you to homecoming, right? I didn't know they were together."

"They got together a few months ago."

"Cool. So, Dave, Cindy, want to go get a beer? I don't know about you, but these kids could drive you to drink."

"Gray, let's just go home," I say at the same time Dave and Cindy! say, "Great" and "That sounds like fun!"

Everyone looks at me—the party pooper—and I say, "Fun! Let's go."

Grayson laughs and slaps my back. "Come on, Allie. You look like you could use a drink."

Dave suggests a place on the other side of the lake where we can get dinner and—his main requirement—cheap beer, and Gray and I take my Z4, while Dave and Cindy! take his Hummer.

That's right. As if the Land Rover wasn't big enough, now he's driving a silver tank—I mean, Hummer.

At the Bait Shop—yes, that's the name of the restaurant Dave has selected—we grab a table on the patio and watch the sunset. The food takes forever to come, and when it finally arrives it's greasy guy food, so I order a fourth margarita and nibble on oily french fries.

Cindy! has like two beers and starts giggling and singing along with the honky-tonk band, playing covers of Jimmy Buffett and Garth Brooks. Every once in a while, she tries to get Dave involved, and he plays along with her, but I can tell he'd rather talk than sing. He and Gray are discussing basketball, doing the play-by-play of every game they've ever attended, seen, or heard about, and "Cheeseburger in Paradise" isn't holding Dave's attention right now.

Cindy! and I tried to talk to each other for the first five minutes. I can see why a guy would be attracted to her. She's blonde, pigtailed, and twenty-three. Add that she just graduated from college with a sociology degree and doesn't have a job yet because she's trying to find herself, and it becomes clear why I'm not enamored of her.

Finally, the band takes a break, and "Blue Suede Shoes" comes on the jukebox. Gray loves Elvis. He's taken Elvis's half-snarl and modified it into model chic.

"Allie, this is our song. Come dance." He hauls me out of my chair, at which point the margaritas go straight to my head, and I stumble.

"Maybe later, Gray."

"I'll dance with you! I'll dance with you!" Cindy! screams, jumping up and down.

"You know how to swing-dance?" Gray asks dubiously.

"A little. I'm a fast learner, though!"

"All right, let's give it a go." He grabs her hand and pulls her into the small group of couples lumbering away to the music. He shows her a few moves and a moment later, they're doing a decent job.

"Your brother's a good dancer," Dave says, moving to the chair next to mine so he can see the dance floor better.

"My grandmother was a hepster. She used to go to the Cotton Club in Harlem. Taught us the jitterbug, Susie-Q, trucking . . . lots of swing moves."

"What, no tango?"

"That, too, but Gray always gets carried away and dips me too low."

We're both watching the dancers, not looking at each other, so Dave surprises me when he lifts my empty margarita glass. "What is that? Four?"

"You watched your Sesame Street."

He laughs. "One margarita, two margarita, three margarita! Ha-ha-ha."

I grin in spite of my intention not to let him affect me. "You're a goof."

"Wow. I don't think I've ever been called that before."

I shrug. "I'm not used to drinking four margaritas on an empty stomach."

"You're drunk."

I think for a moment, stare at Gray and Cindy!, and say, "Yep."

"That bad of a day?"

"Oh, I don't know. I filed, cleaned up after a bunch of messy kids, watched you kiss Cindy, got caught in my underwear, and then spread calamine lotion over three itchy kids. Not my ideal Saturday."

"Why did my kissing Cindy drive you to drink?"

I whip to face him. "I didn't say that."

"Yeah, you did." He's leaning back in his chair, the bar's sting of festive lights illuminating his face in patches of red and gold. "You said you watched me kiss Cindy."

The waitress walks by, and I snag her arm. "Another margarita, please."

"You avoiding the question?"

"I'm not avoiding anything. I'm thirsty."

Another song comes on, I think this one is by Sammy Davis Jr., and the waitress returns with my drink. Dave hands her a credit card and asks her to close out the tab.

"Thanks," I say and sip the margarita. Like the four before, it's too strong and tastes like crap.

"I like that about you."

I frown at him. He's smiling again. He's always smiling. "I like how you don't argue when someone does something for you."

"What do you mean?"

I took my hair out of the ponytail when we arrived, and now he lifts a strand of it and twirls it around his finger. I try to pretend I don't notice.

"Like today when I gave you my shirt. You didn't argue, you just said thanks. Most girls would have argued or been all prissy—telling me not to look. And now when I paid the bill, you didn't argue. I like that."

I shrug. "If you didn't want to do it, you wouldn't. You know I can pay, I know I can pay. What's the big deal?"

I sip my margarita again, feeling the heat of the tequila slide into my belly. I cross my legs and my calf brushes against Dave's leg.

"And giving me your shirt this afternoon made sense. Why am I going to be illogical and argue or make a big deal out of telling you to turn around? I've got breasts. You know it, I know it, and I'm reasonably sure you've seen a pair before."

He doesn't answer, just releases my hair and watches Gray show Cindy! how to Charleston.

"I like *that* about *you*," I say, but I'm not sure I've said it aloud until Dave gives me a curious look.

"Wait a sec. I'm not hearing straight. *You* like something about *me*?"

"I *did*. I liked how you don't say stupid things like other guys."

I reach for the margarita glass, miss, and Dave hands it to me.

"I mean, like just now. You didn't say something stupid like, 'No, I've never seen breasts' or 'I've never seen any like yours.' I hate that bullshit." I drain the glass. "And this afternoon, you didn't make any wet T-shirt jokes or exploit the situation."

He laughs, and Frank Sinatra starts singing "They Can't Take That Away from Me."

"As much as I like being the good guy, I gotta tell you that I exploited your half-nakedness this afternoon as much as I could."

"Yeah. Oops." I wave an arm, knocking over an empty beer bottle that Dave catches before it hits the ground. "But you didn't make it obvious you were exploiting it. I like that."

"You like that I'm sneaky?"

I scowl at him. "Just forget it. I can't even compliment you."

He stands up. "Come on. We can't sit here when Frank's on."

"You like Frank?"

"Who doesn't?" He pulls me to my feet, his hand on my back to steady me, and takes me to the dance floor. I drape my arms around his neck, and he puts his hands on my back, pulling me close to him, just like he did with Cindy! this afternoon.

I let him lead, closing my eyes after a moment and resting my head on his shoulder. Everything is spinning. I hardly feel my legs or my arms.

"Where'd you learn to dance?" I say after a moment.

"Three older sisters."

I glance up at him. God, his mouth is so close. It seems like I've never wanted to kiss a guy as much as I want to kiss Dave right now. "Three sisters?" I force my lips to speak, so I don't kiss him.

"Yeah. They all took dancing lessons—ballet, tap, and ballroom—then graduated to the high school drill team. I was the token male ballroom partner. I can dip and twirl in my sleep." He dips me, and I laugh as my head spins.

"Did you really go to homecoming with Hunter?"

"No. He was homecoming king. I was queen. We never dated."

"Why not? Rory?"

"No, he's just not my type."

"Who's your type?" He glances down at me, and I can't take it anymore. I don't know if it's him, or too much to drink, or me just being an idiot, but I tug his mouth down to mine and kiss him. His hands tighten on my waist, and I feel the muscles of his shoulders bunch when I slip my tongue in his mouth. He responds, meeting me more than halfway, and then my head is really spinning. And then I'm falling because he's pulled away.

"Sorry," I say when everything isn't spinning anymore. "I don't know why I did that. You're just such a good kisser." Did I really say that? His jaw is set, and he's not looking at me, staring instead across the room. Cindy!

"Dave, I'm sorry. I'll tell Cindy it was my fault—"

"Shut up. I'm enjoying this way more than you think." His hand skims across my back. "Did you put your underwear back on?"

"It's in my purse."

"Oh, man." He drops his forehead on my shoulder, then straightens again.

With a laugh, I wrap my arms around him and press my cheek to his chest. I really don't get Dave. We talk like we've been friends for years, he makes it clear he thinks I'm attractive, but he doesn't want to take things to the next level. Okay, so maybe I overreacted a few weeks ago when he said he didn't want to sleep with me. I mean, that was like our seventh date, and I still didn't know where I stood with him. And, okay, maybe I pushed him a little because I wanted to see what he'd do, and because—oh, just admit it—because I liked him, and I couldn't tell if he liked me, and I hate uncertainty.

So now he's with Cindy! but dancing with me, and he's hot and bothered because I'm not wearing any underwear but he won't kiss me. I'm beginning to remember why I was so pissed off with him before. And still, if I had another chance . . .

"Come on, Red. Time to go," he says, and his voice is far away. Then Gray is beside me. The next time I open my eyes I'm in a tank, moving really fast on the freeway.

Gray's next to me, and Cindy! and Dave are up front.

"Where's my car?"

"We decided not to let you drive," Gray says.

"We'll pick it up in the morning," Dave says.

I'm not sure how that's going to work, but I'm at that stage of drunkenness where everything is pretty much okay.

"Right up here. The lofts," Gray says. I lift my head and study Gray's trendy neighborhood. Dave pulls the Hummer over, and Gray shakes his hand, then says good night to Cindy!

"You still going to the lake tomorrow?" he asks me.

"Yeah. I'll be okay."

He leans over and kisses my temple. "Call me in the morning, kiddo."

I lie down in the backseat, lulled by Dave and Cindy!'s voices, and the next time I look around, we've stopped. I sit up, wondering if they've abandoned me in the tank, but when I look outside, I see Dave and Cindy! standing on the porch of a small house. There are five other cars in the driveway and grass, so I'm assuming Cindy!'s got roommates. As I watch, Dave bends down and kisses her. It's not a long kiss, like this afternoon, but it's not exactly short, either.

She turns to go inside, and I flop down on the backseat hastily.

Oh, fuck. I mean, fudge. Mistake. Head fallen off body.

Dave opens his door and looks over the seat at me. "You still alive?"

"I don't know. Is my head attached?"

"Yeah. Want to sit up front?"

"No. Drive on, James."

Dave doesn't turn on the radio, and we're quiet for three minutes. I know this because I can see the little clock on the dash from my position. "When did you get the Hummer?" I say.

"Last week. Bonus from the Y and Y account."

"What was wrong with the Land Rover?"

"Blue, sticky, and smelled like Gatorade."

"Oh." I feel my face heat.

More silence.

"Dave?" *Shut up, Allison. Whatever you say now will make you cringe in the morning. Pretend you're asleep.* "You were kissing Cindy."

He glances at me, then back at the road.

Another minute.

"How come you kiss her but not me?"

"I did kiss you."

"But you didn't want to."

"I don't want to get into this right now."

We slow for a light, and I sit up. "I don't get it. She's like twelve."

We turn the corner, and I recognize the convenience store. We're almost to my town house.

"Look, Allison, you're drunk. You don't want to talk about this stuff now."

"Yeah, I'm drunk, but I know what I'm saying. I think I'd hate myself in the morning more if I *didn't* say all this."

"Okay, let's test it. If you still want to talk about this in the morning, call me, and we will."

"Goddamnit, Dave! Just tell me what the fuck is going on. Are you fucking seeing Cindy or not? Do you fucking like me or not?"

We slow and he pulls in front of my house.

"Oh, just fucking forget the whole thing."

I open the door, fall out, and curse all tanks and their

drivers. When I finally make it to my door, it's locked, and I can't find my purse or my keys. I rest my forehead on the door.

A moment later, Dave nudges me aside.

"Go back to your tank. You might need to invade Michigan Avenue."

Dave unlocks the door, pushes it open, then, without even asking, picks me up and carries me inside. I want to yell at him, but I can't summon the energy to argue. I hear him kick the door shut and drop my purse and keys on the tile floor. He heads upstairs and straight for my bedroom, and when I make a hasty check of his face, he looks pissed.

"Light?" he asks.

"Wall on the right."

He flicks it on with his elbow, and the lamp on my nightstand illuminates the room. Dave stands in the doorway for a moment, staring at my room. "That bed is huge."

As the bed dominates the room, it's a little hard to ignore. "It's a tester bed, king-size."

"It has curtains."

"Just whispy sheers strewn through the canopy."

"Right."

He strides forward, lays me on the edge of the bed, then stands there looking at me. I scrutinize his face, but I can't tell what he's thinking. I'm shaking. I don't know why. I've done this before. With another guy, I'd grab him, pull him down beside me, and rip his clothes off. But I honestly don't know what to do with Dave.

"I don't know what the fuck is going on. I'm not seriously seeing fucking Cindy, and yes, I fucking like you."

I stare at him. He hasn't moved, and his face is still completely unreadable. "So, what are you going to do now?"

He looks around. "Your cat's sitting by her bowl. I'm going to feed her." He heads into the kitchen, and I hear Booboo Kitty meowing for dinner.

I sit up, brushing my hair out of my face, and wait to see what will happen next. I'm completely on edge. Dave might do anything—leave, watch TV, come in here and kiss me senseless. I hear him walking back down the hallway, and then he stands in my doorway, his shoulder against the jamb. "Do I get to ask questions?"

"I didn't sleep with Nicolo," I say, slurring his name.

"Okay." He looks a little thrown by my admission. "Why are you telling me this?"

"Because I don't want you to hate me."

He looks more confused.

"Not that I didn't sleep with him because of you. I wasn't really thinking about you."

He inclines his head. "Good to know."

"No, what I mean is—remember when you said that thing in Rory's bedroom?"

"What thing?"

"You know what thing. What did you mean, maybe you didn't sleep with me because you like me? Is that some kind of prefeminist holdover?"

"Whoa." He holds up both hands and walks toward me. "Don't even play the feminist card, and I'm not going to talk about this if you won't listen."

"Hello? I'm listening." I flop on the pile of pillows.

I expect him to argue, but he props himself on an elbow beside me. "I'm friends with Hunter and Rory. You're friends with Hunter and Rory. We can't have a one-night stand because we're going to see each other again. We can't have a relationship because I don't know if I want that with you yet. I was trying to walk a middle line, but you're sort of a right or left girl."

"I can walk a middle line," I say, flipping on my side to face him. "You're the one who's right or left. You're all friendly around other people, and then you act like you don't know what to do with me. Then I see you kissing Cindy—who's all wrong for you, by the way—and FYI I'm *not* saying I'm right for you, but we've been out half a dozen times or more and you won't even touch me."

He lies back and closes his eyes. "Things aren't that simple with you."

"Why not? I'm a simple girl."

He laughs and spreads his arms as if encompassing the canopied bed, the white chaise longue, cherrywood dressing table, cheval mirror, and silk sheers on the window.

"No, you're not. You're high-maintenance, and I'm not a very good mechanic."

"Oh, poor baby. That's why they have Viagra."

"Go to sleep."

"You're not going to rip my clothes off and make mad, passionate love to me?"

"Not tonight."

"But sometime?"

"No comment."

"Are you going back to Cindy's?"

"No."

"Good." I scoot closer and he turns, fitting me against him. He's warm and solid, and he smells like a man—a man with a hint of pinewoods, lime margaritas, and Frank Sinatra. I'm asleep in no time.

Are You in Love with Me Again?

When I open my eyes, the comforter is tucked around me, Booboo Kitty's sitting on my pillow staring down at me, and Dave's gone. I don't even have to call out or look around for him. A place feels different when it's occupied. People give off certain vibes—casual, neat, artsy—and I'm good at latching onto those when I decorate. Dave's vibe, sort of casual and sexy, isn't present.

I sit up, and Booboo, seeing signs of life, jumps onto the nightstand, wrapping her tail around a glass of water that wasn't there last night. Next to the glass are two aspirin and my car keys. I take the aspirin, drink the water, and pad to the foyer to peek out the curtains. My Z4's parked in the driveway, and I'm betting it has a full tank of gas. I sigh and go back upstairs to feed Booboo, but that's been taken care of as well. Her bowls—food and water—are already full.

Okay, if Dave's taken the trash out, I'm going to propose.

Thank God the trash is still full, and I don't have to start calling myself Allison Tivoli. Later in the car with Gray, I don't have to think too hard to know what Dave's trying to tell me. A guy sneaks out in the morning, doesn't say good-bye, doesn't call, he doesn't want a relationship. See what happens when a guy sees the real me?

I turn on Wrigley Drive in downtown Lake Geneva, and Booboo Kitty wakes from her nap, starts meowing, and scratches Gray's leg in an effort to sniff the vents.

"How does your cat know?" Gray steadies Booboo so she can sniff without flaying his knee to bloody shreds.

"She's smart. Or maybe the air smells different in Wisconsin." Less smog, more patriotism. All the little downtown shops have American flags flapping in the breeze, and up ahead there's a banner stretched across the street that reads "WIN BIG! MEMORIAL DAY AT THE TRACK!" Booboo meows.

"No, Booboo. No track for you. Those dogs will eat you up."

We stop at a light and wave to Kristen Browning. She's on the corner talking to Ashley Smith-Roberts, and both women are flanked by small children. Ashley turns and waves at us, too, lifting the hand of the toddler locked in her grasp.

Gray shakes his head. "Man. I used to date those girls. Now they've got kids. Makes me feel old."

"You *are* old."

He glares at me until Booboo swishes her tail in front of his mouth. "Ashley's your age," he says through a mouthful of fur. "And Kristen is only a year ahead."

"Two," I say, but I know what he means. I *do* feel old

when we come to Lake Geneva. It's part of who I am, my history. As soon as we exit Route 12, my childhood floods back to me: the first time I went sailing, the first time I kissed a boy, the first time I skinny-dipped. I have as many friends here as in Chicago, and over the years those friend-ships have served me well professionally. But there's some-thing bittersweet about coming back. I'm no longer the little girl who did cartwheels on the lakeshore and twirled a baton in the Fourth of July parade. I'm not Allie Bo-bally anymore and yet, I am. In so many ways, I am.

My parents' house on Geneva Lake has a balcony on the second floor, and when I was in elementary school, Rory and I used to dress up in princess costumes—mine was a pink tulle skirt, pink leotard, and sparkly tiara—and twirl about on the balcony, looking out at the lake and hoping a prince (or Jedi, in Rory's case) would sweep us away. My prince would sail in on his pirate ship (he was a bad-boy pirate prince, of course) and rescue me.

I'm not sure what I wanted to be rescued from, since my life was pretty good, but I think I saw enough of my parents' world that I realized my idealized life couldn't last. I would have to grow up, and even at eight, very little about adult life seemed innocent or uncomplicated. My parents' friends di-vorced, remarried, divorced again; lost fortunes, made for-tunes. My dad was always worried about money, and my mom worried about the lines on her face, and then there was all the drama with Gray. Certainly adult life was not as simple as spinning around and around until Rory and I were dizzy and falling down in a heap of giggles and pink tulle.

And how much has really changed? Nowadays, my prin-cess clothes are a bit more expensive and any dizziness I suffer is probably alcohol-induced, but I still want to be a princess. I still want that magical, fairy-tale life. And the stupid thing is that more and more, I know there's no fairy tale. As if the fudging kamikaze show has infected me, I keep trying to fix parts of my life that aren't broken.

But I don't know how to stop. I don't know how to let go of the fantasy. And that really messes up my life. And I know I'm doing it, but it's like I can't see the details as clearly as the big picture. This has always been my flaw as a decorator, and it's my downfall in life and love, too. It's like hanging a picture. I should measure, calculate, use a level, but I never do. I blindly pound the nail in every time, supremely confident— and supremely wrong—that I've eyed it perfectly.

With men, sometimes it seems like I throw the tape measure out the window. I ignore the details, always ready to try a new relationship on for size. And I'm always looking for that dream guy—the one who in my reality probably doesn't exist.

I turn down the drive to Maytag Point, where my parents' house overlooks the lake.

"Ow! Jesus!" Gray yells as Booboo Kitty tries to squeeze through the air vents. Gray struggles to keep ahold of her. "I don't get it. The air downtown can't possibly smell different than the air here. It's only three miles away. How does the cat know?"

"Instinct, I guess," I say, patting Booboo's head. "The same way she always knows who doesn't like her and goes to rub against their leg."

"I wish I had instincts like that."

"Me, too."

"What's with you this morning?" Gray says. "You're really quiet. Sure you don't have a hangover?"

"I'm just—Gray, whose car is that?"

Our parents' house is up ahead, and next to my dad's Lexus in the driveway is a Porsche Carrera.

"I don't know. Cool car, though."

I pull in behind the Lexus, shoo Booboo Kitty into her carrier while Gray gets our bags from the trunk, and we're coming up the walk when my mother opens the screen door.

"You're just in time! We've been holding lunch for you." My mother is wearing a sundress and heels, full makeup, and a hat over her blonde hair. She's not a real blonde, but she tells everyone she's been one so long they gave her an honorary membership.

She kisses Gray and then me, closing the door behind us.

"Mom, why are you so dressed up?"

"I'm not dressed up," she says. "I've had this old sundress for ages."

"Mom, it's Christian Dior, and I was with you when you bought it last month." I set Booboo's carrier down and let her out. She immediately runs for the back of the house and the deck. I'll have to bribe her with tuna to get her back in so we can leave tomorrow.

"Yes, well, it wouldn't kill the two of you to dress up once in a while. Why don't you go change?"

Gray and I are both wearing shorts and T-shirts, the usual code of dress for a weekend at the lake house.

"The only thing I brought was a sundress in case we went to the yacht club," I say.

"Whose Porsche is that?" Gray asks, dropping our bags by the door.

"Oh, why don't you ask your famous sister? She's full of secrets. Allison, go wash your face and put on some lipstick, then come out to the deck and say hello."

Gray and I exchange wary looks, but I pick up our bags and head toward the stairs to our bedrooms. As I pass the guest room on the bottom floor, I notice a leather Louis Vuitton bag sitting right inside the door.

My room is at the top right of the stairs, but I pass it and drop Gray's bag in his room first. Ahead is the master bedroom. The door is open and straight back are the French doors leading to the balcony. I can see the lake and white sailboats dotting the blue water through the glass panes. My room is in the front of the house and has two large windows—one overlooking the drive and the other the strip of woods between our place and the Iversons'. A half-mile down is my aunt and uncle's place. Maybe I'll walk down later and see if my cousin Cassie is around. Back in my room, I set my bag on one of the twin beds, both covered with pretty pink-and-white spreads.

I always slept in the one on the left and my friends—Rory usually—slept in the one on the right. The bathroom I share with Gray is across the hall, so I head there next. I don't put on lipstick, but I do wash my face and drink another glass of water. When I step out of the bathroom, Nicolo is standing in the hallway.

"Oh, my God!"

He grabs my shoulders. "It is okay. Do not be frightened."

"What are you doing here?" I shake his hands off me. "Get out!"

"I am here for work."

I gape at him. "That's your Louis Vuitton bag downstairs?" Piece of advice: No matter how freaked out you are, never miss a chance to say Vuitton.

"Yes. I wished to speak to you before you saw your parents."

I narrow my eyes. "Why? What have you done with them?"

"Nothing." He spreads his arms. "As you see, I am harmless. Might we go into your bedroom and speak?"

"You're not that harmless. Right here is fine."

He sighs. "Very well. Again, I am sorry I frightened you."

I nod, waiting for him to go on.

"When you signed the contract, you agreed to all access. I wanted to get to know your family, maybe take a little footage."

"No cameras here, Nicolo. After what we did to that poor family's house Wednesday, I don't know if I even want to be part of this show anymore. But I do know that I don't want to see you. Just take your Louis Vuitton bag"—see, lots of opportunities to get that in—"and go play reality TV with some other family. Leave me alone."

"Allison—" He reaches out and touches my shoulder, but I shrug him off. "Very well. I will leave if that is what you wish, but the consequences may not be to your liking."

"Is that a threat?"

"You signed a contract that stipulated all access. Are you reneging on the terms of that legally binding document?"

I glare at him, feeling like a cat on her way to the vet for shots. No escape. "You don't care about footage. You're just trying to weasel your way into my life."

"That is not true."

"Fine. Then send a camera crew, but you and your Louis Vuitton bag can go."

"Allison"—he reaches for my shoulder again, but I give him a warning glare—"please, allow me to apologize for what happened at the fashion show. I am so very, very sorry. It will not happen again."

"You're right about that. Get out."

I watch him closely. His face is so sincere—eyes puppy-dog–pleading, brows crumpled, mouth turned down at the corners. That soft, sensual mouth—damnit!

"Allison." He puts his hand on my shoulder, and this time

when I remove it, he manages to keep hold of my hand. "Can you forgive me? You were just so beautiful, so sexy, I was overwhelmed."

Okay, now this is a load of bullshit, but it's nice bullshit. I mean, it's not every day a girl's told she was impossible to resist. But it's going to take a hell of a lot more than words to win me over.

"If you pull any crap like the other night—"

"Allison!" My mother rushes up the stairs, probably picking her moment after eavesdropping from the first floor. She's balancing a tray of deviled eggs in one hand and holding her hat securely with the other. "What is wrong with you? The prince is our guest, and"—she lowers her voice—"he came to see Y-O-U!"

I cross my arms. "Perfect." I forgot how my mother can be. When she gets emotional—nervous, excited—she reverts back to when Gray and I were kids and she would spell all the words she wanted to keep us from understanding.

Nicolo smiles, all charm. "Thank you again for your graciousness in allowing this intrusion on your holiday, Mrs. Holloway. I have just been telling your daughter that if she does not want me here—"

"Of course she wants you here!" my mother protests loudly. "Allison is tired from the drive. Please, call me Mitsy, and come back out on the deck. Lunch is almost ready. Allison, why haven't you changed yet?"

I roll my eyes and follow Nicolo and Mitsy downstairs. Nicolo's taken the tray of eggs from her, and she's looking up at him as if he's her prince in shining armor.

"Allison, you didn't tell me Prince Parma was so handsome. Of course, you didn't tell me he was royalty, either." She glares at me, but Nicolo just smiles.

"Please, it is a courtesy title, nothing else," he says as we near the sliding glass doors.

Through the glass, I see that the weather is truly gorgeous today. The sky is as blue as the lake, no clouds speckle the sky, and a pleasant breeze teases the spires of the blue spruces and the leaves of the maple trees.

I follow my mother through the patio door and onto the deck. On the left is my dad's grill, smoking with what smells deliciously like hamburgers. To the right, with the best view of the lake through the trees, are three chairs. Grayson's already in one, and my mother motions to Nicolo to take his choice of the others. Gray glares at me, looking like he'd rather sit with Saddam Hussein than Nicolo.

Dad's trying to affix a large American flag to the center rail of the deck. He's already got Illinois and Wisconsin state flags up and flying.

"Allison's here!" my mother announces.

My dad doesn't turn from the recalcitrant flag, but calls, "Hi, darlin'."

I leave Nicolo and wander over to my dad. "Hi, Daddy. Sorry about the unexpected guest."

"No problem. Your mother practically asked the guy to move in. This is exciting stuff for her."

"I noticed. She's spelling again." I glance over at my mom. She's arranging the table just so. With Mitsy Holloway, everything is about appearances. She's Miss Manners and Martha Stewart rolled into one. But get her on a bad day, and she can turn into Joan Crawford with an attitude.

"So what's up, Dad?"

He's about secured the flag and says through teeth gritted with effort, "Trying to get this flag up and flying. There we go." He dusts his hands together, dislodging invisible particles of dirt. He slings an arm around my shoulders and stands back to admire his efforts. "So how do they look?"

"Who?" I glance around. My mother has enlisted Nicolo's help in pulling the table forward on the deck to make the most of the light.

"The flags? How do they look?"

I study the flags. What answer to give here? They look like flags. "Um, they look . . . patriotic."

"Mmm-hmm." He nods. Obviously more is expected.

I draw on my interior design experience. I should really call Columbia College and suggest they add a course to train the Interior Architecture students for moments like these. They could call it "Bullshitting 101: The Art of Saying What the Client Wants to Hear."

"Um . . . I love the way you've spaced them. The two state flags flanking the American one."

"You'll notice I've left gaps." He gestures proudly to his creation, arm still around my shoulders, we two facing the vast horizon and three flapping flags bravely.

"The spacing is great. It creates the illusion of size." Actually, the spaces pretty much look like big gaps between the flags, but you couldn't pay me to tell my dad that.

He gives me an incredulous look. "Really? That's what I was going for." He points around a bend in the lake. "See the Boyds' place?"

I stand on tiptoe and peer through the towering spruces. "Yeah."

"See his flags?"

"Yeah." The Boyds are from Dallas, Texas, and they're flying not only the American flag, but the other flags that have, throughout history, flown over Texas. There's the Lone

Star, Mexico, France, Spain . . . "Dad, what's that one with the circle of stars?"

"The Texas Confederate flag."

We both frown and narrow our eyes.

"I don't know what Luke's thinking. This is Yankee country. I talked to Dick down on the city council, but he said much as he supports my line of thinking, there's no restriction against Luke flying those Texas flags. So it's up to me to shame him into taking them down."

I glance at my dad. "How are you going to do that?"

"Put up bigger flags. More flags. I think it's working, too. You just said my flags look bigger. I need to go into town and shop for a few more. Luke's got—what?—six flags? We'll fly seven."

I do a mental eye roll. I've heard of penis envy, but flag envy? Everything is a competition to my dad. That's probably why he's so good at what he does and makes like five million dollars a year. I'm not sure what my dad does exactly. I never cared much, but a few years ago when Rory was at Northwestern studying accounting, we were here for the Fourth, and she asked him. I listened in, but all I got was that he makes money out of money. Rory had nodded sagely, and when I asked her about it later, she said—well, I don't know what she said—but I think it boiled down to investing.

"Donald, are the B-U-R-G-E-R-S ready?" my mom asks as she brings glasses and silverware onto the deck.

Dad starts. "Oh, uh, I'll check."

I shake my head. He's totally forgotten them, of course. Flags will do that to a man, you know. I give my dad a kiss on his cheek and watch him walk away. He looks older, his hair almost completely gray now. My grandma used to tell me that growing up he had red hair like mine, but I can't remember it being any color other than steel gray.

"Lunch is ready," my mom says. We sit down, and my mom, in her best society mistress role, passes the plate of burgers around and begins the conversation. "Allison, darling. How is your job at one of the T-O-P interior design firms in Chicago?"

I give her my please-don't-embarrass-me look, which I thought after the age of seventeen I'd never have to use again. "Well, Mom, it's pretty much the same as always. I'd love to tell you about the show, but I'm not allowed to."

"A little bird told me there were TV vans at Lucinda Chippenhall's place. Is she getting something I'm not?"

"No," I say firmly. I don't know whether it's good news or bad that my mom hasn't spoken directly to Mrs. Chippenhall yet.

"And are you working on any big projects?" She looks at Nicolo. "Last year you redecorated Oprah's studio."

"The show's pretty much taking all my time," I say, putting lettuce and tomato on my burger.

"What about you, Grayson?" Mom trills. "How is your career as a supermodel going?"

I glance at Gray. He's got that sulky model look on his face, which means he's annoyed at her act. He doesn't answer, but my father steps in. "This potato salad is wonderful, Mitsy. Have you ever eaten potato salad this good, Nicolo?"

"Ah, no," Nicolo says. I glance at his plate. He hasn't taken a bite of anything. "It is delicious." He glances at me, and I raise a brow.

He clears his throat. "Mrs. Holloway, tell me a little about yourself. What was it like raising two children who have grown to be so successful?"

My mother beams, and we're off. Embarrassing stories of my childhood aside, the rest of the afternoon goes pretty well. After a while, my family forgets Nicolo is a prince, and we end up having a pretty good conversation. Nicolo is naturally charismatic, and he makes everything easy. He smoothes the rough spots, asks all the right questions, and steers the conversation in the direction he wants it to go.

I hold up my end, but mostly I watch him. Since dating Bryce, I'd almost forgotten how uncomplicated it is to be with a guy who can hold his own with my parents—hold his own socially.

Nicolo knows the unspoken rules, the intimations, what questions are really being asked behind the pretty veneer of light conversation. He knows and he plays his part. At the end of ninety minutes, my mother is in love with him, Gray's comfortable, and my dad's slapping "Old Nik" on the shoulder.

I'm impressed at how easily Nicolo charmed my family, especially my dad, but overall my feelings are still mixed.

The conversation settles into a relaxed after-lunch lull, and I allow my mind to drift. Sitting here on the deck, I feel young again. It's partly the association this place has with my girlhood, and partly Nicolo being here. He reminds me of all those childhood dreams and imaginings.

And so much of what is around me churns up those fantasies. The view of the lake is the same, blue and vast, now crowded with boats and Jet Skis. Our deck juts out, my dad's varnished mahogany boat, *The Lady Is a Tramp,* with its blue and red Chris-Craft flag, bobbing in the water at the end. I'm surprised he's gone to the trouble of taking it out of the boathouse, but my mom probably nagged him to do it because of Nicolo.

The house is the same, big and bright and comfortable; the neighbors, always friendly, stop by to invite us to a party or to play golf or to go out on their boats tonight. And my parents are the same: My dad made the traditional hamburgers on the grill and my mom put them on low-carb buns with sides of low-fat potato salad and reduced-fat potato chips. Nothing has changed except Nicolo's presence.

When we're no longer stuffed full of lunch, my mom brings out dessert—fruit or sorbet—and the eating and drinking and promising the neighbors we'll play golf and tennis and stop by for a party catches up with me. It's already afternoon, and I'm feeling my late night.

"Allison?" my mother says, and I blink several times, shaken out of my drowsy state. "Are you sleeping?"

"No."

She frowns at me, her lips thinning in a way that means she thinks I'm neglecting my guests. I glare at her, my eyes narrowing to communicate to her that he's *her* guest, not mine, and I'll be as neglectful as I want.

But Nicolo has other ideas. He asks me to play tour guide, and my mom glares at me until I agree. By the time we get back from viewing all the mansions, the town, and the Riviera Ballroom, where Tommy Dorsey and Louis Armstrong once played, there's a group going to play tennis and we get roped into that, too.

All in all, it turns out to be a pretty fun day. Nicolo kept me entertained with his dry sense of humor and his stories of an adventurous life, and as we step on my dad's antique Chris-Craft to head for my aunt and uncle's house and their party, I realize Nicolo is right back in my good graces.

Maybe I really did misunderstand him before. He seems like such a nice guy—my kind of guy.

Let's Misbehave

Later that night, I'm lying in bed, the window open to the moon and stars, the ruffles of the white cotton curtains swaying in the breeze, and my head full of Nicolo.

The party was fun. For the second time today, Nicolo was fun. He was witty and exuberant and so charming. Normally I like to mingle at parties, but tonight I didn't want to leave Nicolo's side. I wanted to see what he'd say next, what he'd do.

And I wanted to know who he knew. We hadn't yet played that tedious "who-do-you-know" game, but Kristen Browning and Ashley Smith-Roberts wasted no time. Pretty soon names like Rockefeller, Kennedy, Hilton, Blair, and Spielberg are being tossed around, followed quickly by J. Lo, Brad, Ashton, Justin, and Madonna. I'm not buying Kristen's story about Madonna, though.

It seems like Nicolo knows everyone and has been everywhere. He speaks English, French, Italian, Greek, and a bit of Japanese. He can converse about events as varied as the Crimean War and the Crusades as if they happened yesterday and involved his close family friends. And when someone asked what our favorite opening line for a book was, Nicolo had the most intriguing answer.

He quoted a line from *The Odyssey. In the original Greek.* Okay, now that's pretty sexy, right? "Tell me, O muse, of that ingenious hero who traveled far and wide after he had sacked the famous town of Troy."

Watching him wrap his full lips around those ancient words, his voice seductive and velvet, left me slightly breathless.

Just thinking about it again makes me restless, and I roll over onto my stomach. Nicolo and I walked home from the party, and now I can't seem to shut out the feel of his hand in mine, the silk of his shirt as it rubbed against my bare shoulders, the light kiss he gave me at the bottom of the steps as we parted—me to my room and he to the guest room.

I sit up and bury my head in my hands. I need to get some sleep or I'll be a zombie tomorrow. I'm about to lie back when I hear a creak. I sit very still, listening. The house is dark. My parents went to sleep hours ago, and Gray stayed late at the party, but surely by now he's home and asleep. It could be him, but I know it's not.

I listen again, staring into the darkness. My heart's pounding, and I feel like I'm fourteen again. I glance down at my tank and boy shorts, wishing I'd worn something sexy to sleep in. And then the door handle turns silently, and Nicolo is standing in the entrance.

"May I come in?" he murmurs, and at the sound of his sexy voice, I shiver.

"For a moment," I answer, then scoot over to make room for him on the edge of the bed. He sits and for a long time we don't speak. I stare at his face—the dark eyebrows framing shadowy blue eyes, the patrician nose and cheekbones, the mouth with its European sensuousness. He's wearing silk boxers and nothing else, and I put my hand on his chest, the bright pink La Paz-itively Hot OPI shade gleaming on my nails in the moonlight as I make a figure eight over his heart.

He's not built like American boys from the Midwest. His chest and shoulders aren't broad and muscled and brown from the sun. He's slim and fine-boned—a true aristocrat. He's not weak or puny; there's power and strength under that long, slender physique.

I look into his eyes again, prepared for chatter about how neither of us could sleep or what a great party it was or whether we should go out on the boat tomorrow. What I'm not prepared for is Nicolo's hand sliding into my hair, cradling my neck, and pulling me gently to him. His mouth, warm and skilled, closes on mine. I don't kiss him back at first. I let him take control, let him kiss me at his own pace, run his hands over me and linger where he wants.

He's slow and thorough and enticing. And when we break apart, I'm breathing hard. I push him back and slide over him, feeling the silk of his boxers on the inside of my thighs, the heat of the flesh at his waist against my knees. He's hard where our bodies meet, sleek where I bend down to press my breasts against him. I feel his warmth, his strength through my thin tank, and tighten my legs around him.

Then I look up, into his half-closed eyes, and I kiss him,

my hair forming a curtain around us. His arms come around me, pulling me closer, eager to divest me of the layers of material keeping us apart. But we're moving at my speed now, my level of intensity, and I don't break the kiss until I have his full attention, until he's kissing me back with unreserved focus. Only then do I pull away, dragging my lips over his jaw to kiss his neck and touch my tongue lightly against his earlobe.

He groans softly, and I smile, breathe in his scent. There's nothing remarkable about it—expensive cologne and French-milled soap. He smells like I imagine a prince would—money and privilege and pride. It's a scent I'm not altogether unfamiliar with, considering some of my previous lovers.

Somewhere in the house there's a light thump and a bang, and Nicolo and I freeze, listening for footsteps on the stairs. When it's silent again, I peek up at him and we both laugh.

"I feel like I'm seventeen again," I whisper, laying my cheek against his chest. "I was this close"—I hold my hand up, two fingers a millimeter apart—"to getting caught a half dozen times."

"The danger can be its own aphrodisiac."

"Hmm." At seventeen I would have agreed, but I'm beginning to think I'm too old for that kind of adventure. Maybe a long leisurely night rather than a fast fuck is more appealing to me at this point. Or maybe I'm just tired of sex without emotion. I want to feel more than attraction. I want the connection, the knowledge that the man I'm with knows and wants the real me. I want something more, something real.

The house is quiet, and I listen to Nicolo's heart beating. This is nice, very nice. My body's reacting as it should, and I'm going through the motions, but my head is somewhere else.

I don't know what Nicolo feels, but he doesn't look pleased when I roll off him. "I want you to go back to your room."

"Why?" He watches me back away, but the room is too dark to read his eyes.

I shrug. "I don't know. This doesn't feel right."

"I can change that." He pats the mattress next to him. "Come here. Let me show you."

"Not tonight." I shake my head. "Sleep well."

His face seems to darken in the moonlight, and he finally murmurs, "You, too."

He leaves, closing the door behind him, and I tug the covers snug around me. I adjust them, pull them tighter, but they still don't feel like a man's arms. And for the first time in thirty-two years, I feel lonely in bed by myself.

I don't come down until almost noon on Monday, and by then everyone has progressed from coffee to beer and mimosas. I make a fresh pot of coffee and settle in a chair between my mother and Nicolo.

The atmosphere is kind of gloomy today. My father's unhappy because he didn't find the flags he wanted yesterday, and now he can't prove to the neighbors that if size matters, the Holloway flag is biggest of them all. My mother's unhappy because my aunt, her sister-in-law, was showing off the results of her liposuction at the party last night, but my dad told Mitsy he wasn't paying to have her nonexistent fat sucked out. And Gray—Gray's a model, so he always looks pissed.

Only Nicolo appears happy, though from the detritus around him it looks like he's already smoked a pack of cigarettes and drunk three beers. That might account for the absence of his usual ennui.

"Well"—Grayson rises and stretches—"not much going

on here. Why don't we take the boat out and show Nicolo some of the lake?"

"More coffee first," I say, begging off.

My mother only rides in the boat when no car is available, and my father is about to leave for the neighbors' house two doors down. He's thinking of buying their catamaran, so Gray says, "I can take the boat out. Where are the keys, Dad?"

My father frowns, glances at my mother, and then down at the dock and his antique wooden baby. "Why don't you wait until I get back from the Goldbergs? We can all go then."

"I'll take him for a ride, and on the way back we'll pick you up from the Goldbergs." Grayson turns to Nicolo. "You should see how *Lady* moves when we get on the open water. That baby's a 1941 Chris-Craft Deluxe Runabout, made in Holland, Michigan. We'll take it for a spin, then head over to the Coral Reef for a beer and be back for an early dinner with Mom and Allie."

"Honey," my mom says, "why don't you just wait for your father? Or maybe Allison could drive the boat?"

Gray's face darkens, and everyone tenses. I set my coffee mug down and place my feet on the deck. Oh, fudge. Here we go.

"You don't want me to drive the boat," Gray says, his voice dangerously calm.

My dad holds out a hand. "It's not that, Gray, it's just—"

"You don't trust me. What do I have to do to make you stop treating me like a juvenile delinquent?"

"Gray," I say, "not now."

"Why? Because royalty's here? He'll stick around if you let him in your pants."

"Grayson!" my father bellows, while my mother's jaw drops.

Nicolo stands. "How dare you talk to her like that!"

As much as I'd like to smack Gray right now, that would only make things worse, so I grab Nicolo's hand and pull him down.

"We do trust you, Gray," my mother says. "But your license was revoked, and we don't think it's a good idea for you to take the boat."

Gray crosses his arms. "I get it back in two months. Even the government forgives after a year. It's been a decade or more since I was arrested, and you two are still acting like I'm a criminal."

"Gray." My dad stands. "We don't think that. The past is the past, but you've been drinking today and—"

"One beer, Dad. One. You've had more than that. Shit. You should have seen Allison the other night. She was drunk off her ass and making out with some guy from the basketball camp."

My eyes widen. How dare he say that in front of my parents? "Fuck you, Grayson. Don't take this out on me."

Nicolo stands and holds out the keys to the Porsche. "Have you ever driven a Porsche, Gray? I find the speed, the roar . . . therapeutic."

Gray narrows his eyes. "I wouldn't know."

"You should drive one. It's good for the soul, yes?"

"My license is revoked."

Nicolo shrugs. "Eh. Your laws do not apply to me or my property. Let's drive."

I hold my breath, ready for Gray to take a swing at Nicolo, but Gray only nods, catches the keys when Nicolo tosses them, and follows him off the deck and around to the front of the house.

My parents look torn. Object or keep quiet? Thankfully,

they elect to keep their mouths shut. Nothing like male bonding to make everything right with the world. Only, what right does Nicolo have to bond with my brother? The whole argument wouldn't have happened if Nicolo hadn't come in the first place.

I sigh as the men retreat, leaving my mother, father, and me behind. I had thought we'd finally gotten this tension between our family worked out.

"I don't understand that boy," my mother says. "Why does he get so angry?" She looks at me.

"Because he's thirty-six, and you treat him like he's sixteen."

"I wish we'd treated him like this when he was sixteen," my dad growls. "Maybe then he wouldn't have spent a year in jail." He rises and stalks away, presumably to spend twenty thousand dollars on a sailboat. Who said retail therapy is a woman's-only sport?

My mother turns back to me. "What was Grayson saying about you being drunk and kissing some camp counselor?"

I sigh. "Nothing. He's mad and lashing out."

She sips a mimosa—how else does one cope when told liposuction is not an option and your son blows up at you?

A while later, I go for a walk. Out of habit, I take the path dotted with trees and flowers. Rory and I used to play hide-and-seek back here, and Gray used to scare me with ghost stories about a man with a hook lying in wait for me.

As I walk, I keep thinking about Gray's blowup and all the years of tension and fighting among all of us. Is it normal? Is any family normal? I glance down, studying the pine needles underfoot, then walk down to the trees where they meet with the sand, plop down, and stare at the water, at the vista I've seen a thousand times before. What is wrong with me? Why am I so reluctant to take what I've always wanted? I mean, Nicolo's what I've always wanted, right?

I hear the brush behind me crackle and see Nicolo tramping through the foliage in his jeans and loafers. He looks casual, relaxed, very handsome.

"Your mother said I might find you here."

I rise, running an appreciative eye over him. "Where's Grayson?"

"At the house, but I think he got rid of his anger." Nicolo takes my hand and leads us down toward the lake. "After the TV show is finished, you must come visit me in Roskilde. No expectations."

"You're being very nice."

"Why not?"

"Well, for one, I said some pretty harsh things at the fashion show. And two, you couldn't have been happy when I sent you back to your room last night."

He stops and turns to me. "As for the first, I deserved all you said that night. I do not apologize often, but I am sorry. You were right." He lifts my hand, kisses it. "As for the second, I await your pleasure. When you are ready, you will come to me."

A group of kids in a paddleboat wave from the lake, and we wave back.

"I like this place," Nicolo says, standing with arms akimbo, like a king surveying his dominion. "I like your mother and father. They are good people, and even your brother. Tell me, why was he so upset this afternoon?"

The sun is warm, but the water laps softly against the docks and the shore. We follow the gentle curve of the lake, Nicolo still holding my hand. His hand feels good in mine, familiar, like that of a longtime lover.

"Grayson got in some trouble when he was young. He was hanging out with the wrong kids, and he got arrested for stealing and drug possession."

"I see. What did he steal?"

I keep my eyes on the paddleboat, the paddlers stirring the blue silk water. "A car."

"That's rather serious. How old was he?"

"Seventeen."

"And he was also arrested for drugs?"

I sigh. "That was later. He went to juvenile detention for the car incident. He got arrested two years later for possession of heroin. He did nine months for that—real jail."

"Your parents must have been very embarrassed."

I turn to look at his face. No wonder my mother likes him. "My mother was. She got him accepted into Northwestern when he got out, but Gray didn't want to go to college. He loafed around a lot, then he started modeling, and now he's doing really well for himself."

"Why was his license taken?"

We stop walking, and Nicolo gives me a long, direct look.

"DUI last year. He totaled his car when he hit a tree. No one else was hurt."

Nicolo shakes his head. "I think it is good you told me. I do not want to be seen in public with your brother."

I stare at him. "Why? Because it might be bad press? That's a pile of crap."

He looks at me as though I'm a naive child. "It is a practical matter. You do not want Grayson's past dredged up in the media any more than I do."

"Then maybe you shouldn't be seen with me, either."

"Perhaps not, but I do not want to give you up. And I have ways of suppressing certain stories."

I laugh. "God, you sound like the Italian version of Juan Perón. What do you do, run around the globe producing weird TV shows, wooing women, and paying off reporters?"

He shrugs.

"Oh, my God. I do not want to know this. I feel like I'm dating Al Capone."

"Who?"

I shake my head. "Look, Nicolo, in case you haven't noticed, I'm a bit"—high-maintenance?—"*complicated*. You don't want to get involved in all this."

He makes a gesture of protest, but I cut him off.

"Not only that, but between the kamikaze show, all my other clients, and my family, I just don't have time for dating games."

"This is not a game." He draws me into his arms then and kisses me. It's long and slow and calculated to leave me panting. I give in to the experience, wondering what it would be like to kiss this man every day, go to bed with him at night, wake up with him in the morning. I could be happy. I could be a princess.

He ends the kiss and pulls me into his arms, whispering something in one of his many languages. He's strong and solid. My head fits perfectly in the crook of his neck. He strokes my hair and lavishes endearments, and I want to believe all this is real. I want to believe the fantasy is now reality, but can I trust Nicolo? What happens between us if life isn't all roses?

"Give me a chance," he whispers.

It would be easy to grant his request. I could have everything I ever wanted. I could live in the fantasy. But what about the real me—the imperfect me—where would that Allison fit?

Nicolo pulls back. "This is not a game." He opens his

hand and there's a diamond tennis bracelet in his palm. Even in the shade of the pines and maples, the diamonds sparkle, creating the illusion of a hundred tiny fires.

He clasps it around my wrist.

"It's beautiful," I say.

"This is only the beginning."

11

It Don't Mean a Thing (If It Ain't Got That Swing)

The next few days are pretty good. I see Nicolo almost every day, and he takes me to dinner, the theater, parties . . . After more time with the new and improved Nicolo, I start spending a few of my nights at his luxury penthouse overlooking the lake. It's great, but Booboo Kitty is mad that I've been away so much.

Maybe that's why princesses in fairy tales don't have pets. I miss Booboo, but my life sure feels like a fairy tale. I'm up to my OPI Marquis d'Mauve nails in affection and gifts. Every day there's a surprise—flowers in my office, a jeweled barrette, a painting by an up-and-coming artist, a pearl choker. He's courting me in every sense of the word.

It's not all glass slippers and fairy godmothers, though. I never realized how relentless the media can be. We're in all the local papers as well as some of the national ones, and they're calling me Princess Allison, which I kind of like, even if it's not accurate. The press is another reason I've been staying with Nicolo—reporters, mostly European, have been sitting outside my house for the last few days, and I'm afraid I'll open the door and find one of them going through my trash.

Last night I stayed at home, and I woke up in the middle of the night, stumbled into the bathroom, and looked up from my seat on the toilet to see a reporter peering in my bathroom window. This morning when I went out to get the paper, a dozen flashbulbs went off in my face, and when I tried to drive away, my car was swarmed. I shook for an hour afterward. I'm not used to that much stimulation before nine A.M.

As for the office, I'm getting used to splitting my time between the show and real work. We've still got two more shows to film. Then next week the vibrator show airs, and while Rory is planning a big viewing party, I'm trying to think of a way to keep my parents from seeing it.

But this morning, I start hoping no one sees the show. Any of the episodes. We're in a tiny apartment near the now-defunct Robert Taylor Projects getting miced. The family who lives there is staring at the motley group of cameramen, designers, and Japanese guys mulling about their house. Watanabe is on a cell phone, screaming something in Japanese, which Yamamoto translated as, "This show very exciting."

Right.

When the sound guy finishes, I lift my clipboard and double-check the list of supplies we've brought, drowning Watanabe out by humming "They Can't Take That Away from Me."

Yamamoto has taken the phone from our director, and now he's screaming into it as well. I plop down on top of one of the boxes we lugged upstairs and watch Miranda talking to the Ron Howard producer.

"Should we ask what the problem is?" Josh asks.

"No. He'll only tell us Yamamoto is very, very happy to work with us."

Yamamoto screams again and holds the phone out to Takahashi, one of the Japanese designers. They're going to be doing the apartment next door. Takahashi scurries over. "Hai."

"Where's the princeling?"

"I don't know. He's not talking to me because I didn't go out with him last night."

Josh gapes at me. "We were working until nine."

I shrug. "I know."

"Are you sure you're okay?"

"Who are they talking to?" I ask instead of answering Josh's question.

"No idea."

Then we both stare as Takahashi begins to sob loudly. The door opens, and I stiffen but, thank God, it's not Nicolo. I can't deal with him right now. Fukui, the other designer, enters, wearing a blue tuxedo shirt with ruffles. Strange decorating outfit, but I guess Hildi on *Trading Spaces* wears Prada pumps.

"I wish someone would tell me what's going on," Josh moans.

"He is talking to Mr. Kobayashi in Tokyo," Fukui says.

Josh and I stare at Fukui. Josh recovers first. "You speak English?"

"Of course."

"But why didn't you say so before?" I ask.

Fukui smiles.

"So, who's this Kobayashi?" Josh asks. "Why's Takahashi crying?"

Fukui sighs. "Kobayashi is CEO of Dai Hoshi. He is angry that first show not on air yet."

"It's airing next week," I say.

"We are behind schedule. We should have film last show today. Lose money."

"Oh. But Nicolo set the filming schedule."

Fukui gives me a long look. "Your prince cause more trouble than good."

Josh glances at me. "How?"

"You read contract?"

"What does that have to do with anything?" I say.

Fukui looks like he might answer, then Yamamoto motions to him, and he walks away.

"What's that about?" Josh asks.

"I don't know, but do you ever get the feeling we're on *Survivor*?"

Finally the phone calls end, and we all get to work. For this project, Watanabe gives both groups twenty rolls of duct tape. I glare at Miranda, but she doesn't say anything. Here we go again. Fix something that isn't broken. I look around the tiny apartment. The family who lives here seems so nice. I'd like to do something really great for them; instead, I'm going to cover their home in duct tape.

None of this feels right. But I have the duct tape, and I have a job to do. I look at my rolls of tape. The last thing the apartment needs is duct tape, but I try to think creatively. What about all those kids who make prom dresses and tuxedos out of duct tape every year? Maybe I can make household items out of duct tape.

But after three or four hours of working with the duct

tape, I have new respect for the prom kids. This stuff is hard to work with, and if you mess up, there aren't any do-overs. This stuff sticks—to everything. My hands are sticky, my scissors are sticky, and I have pieces of silver duct tape in my hair and on my jeans (my Michael Kors jeans, which I wore because after the Chippenhall house, I didn't anticipate another foray into the ghetto). I am never going to get this stuff off.

Finally, with only about two hours left, I've made some progress, and I'm painting over the duct tape I've fashioned into trim for the kitchen cupboards and thinking about how much I hate this stupid show when I hear a *thump*.

The Japanese designers' apartment is next to this one, so at first I ignore it, figuring they've dropped a ladder or something. But then I hear another thump followed by a sharp cry, and I run for the living room. Watanabe is watching our camera crew film Miranda patching a torn sofa cushion with the duct tape, but they turn when I run in.

"I heard something next door," I pant. "A bang and then a scream."

We rush into the hall and pause when we see the faces of the Iron Designers' production team. They look stunned. Watanabe asks something in Japanese, and one of the team answers, motioning us inside. Takahashi is lying on the floor, his hand to his forehead, and Fukui is kneeling beside him.

There's a long conversation in Japanese, and finally Yamamoto tells us what happened. Drug dealers came by looking for the owners and thought Takahashi and Fukui were lying when they said they didn't know where they were. One of the drug dealers hit Takahashi with a lamp, and now Fukui is taking him to the hospital as a precaution.

And since Josh and I don't really want to hang around our

unfinished apartment, waiting for a drug dealer to come quiz us, we start packing up to go. The camera crew helps, and we're climbing into the van when Watanabe and Yamamoto come over. Watanabe says something, which Yamamoto translates as, "Work not done. You go back and finish."

I glance at Miranda. She looks ready to capitulate, so I step in. "No way, Mr. Watanabe. I'm only going in there if you have security."

Josh nods, and Watanabe's face flushes when Yamamoto translates. "Then you lose."

"Only if they lose, too," Miranda says, pointing to the ambulance taking Takahashi away.

Grumbling in Japanese, Watanabe and Yamamoto walk off and Josh and I glance at Fukui, standing nearby, watching the ambulance pull away. "What'd they say?" I ask.

Fukui shrugs. "Same thing he always say, but Yamamoto usually make it sound nice."

Josh narrows his eyes. "What's that?"

Fukui thinks for a moment. "Hard to translate, but I think something like, 'You Americans are more stupid than water buffalo and uglier, too.'"

Josh and I gasp. "He didn't say that!"

Fukui smiles enigmatically and climbs in the van.

The day before the first show airs, we're filming the last show back where the Robert Taylor projects used to be. This time Watanabe has security, though, and both teams are working practically side by side. Interiors by M has the apartment complex's laundry room, while the Japanese designers are assigned the rec room.

Our goal is to use about a hundred rolls of plastic wrap in various colors, including holiday green, red, and, just for fun, blue. It's very hard to decorate with plastic wrap. I can't even get it to stay on my bowls at home, so this task is nearly impossible. Even the intrepid Fukui isn't quite sure what to do with it.

Our main problem has to do with heat and plastic wrap. Apartment tenants are in and out, dropping clothes from the washers into the dryers, and the heat from the industrial-size dryers makes the room feel like a tropical rain forest. The warm metal dryers also act as magnets for the plastic wrap, so that every unattended or unsecured piece of wrap gets sucked onto the dryers, melted by the heat so that we have no hope of ever removing it.

I'm sure this is a major fire hazard, and I'm about to say so, when the dryer I'm peeling plastic wrap from suddenly makes an unfamiliar noise, and there's a *whoosh*! I peer around the back, and a flame of searing fire licks at me. "Oh, fudge!" I scream.

"What is it?" Miranda says, turning from her plastic-wrapped clothing hangers. The cameras turn with her, and I suddenly realize this could be very bad if it's caught on film.

"Oh, nothing," I say with a smile.

Miranda glares at me for interrupting her for no reason, but I ignore her, scanning the room for a fire extinguisher. I spot one and try to sidle over to it without drawing the attention of the cameras. Meanwhile, I can see the fire poking hot fingers over the top of the dryer. I take the fire extinguisher from a wall, pretend to examine it for possible decorative value, then scoot back over to the dryer, pull the extinguisher's pin, stand back, and aim. I squeeze with all my strength. But nothing happens.

What the fudge!

"What's that smell?" Josh says from the other side of the room. "It smells like smo—"

"It's nothing!" I snap, cutting him off and becoming much more frantic now. I try the extinguisher again, and still nothing happens.

Across the room, Josh gasps as fire rises on the wall behind me. I shake my head, appealing desperately with my eyes for him to keep his mouth shut, but then I glance at the round indicator on the extinguisher's nozzle. There are two pieces of colored pie labeled full and empty. The pointer on the indicator shows empty.

Fudge!

And that's the last thought I have before the fire alarm goes off and water rains from the sprinklers in the ceiling.

By the time the fire department leaves, I've almost forgotten the reason we were here. If I'd known firefighters were so cute, I would have started more fires. But not here. The residents forced out of their apartments for the past three hours look less than happy to see cute firemen.

And when we're all allowed back into the laundry room, I wish the fire had done some damage. Now not only is there plastic wrap everywhere, there's smoky, wet, singed plastic wrap everywhere.

In the end, after twelve hours of wrestling with plastic wrap, fire, and irate residents, we've ruined another perfectly good room. Before leaving, we peek in at the Japanese designers' finished product. Thankfully, their sopping-wet made-over rec room isn't much better than our laundry room.

I never thought I'd say this, but at the end of the last show, I'm thoroughly sick of reality TV. I'm so glad the show is over, and if I never watch another reality TV show again, I won't shed a tear. I hope I don't shed too many at my television debut tomorrow night.

* * *

Since it's been a long week amid a series of long weeks, I'm capping this one off with a party at the Ritz-Carlton for Nicolo's friends, who have flown in for the *Kamikaze Makeover!* premiere tomorrow. Nicolo reserved the hotel's greenhouse—a gorgeous room with a view of the city. All around me men and women are reclining on plush antique-styled divans and chairs, standing on thick oriental rugs, placing glasses of Napoléon brandy and Krug 1990 Clos du Mesnil Blanc de Blancs champagne on gilded cut-glass tables. Everyone is laughing and talking. And I'm miserable. Before the party even began, Nicolo and I had a huge fight. Huge. I'd put on my favorite vintage Valentino, but Nicolo had bought me a bland beige creation by Alexander McQueen and insisted I wear it.

We finally agreed on a sexy black Alaia, but it pisses me off that I should have to even discuss my fashion choices with a man. I've got my own style. I know what's being shown in the couture shows on the Paris runways, but I don't want to be like everyone else. I want to wear a romantic silk Galliano, a vintage layered tulle by Schiaparelli, or something slim and gorgeous by the defunct Augustabernard house.

Now, I'm standing at one of the windows overlooking the city, partly shielded by a large tree, trying not to cry. I hate the stuffy, pretentious Ritz-Carlton, and I hate the Alaia I've been forced to wear. Okay, I love the Alaia, but I hate the idea of it. And I especially hate Nicolo's friends, standing around blathering about how much Chicago sucks, how boring Cannes is at this time of year, and how stressed they all are, jetting about the globe and looking chic.

I mean, are any of these people real? Do they ever worry that the guy they like won't call for a second date, or that they'll multiply wrong and the whole budget will be off, or that they'll set an apartment building on fire? Are these people for real? Is Nicolo?

I want to go home, but if I do all the reporters will write that Nicolo and I are having a fight. Which we are.

"What are you doing here all by yourself?" Nicolo says, coming up behind me. "You are not still sulking?"

I watch his reflection in the glass—a tall, regal man, a prince, standing beside a little girl pretending to be a princess.

I take a breath and turn. "I don't sulk. I was thinking. You might try it sometime."

"Ah, yes. That coming from you, whose big decision is the red nail polish or the pink?"

Before I can retaliate with my own scathing commentary, Nicolo holds up a hand. "No. I am sorry. I do not want to argue with you. We put all that aside, yes?" He scans the room, his gaze critical. "Come. Sixte has been asking for you."

Nicolo leads me across the room, where a small group of Europeans including Sixte, Valencia, and Maxmillian have gathered. We embrace and kiss as though we haven't seen one another in years. When I sit down, they continue their conversation.

"I refuse to ride in a white limousine," Valencia says. "I look fat in white."

Valencia is wearing a gown by Badgley Mischka, and if she's larger than a size zero, I'll eat my Emilio Pucci bag.

"Black is the only color for a chauffeur-driven car," Maxmillian adds.

"Well, I for one intend to take a Rolls back to the airport," Valencia says. "I cannot abide these dinosaurs some people consider cars."

I hear a muted sound and glance around until I notice one of the bartenders has a portable TV. He and a waiter are watching the Bulls play-off game surreptitiously. The cameras flash on Benny the Bull, and I can't suppress a smile. God, that Gatorade incident was horrible. Horrible and crazy and real. I glance at Nicolo, seated beside me on a divan. His expression is blank, the perfect mask of ennui.

My purse vibrates, and I jump in surprise. "Excuse me." I walk away, feeling Nicolo's frown burning into me.

"Sweetie, where are you?" It's Josh.

"The Ritz." I retreat to my corner behind the plant and stare at the lights of the city behind the windows.

"Ooh, swanky. Okay, quick question, since I know you've got all those royal affairs to attend to. Do we have everything ready for the next Wernberg meeting on Monday, or should we go in tomorrow?"

I close my eyes. "Josh, I don't even know. My brain is so fried right now."

"Sweetie, go home and turn in early," Josh says. "You sound exhausted."

"Nicolo has been dragging me out every night. I've gotten like no sleep."

"So tell his royalness you need a night off."

"We already had one argument today. It's easier just to humor him." I touch my fingers to the glass, tracing the outline of a building a few blocks away.

"Well, be a martyr, then."

"Look, I can meet tomorrow to double-check everything, but it has to be either early or late. I'm going with Gray to basketball camp."

"The princester's letting you out?"

"Josh."

"Sorry. Well, look at it this way: The sex is good, right?"

"Yeah. I'm just tired. I want a break from my life."

"Not next week, sweetie. We've got a show to watch, and a game to win."

I groan.

"Come on, girl. You were the cheerleader." I can almost see him jump up and strike a pose. "Give me a J."

"Josh, the Village People do that, not cheerleaders."

"Come on! Gimme a J!"

"J."

"With spirit!"

"J!" I growl.

"Ooh! Give me an O."

"O."

"Give me an S and an H."

"S, H."

"What does it spell?"

"Idiot."

Josh huffs. "You are no fun. I say you ditch the princelet and come out with me and Carlos tonight. We're going salsa dancing."

I glance at Nicolo across the room. He's frowning at me. "Better not, Salsa King."

"Speaking of kings, what's it like sleeping with royalty? Are you like, 'Oh, Your Majesty! Oh, oh!'?"

"Hey, when you tell me about Carlos, I'll tell you about Nicolo."

"But there's nothing *to* tell about Carlos. Yet."

"Well, then you better get moving, Salsa Boy, or he's going to mambo off with someone else."

"So, how are things with the prince?" Gray asks on our way home from camp the next morning.

Oh, good. This question again. "Fine. Except he'll probably be pissed that I'm staying in tonight, but I'm too tired to deal with his bullshit friends."

"Better get used to it." Gray slips a Nickelback CD in the

player and turns the volume up. "You're going to be almost royalty. That's a job that entails a lot of partying."

"Hmm."

"That guy Dave asked about you today."

I swerve. "Who?"

"Nice try. I told him you were a princess in training."

"Oh."

"He said to tell you the prince is a better mechanic than he is. Does that—hey, you ran that stop sign."

"This music's too loud. I can't concentrate." I punch the power button on the CD player and we're cast into silence. I don't know why I'm annoyed at Dave's comment. It's probably true, and what do I want him to say, anyway?

"Look," Gray says. "Nicolo's an okay guy. If you like him, I like him."

Wow. Big praise for Grayson. "Thanks."

"And I'm sorry about what I said at the lake house. I didn't mean that."

One more emotional comment like that, and I'm going to start believing the alien body-snatcher theories. "It's okay."

"No, it's not. I shouldn't say stuff like that to you—about you. I pretty much suck as a big brother."

I brake at a light, shifting into first. "No, you don't."

"Jesus, Allison"—he runs a hand through his long hair—"do you know how sorry I am about everything I've done? I'd give anything to go back and do it over again."

I squeeze his hand, wishing I could make things better, make the pain etched on his face disappear. I can see the fine lines and beginnings of wrinkles when he looks like this.

"Mostly I wish I could go back to that summer. I knew what was going on with that asshole Chris, but I was so strung out I didn't care."

"I've got as much to be sorry for as you do. It's my fault

you went to jail." The light turns green, and a car behind us honks. I jump, releasing the clutch too fast so that the car lurches forward.

"No, it's not."

"Gray, let's not talk about it. What happened with Chris is no big deal."

"He raped you."

I shift from second to third. "No, he didn't." We're going seventy in a fifty-five zone, but it's still not fast enough. "I had a huge crush on him. I didn't say no."

"You were fifteen. He was nineteen. That's rape."

We hit eighty, and I shift into fourth. It doesn't matter how fast I go. I can't outrun the poisonous black pit that opens when Gray brings Chris up. Usually I don't notice it gnawing away at me. Sometimes I think it's gone, then something happens and the canyon yawns and I plummet down, down, down.

"Slow down. You're going to get us killed."

I put in the clutch, brake hard, and turn, tires squealing, into a McDonald's parking lot. The car shudders.

"Gray." I turn to him. "It's not your fault. It happened. I regret it, but we all do stupid stuff when we're kids."

"And some of it messes us up more than others. Allie, I look at you now, and I think, man, if I'd just stopped it—"

"If you'd stopped him, what? Everything would be the same." My heart is beating fast, the blood is rushing in my ears, and the roar of the bottomless chasm in my belly is deafening.

"I don't think so. You'd be married or at least serious with some guy by now. You wouldn't be so afraid of getting hurt that you hide behind childish fantasies and designer clothes."

I recoil, feeling the verbal punch in my gut. My defenses

spring forward like porcupine spikes. I roll my eyes. "Please. What do you know about it?"

He sighs. "More than you think. I've got my own barricades."

I'm sort of speechless at that comment. Am I really that much like Gray? Afraid to commit, changing men as often as my nail polish?

Gray glances toward the McDonald's playground. The sound of laughter and the smell of french fries and Big Macs seeps in through the car's vents. "You're so cool, Allie. You never let anyone see you—the real you."

"That's not true."

"Allie, you go through guys like—"

"Nail polish?"

"I was going to say disposable razors, but the idea's the same."

His tone is lighter, and now that we're past the subject of our past, I can see the bridge out of this desert wasteland. My heartbeat slows and returns to normal. "Hey, maybe I just haven't found the right guy."

"Allison, you're thirty-two, smart, successful, gorgeous— not as gorgeous as me, but—"

"What's your point?"

"I've met some of your boyfriends. They're good guys, but as soon as it gets serious, you ditch them."

"Ha! Not true. They break up with me almost as often as I ditch them."

"Because you make it happen. You won't let them get close. If they start to get past the perfect exterior to the broken interior, you back away." He puts his hand on my arm. "But you know what, you're not broken inside. It's like that useless show you're doing. Stop trying to fix something that's not broken."

"That's a lot of philosophizing. Have you considered that maybe Nicolo's not the right guy for me?"

"Maybe not. He comes with a hell of a lot of baggage, but if you're not sure about this thing, you'd better break it off before you're in too deep. Before your entire life is fodder for the tabloids. Now I'm going to shut up and buy you an ice cream cone." Grayson hops out, walks around, and opens my door.

"I'll have a Diet Coke."

"No, you won't." He pulls me out of the car. "I'm the model, and if I can eat an ice cream, so can you."

12

Ev'ry Time We Say Good-bye

When Nicolo and I arrive at Rory's, her apartment is packed. Hunter, Grayson, and Grayson's flavor of the month are playing with a big-screen TV that Hunter must have hauled over; Josh, Carlos, and Stormy, Rory's sister, and Stormy's latest boyfriend are in the kitchen getting the hors d'oeuvres ready; and Court-ney and Christina, two of my friends from college, are sitting on the couch.

I introduce Nicolo to everyone he hasn't met, and he's relatively civil, which means he shakes the hands of the TV group, nods stiffly at the kitchen group, and kisses the hands of Court and Tina. By the time Rory comes back from the store, where Hunter told me she ran to fetch more ice, Nicolo's sitting between my college friends, ensconced in conversation.

"Allie! You're here." Rory hugs me, which isn't typical for her, but it's sweet.

"Thanks for doing all this," I say, indicating the streamers and balloons and party hats that no one except Hunter and Rory are wearing.

"It was fun." She glances at Nicolo, still flirting with my friends, and I roll my eyes, then follow her into the kitchen.

"Want a wheatgrass smoothie?" Stormy asks, holding out a glass filled with bright green liquid.

"Um, I already grazed today. Got any wine?"

"Sure." Rory pulls out two bottles. "White or red?"

"White."

She reaches for a glass and pours the wine.

"Sweetie, are you as excited about the show as I am?" Josh asks. "Carlos did some strong mojo before we came."

"That's right. I got a chicken—"

"Okay!" I say before Rory or her animal rights sister catch on to Carlos's anti-SPCA practices. "Let's go."

Everyone settles in front of the TV—Hunter's big screen. I give him a hug and a kiss on the cheek, then rinse and repeat with Grayson. "Thanks for hauling that over. You're very sweet."

I do wish they'd asked me before going to so much effort, though. I'm not so sure I want to see me and the box o'vibrators on the big screen.

Tina moves over, and I settle next to Nicolo on the couch. Josh sits directly in front of the TV, his eyes riveted on the Charmin commercial. Someone is ready for *Kamikaze Makeover!* and his close-up.

The show starts and a slick piece of eye candy stands in a studio and explains the concept of the show.

"Who's that?" I ask Nicolo. "I never saw him."

The screen flashes to a shot of the Japanese team in an

office, talking and examining various fabrics. They look really industrious, like serious, skilled decorators.

The host introduces them, accompanied by a headshot of each, then flashes to a scene of the challengers.

"That's us! That's us!" Josh yells. "We're the challengers!"

But the rest of the room is silent. Where the Japanese team looked busy and successful, we look like a bunch of losers. Watanabe chose footage from the first house, when Josh and I collapsed on the floor. We look like we're lying around with nothing to do. Even Miranda, relaxing in the chair, her eyes half-closed, looks like a bum.

Nicolo laughs. "You keep telling me you are so tired. Look at you. Very lazy."

I don't particularly want to look at me. The khaki capris and white T-shirt I'm wearing on-screen are wrinkled, splattered with dirt and grime; my hair is tangled, stuck on top of my head and secured with two pencils; and the angle of the shot is not as flattering to my hips as I would have liked.

"That was at the end of the day," I tell no one and everyone. "We didn't know they were still filming." I bite my thumbnail, chipping my Shootout at the O.K. Coral OPI polish. I'm more than concerned now about Watanabe and his cronies' selective editing.

The shot goes back to the slick host, and he intros the first segment, leaving off with shots of the houses and a cliff-hanger with footage of me arguing with the gang member. As soon as the ad for Sherwin-Williams comes on, everyone starts talking. Josh whines that he looks horrible on-screen, that his skin was ashy and he looked so fat—more so than the extra ten pounds the camera adds can account for.

"Carlos, why didn't you tell me I was fat? I'm a cow—no, a hippopotamus." He runs into the bathroom, and Carlos follows.

"No, honey. Jou look good."

The show starts again, and we get a look at the house the Japanese team had to redecorate. It starts out looking as bad as ours, so at least that's fair. The camera shows them scraping away old wallpaper and wrestling the vibrator into a tasteful-looking objet d'art. The host refers to the vibrators as personal massagers, but we all know what they really are.

"You had to decorate the house with vibrators?" Gray chokes back a laugh. "You are so going to get it. Mom and Dad are going to freak."

"Maybe they'll believe the personal massagers thing." Unfortunately, I remember one incident all too clearly and if the film crew has decided to show that footage, which they probably have as they seem determined to make us look like idiots, there won't be much question what the vibrators are used for.

"Are we back on yet?" Josh calls from the bathroom.

"Next commercial," Rory answers. "Come out and watch. I'll pour you another glass of wine."

"Half a glass. I have to watch my figure, since I'm such a blimp."

There's another commercial break and Josh, dabbing his eyes with Kleenex, reemerges. "Oh, God. It's coming back on."

Kamikaze Makeover! flashes on the screen, accompanied by the sound of Japanese drums, and our host intros our house. There it is, and there's the three of us in the conference room at the office. "Look, Josh," I say. "It's not that bad. We come across really serious there."

"The American team did have a few distractions to contend with," the host announces. Flash to a close-up of Lila.

She says, "We'd better get on that or we'll be late and end

up having to cut corners like we did at Harpo Studios." Flash to a shot of me, looking very guilty.

In Rory's living room, I shake my head. "Wait. We weren't even talking about the show there . . ."

I trail off as footage of Nicolo and I going into a restaurant together last week begins. I glance at Nicolo, but he looks unconcerned. The host starts talking about me, about the romance that bloomed on the set between Nicolo and me kissing in the office one day. When I thought there weren't any cameras around. I'm so mortified to see myself like this. I want to ask Nicolo if he knew about the cameras, but before I can, there's another shot of me at Mrs. Jackson's house. I'm talking to Josh and holding the box o'vibrators.

On-screen Miranda says, "I thought you liked a challenge."

"This isn't a challenge," I say, holding a purple vibrator aloft. The scene then shifts to a few hours later. Josh and I are kneeling next to a table, trying to figure out how to fashion a vibrator into a lamp stand. We pull one out, and I accidentally turn it on. But instead of just vibrating, this one swivels and dips. The screen then flashes back to the earlier scene.

Josh says, "I think we're screwed," and I say, "Well, we've got the right equipment." Flash back to the gyrating vibrator.

I put my head in my hands. I'm not so much embarrassed as dreading the fallout. Right on cue, my cell phone rings. I glance at the display, then at Gray. "It's Mom and Dad."

"Don't answer," he says. The ringing stops and the phone goes to voice mail. A minute later, Grayson's phone rings. "Shit." He answers, "Hello? Oh, hi, Dad. No, I don't know where—"

I stand. "Just give me the phone. I better get this over with." I start walking toward the door. "Hi, Daddy. You were watching? It wasn't my choice. You heard what I said . . . I know but . . . Mrs. Chippenhall called? . . . I know, but I signed the . . . Daddy, I'm sure no one we know saw—okay, sorry."

Everyone is watching me, pretending not to listen. I give a little wave and step into Rory's hallway. My dad continues to yell, and nothing I say calms him down. Finally, I hear the door behind me open.

"Daddy, why don't we talk about this tomorrow when you're not so upset, okay?"

He says something else.

"Okay, love you, too. Bye."

I turn to see Nicolo. "Your father is upset?"

"Do you blame him? It's not every day he gets to see his little girl on national television playing with sex toys. Did you know they were going to make us look so stupid?"

He shrugs. "It was not hard to do."

"You really are a bastard, aren't you? Why would you do that to me? And what about those scenes with us? Did you know they were filming?"

"You did not?"

"You know I didn't! What am I to you? A publicity tool?"

He shrugs again.

"You fucking used me."

"Again, you make it so easy."

"Get out of my sight."

He opens Rory's door, presumably to get his jacket and keys, and go. I follow him indoors, my insides roiling with anger.

"You know what, Nicolo, I used to think I was a snob, but

you take the cake. I should have thrown you off a boat when you showed up in Lake Geneva."

He turns and glares at me, hand still on Rory's door handle.

"What?" I say. "Do you think I'm going to break down in tears and beg you to take me back? You're the one who should be begging me."

"Stop shouting at me. You act like a peasant."

"Oh, you think this is shouting?" Actually, I had been talking rather loudly, i.e., shouting. "I'll give you shouting."

"You are not worth this. You with your peasant friends— fags and freaks all of them. I cannot wait to leave this country."

"And I promise you that we can't wait to see you go," I hiss.

Nicolo whirls and glares at me, face red with anger. "You bitch." He steps forward and Gray and Hunter rise simulta- neously. Nicolo eyes them, then me. "You will pay." He stomps out and slams the door. As the echo vibrates through the room, I put on a wobbly smile. "Well, that's that," and then I burst into tears.

On Monday I arrive at the office five minutes before nine and am ready to go home again by nine-thirty. Several clients call to tell me they no longer require my services, and the front page of the Lifestyle section has a picture of me and Josh holding the gyrating vibrator. The head- line reads, "DECORATORS GET THRUST OF NEW SHOW." I want to cry, I want to hide under my covers, I want to kick Nicolo's ass.

And then my mother calls to yell at me. You'd think that at a time like this, my mother would be supportive, but she doesn't care about how I feel, only how all of this looks.

Everything is going wrong. My life has become a bad episode of a reality TV show, and I can't shut the TV off.

The only bright spot in my day is when Rory calls to ask how I'm holding up. She offers to cut out of work early so we can have an extended happy hour. But even a mojito and Rory's sympathetic ear don't ease the impending sense of doom. Two mojitos and several baskets of tortilla chips (yes, that's dinner) later, I'm painting my toenails with the TV on for noise. The world news coverage is over, and I hear the anchorwoman say, "In local news, a possible lawsuit against the prestigious Interiors by M."

I scramble for the remote and hike the volume to max. I've smeared OPI's A-Rose at Dawn . . . Broke by Noon polish, but I don't care.

"Sources report that Dai Hoshi, a major Japanese media conglomerate that produces, in part, the television show *Kamikaze Makeover!* will sue the Chicago-area interior design firm. *Kamikaze Makeover!* premiered on KCHI Saturday evening and features competition between three top Japanese interior decorators and three American designers from Interiors by M. Ramosu Kobayashi, CEO and founder of Dai Hoshi, alleges that an employee at Interiors by M violated several stipulations of the contract between the two firms. More on this as the story develops.

"In sports, the Houston Rockets mascot is in court—"

I throw the remote and the TV flashes off. Shit. It's got to be me who's violated the contract. How would Josh or Miranda have violated it? I don't know how I could have, either, but I know it's me. I *know.*

I grab my laptop case, open it, and dig through the files I've stashed there. No contract. I must have left it at the office. I don't remember filing it, so maybe it's still on my desk. Unless I had Natalie file it for me . . .

The phone rings, and I snatch it up, hoping it's Josh or Rory.

"Hello?"

"Miss Holloway? This is Marti Kristynik from *USA Today*. Can I ask you a few questions about your involvement in the show *Kamikaze Makeover!* and your relationship with producer Nicolo Parma?"

"No." I hang up, and then my cell phone rings. The display reads "Evelyn Shephard."

"Hello?"

"Allison Holloway, this is Evelyn Shephard from the *Houston Chronicle*. I'd like your comment on—"

The *Houston Chronicle?* People from Houston are calling me? Oh, my God. The phone rings again, and I unplug it and turn my cell off, too. Booboo Kitty is stretched out on my bed, and I decide she has the right idea and climb under the covers. I lie there, Booboo curled around my head and hogging (catting?) most of the pillow, until five A.M., and then I get up, get dressed, and drive to work.

When I arrive I'm surprised to see the light in Miranda's office. I tap on her door quietly and push it open. She looks as haggard as me in her velour tracksuit, hair in a clip at the back of her head, and no makeup. She's sitting at her desk staring at a pile of papers and doesn't see me at first.

"Miranda?"

She glances up. "Good, you're here. I thought you might call in."

"Why?"

"You didn't see the news?" She beckons me forward, and I take a seat in the chair opposite her desk. Five years ago I sat in this same spot, in this same office, although it wasn't decorated the same, spouting off about my experience and credentials while Miranda flipped through my portfolio and résumé.

I wanted this job so badly. I'd spent almost four years working my way up the ladder at Enger and Associates, a large design firm that's respected in the industry, but I wanted to work for the best. In Chicago, Interiors by M was and is the best.

"I saw it, and I guess everyone else, too, because people were calling me all night. I have nineteen messages on my voice mail at home, and I haven't even checked my e-mail or my voice mail here. What's going on?"

Miranda lifts a thick, legal-size document and passes it over. It's a copy of my contract, exactly the reason I came in this morning. I start reading and Miranda says, impatiently, "Page seven, section twelve."

I flip to page seven and scan the legalese. I have to read it twice before I understand, and when I do, I feel like I'm going to throw up. I glance at Miranda.

"You didn't know?" she asks.

"No. I didn't read it that carefully."

She sighs. "Me either."

We stare at each other for a long moment, then I say, "But surely Nicolo would have known. Why did he—"

Miranda scowls. "Maybe he knew, maybe he didn't. My question is how a copy of the contract got leaked to the media."

"Our relationship hasn't been a secret. Dai Hoshi had the contracts and once they filed suit the media—"

"They haven't filed yet."

I frown. "But the news said—"

"I got a call from one of the lawyers at Dai Hoshi. They're willing to negotiate."

"What do they want?" I press a fist into my belly, forcing the nausea down.

"They want your employment at Interiors by M terminated, effective immediately."

"What?"

"Allison, I have no choice but to let you go. If I don't, they'll run us into the ground."

I start to speak, but she waves a hand.

"Allison, we are in the wrong. You violated the contract—there is to be no fraternization between contestants and the employees of Dai Hoshi or Carpathian Enterprises—that's Parma's company, if you didn't know."

"But maybe if I talk to Nicolo, he'll speak to Ramosu Kobayashi, and they'll drop it."

Miranda gives me a patronizing smile. "Are you on good terms with Parma at present?"

The reality of the situation hits me, and I almost double over from the slash of pain in my belly. "No, not really. Are you sure he knows?"

"He *knows*. Dai Hoshi didn't decide to sue a little firm like us for a minor breach of conduct for the hell of it. They'd spend more money on lawyers than they'd win in court."

I nod. She's right, of course. She's completely right. And can it be a coincidence that it's all come out only twenty-four hours after I told Nicolo off?

"They've offered to settle if I fire you," Miranda says. "This isn't about Interiors by M, Allison. You messed up, and he's using it against you."

The office is quiet, just the rush of the air conditioning and the hum of Miranda's computer. Finally she says, "Why don't you clear your things out now before the reporters get here. Keep a low profile. I'm sure your parents would like it if you kept this as quiet as possible."

I nod and rise. I'm in a daze and don't see Miranda come around the desk. She puts her hand on my shoulder. "Allison, you're a gifted designer. Take a few months off, let all this die down, then look for another job. If not in Chicago, maybe New York or Washington. It's a big world out there."

I swallow my tears and say, "Thanks, Miranda. Tell Lila and Natalie I said goodbye, and I'll miss them."

"I will."

I close her office door behind me for the last time and stare at my own office. Pale gray light filters through the blinds on the outer windows, transforming the desk and furniture into phantoms haunting the dark office.

I stare at it—at what was my office—and my stomach heaves violently.

Okay, so maybe shopping isn't the best thing to do under these circumstances, but how else am I to keep occupied all day Friday? I don't feel like talking to anyone, even if my phone would stop ringing. I'd like to bury my head under the covers, but I did that the last couple of days. There's nothing to watch on TV, nothing good to read, and I'm not hungry. I thought I might work on organizing my desk area and making it more feng shui, but I didn't have any purple cloth for the wealth corner. No wealth corner was a crisis I didn't want to consider, so I rushed out to purchase beaucoup purple cloth (more cloth = more money, right?). Somehow I ended up at Neiman Marcus.

I stroll through the departments, touching silk scarves, velvet tops, chiffon dresses. I buy a pair of Manolo Blahniks that I probably can't afford anymore, slip them on, and listen to the way they tap when I walk. At four in the afternoon, I drive to Rory's office. I've never been inside, but I know where she works. The receptionist for the Yates and Youngman accounting firm asks if I have an appointment with Ms. Egg-lehoff and when I say no, she tells me Ms. Egglehoff can't see me today.

"Look"—I glance at the gold plate on her desk—"Meredith. I'm her sister, and it's a family emergency, okay? Please call her and say I'm here."

Meredith's eyes narrow. "You're her sister, huh?"

"Yes."

"Her sister was in here a few months ago, and you look nothing like her."

I close my eyes and press my hands on Meredith's desk. My OPI Don't Socra-tease Me! polish stands out against the tense white of my fingers.

"Okay, I'm not Rory's sister, but I *need* to talk to her. I called her on my cell, and I got her voice mail. Why don't you just tell me which one is her office, and I'll wait for her?"

"Ms. Egglehoff is in a meeting, so you will have to come back another time."

The phone rings.

"One minute."

I frown, pace, and glance down the hallway behind Mer-edith's desk. It's absolutely silent in here. No one's chatting, no one's got the radio on. It's so quiet I hear the hum of the fluorescent lights. I glance around the lobby. Horrible deco-rating. How can anyone get any work done in a place like this? The lights alone make my head ache.

A typical accountant-looking guy steps out of an office and starts walking down the hall toward the reception area. His pants are too high, his hair looks uncombed, he's wear-ing glasses and a pocket protector, and his arms are laden with files. One almost slips, and he tries to catch it, losing all of the files in the process. They spill on the carpet—burnished orange, cheap, stained—the papers fanning out against the wall.

He bends down to retrieve them, and I notice he's wearing a Tasmanian Devil tie. Where have I seen that before? I don't know anyone who'd wear—

Tedious Tom. Rory's ex-boyfriend.

"Tom!"

The receptionist glances at me at the same time Tom's head pops up. He squints at me.

"Excuse me," I tell the receptionist and start down the hall.

"Wait! You can't—"

"Tom, hey! I haven't seen you in a while. How are you?" I bend down and gather some of the errant files together, making sure to bend over enough that Tom gets a good look at my cleavage without having to try too hard.

"Um, do I know—"

"Tom. Don't tell me you don't remember me."

He straightens and I follow, handing him the files. He shifts from foot to foot, obviously not knowing what to do. God, how did Rory put up with this? I hear Meredith calling out behind me, so I link my arm through his and say, "I'm Allison Holloway. Rory's friend."

He stiffens. "Oh."

"Miss! Miss! You can't just barge on through!"

Okay, time to wrap this up. "Tom, would you be a sweetie and take me back to Rory's office? I need to see her, and I think she forgot to let that lion back there know I was coming." I look into his eyes, blink coyly once or twice—I hope my eyeliner isn't smeared. "Can you help?"

"Okay."

The receptionist finally reaches us. "Miss!"

Tom turns to her. "It's okay, Meredith. Allison's a friend of mine. I'll take her back."

"But Mr. Thompson, are you sure?"

He nods. Twenty minutes later, I've gone through all the books on Rory's shelf, finished off her stash of M&Ms and her can of Diet Coke, played with her computer—but everything that looked interesting is password-protected—and finally decided to balance my checkbook. Hey, there's a first time for everything. And after being surrounded by calculators and adding machines for almost a half-hour, I feel like I should do something mathematical.

I remember feeling this way in school a lot, too. Like if I was just around beakers and Bunsen burners, somehow chemistry would seep into my brain. I learned early on that atmosphere is everything. If I was surrounded by scientific, professional-type things, I *felt* scientific and professional. Hmm. Problem is, it didn't work then, and it's not working for me now.

I've added up about three columns in my checkbook register, but then I pressed a wrong button on the calculator, and now every time I try to add any numbers arcs and lines pop up on-screen. I open Rory's top drawer. Doesn't she have a normal calculator?

"Hey!" Rory rushes in. "Tom told me you were here. What's wrong?"

I frown. "I can't figure out how to work this stupid calculator. I just want to add up my checkbook, but it keeps asking for the X value."

Rory reaches over, hits a key, and turns the calculator back toward me. "Here."

The screen looks normal again. It's even showing my last total. "Thanks." I lean back in her leather chair. "Nice chair, but your office could use some help. You don't have any artwork, no knickknacks, not even a fake plant. And this arrangement is all wrong. The desk would be better near that wall."

"You came here to redecorate my office?"

"No. I came to give you this." I pull the Kate Spade clutch from the shopping bag and hold it out to her. "This is totally your style, and it will go perfectly with that black dress you wore to the reunion."

She takes it, her expression bewildered, then shocked. "Creator! This costs a hundred and forty dollars!"

"It's a Kate Spade."

"I don't care if it's the plans to the Death Star, that's too much. Where am I going to take this? I never get dressed up."

"So, tell Hunter to take you out. I saw this cute dress by Jones New York, and I know you'd love it. I would have bought it for you, but I wasn't sure which size. We can go back and—"

"Stop." She plops in the chair across from me. "What's going on? Is it the *Kamikaze Makeover!* show still?"

I shake my head. "Worse."

"What?"

"Miranda fired me."

Rory's eyes pop open. "What? You are kidding me. How the Dark Side could she fire you?"

"She said, 'Allison, I have no choice but to let you go,' so I went."

"But what does that mean, no choice? Because of the vibrator thing?" She lowers her voice on the word *vibrator* because the door's still open.

"No. I violated my contract. There was a provision against any of the contestants fraternizing with the bosses. I broke that by going out with Nicolo."

"But why didn't Nicolo say something? Why did you go

out with him if you knew it would be in violation of the contract?"

I glower at her, and she sits back. "You never read the contract."

I look down.

"Okay, I'm not going to be a nerf-herder and say I've told you three thousand seven hundred and twenty times to always read paperwork, but maybe if you call Nicolo—"

I shake my head. "He's the one who did this."

"Oh, no."

"Yeah, and isn't it convenient that they'll drop the whole thing if I'm terminated?"

"That Mynok! We can't let him get away with this."

"Slow down, Rebel crusader. He's a prince. We won't win."

"But we can't let the Dark Side win."

"Rory, I don't want this in the news. I'll get another job, but in the meantime, I don't want to embarrass my parents more than I already have. Okay?"

"Okay. But I want to do something to help. What can I do?"

"I know you probably have plans with Hunter."

She waves my concern away. "He'll understand."

"Okay, then, can I stay with you this weekend?" I say with a weak smile. "My phone won't stop ringing, and when I stopped home to drop off my stuff from work, there were a couple of reporters hanging around. It was bad before, but now . . ."

Rory stands. "Of course you can stay with me. I need to shut down my computer and get some files to work on, and we're out of here."

"You won't get in trouble?" I scoot out of her way.

"No. Mr. Yates is at a conference this week. Everyone's been cutting out early." She starts stuffing files into her bag.

"This is going to be fun—a slumber party! Should we order pizza? You need pizza and ice cream after all this. I couldn't stand being the center of attention. I'd have a panic attack if a bunch of reporters were waiting outside my door."

"Yeah. Rory, I kind of need you to do one more thing for me."

"What's that?"

"Brave the reporters in front of my house, go in, and feed Booboo Kitty."

Her face crumples, then she takes a fortifying breath. "Okay, this is like in *Return of the Jedi* when Han, Luke, and Leia needed to disable the shield generator on the Endor moon so the Rebel fleet could blow up the Death Star. They went in the back way. Of course, there was an ambush, but that's only because Darth Vader sensed—"

"Rory! What are you talking about?"

"Don't worry, Allie. The Force is with me."

I sigh. Sometimes I'm not altogether sure whether Rory is living on this planet or a galaxy far, far away.

Flat Foot Floogee

Rory drops me off at her place and comes back two hours later with my pajamas, my toothbrush, and a pizza. She tells me she got into my house "undetected" and not to worry. If she'd quit saying things like "shield generator," "endangering the mission," and "undetected," maybe I wouldn't worry.

I don't think I'll be able to sleep, but I pretty much pass out as soon as my head hits the pillow. I don't move until Rory comes in, sits on the bed, and says, "Allie?"

I crack one eye open. "What time is it?"

"After ten."

"Hmm." I close my eyes again.

"Allie, something bad happened."

My eyes snap open. "Was it another of your missions?"

She shakes her head, and I notice she's holding the newspaper.

"More about the lawsuit or me getting fired in the paper?"
She shakes her head again.

"Then what?" I sit up and push the hair out of my face. I
hold my hand out, but she doesn't hand the paper over right
away.

"Did you go to a fashion show for"—she glances at the
paper—"Cara St. Loren?"

"It's Ciara, and yes. Why?"

"Were there any photographers there?"

"Probably. Why?"

"I think it might be bad."

"Give me the paper." I hold my hand out again. Rory hesi-
tates. I scramble to my knees. "Give me the paper!"

She hands it over and I stare at the picture on the front
page. It's me and Nicolo at the fashion show. The picture is
grainy and slightly unfocused, but there's no question his
hand is between my legs. I don't move. I don't breathe. I
don't speak. I just gawk at the picture and wish I were
dead.

I force my eyes to the caption beneath: "Prince Nicolo
Bourbon-Parma entertains Chicago socialite Allison Holloway."

"Allison, are you okay?"

"Am I dead?" I croak.

"No," Rory says, sounding worried.

"Then I'm not fine."

She grabs my hand. "Allison, it's not the end of the
world."

I stare at her. "Rory, I was on national TV playing with a
gyrating vibrator, I violated my contract, I was fired, and
now I'm in the paper with a guy's hand up my skirt. How
much worse can it get?"

"The photographer was on TV."

"Oh, my God."

"Just now on MSNBC he said he was taking pictures of the models and when he developed them he noticed a pretty face in the background. He blew up that section of the photo, and got this."

"Bastard. Why didn't you wake me up?"

She shrugs. "I was trying to think how we could fix it."

"I know how to fix it." I glance around the room for my cell phone and remember I dropped it on Rory's table. Probably under the box of pizza now. "I'm calling Nicolo and—" I break off as Rory begins shaking her head.

"On CNN the photographer said—"

"He was on MSNBC *and* CNN?"

"Yeah. And, um, he said he offered to sell the photos to Nicolo, figuring the prince wouldn't want a picture like this to come out, but the prince told him to go ahead and print them. He didn't care."

I jump off the bed. "I'm going to fucking kill him. I'm going to get a corkscrew, shove it in each and every one of his bodily orifices, and screw him!"

"Allie, I don't think—"

"Who the fuck does he think he's dealing with?" I pace the room. Back and forth. Back and forth. "Does he think he'll get away with this? I'm going to skewer him on national TV. I'll call *The Enquirer* and tell them he has a small dick, that he sexually abuses young boys, that he likes to wear women's underwear."

"Is that true?"

I halt. "No. But neither is it true that I'm a slut who let him feel me up at a fashion show! I bet the reporter didn't mention that one second after that picture was snapped, I got up and walked out. I bet the paper"—I pick it up and throw it across the room, so the pages fly up and out, settling on the floor and the bed in a heap—"I bet it didn't report that we had a huge argument outside the club, and that I told him he could go fuck himself. No, all you get is me with my legs spread."

"You can't see anything."

"That's not the fucking point!"

Rory flinches.

"Oh, God, I'm sorry." I crawl on the bed and hug her. "I don't mean to yell at you."

"It's okay," Rory says, hugging me back. "But that's not all."

I freeze. How can there possibly be more.

"There was a lady, a Mrs. Chippendale—"

"Mrs. Chippenhall."

"Yeah. She was on right after the reporter. She's suing your firm for shoddy workmanship. You, in particular, are named in the suit."

"Oh, my God." I'd expected something like this from Mrs. Chippenhall, but coming right on top of the rest of it, it's too much to digest. I bolt upright. "What time did you say it was?"

Rory glances at the clock. "It's almost eleven now. Why?"

"I have to drive Grayson to basketball camp. Today is the last day, and there's a big party. If he's not there, the kids will be really upset."

I start digging through the bag Rory packed for me and pull out a long, black silk skirt and a beaded top. I give her a confused look. "What is this?"

"You said to grab you some clothes."

"Yeah, but why did you bring this? This is for formal occasions."

Rory shrugs. "It looked like something you normally wear, and I didn't know what you'd be doing today."

"Well, I'm not going to a dinner party at the governor's." I go through the bag again and pull out flip-flops. Red flip-flops from Target with blue Gatorade stains. I stare at them.

"They've got pretty red flowers on the toe strap. I thought they'd look cute," Rory says.

I nod. Did Dave see the story? Is he thinking he was lucky to get rid of me, that he got off easy with a pair of cheap flip-flops?

"Allie?" Rory says. "Honey, just stay in your pajamas. I'll drive Grayson. You can't go out to the basketball camp."

"I need to see Grayson."

"Allie—"

I hold up a hand. "He's my brother, and I need him. Do you have a pair of shorts and a T-shirt I can wear?"

"Sure."

Twenty minutes later I'm in the car, on the way to the basketball camp. Gray wasn't home, so he must have gotten another ride to the camp. The smart thing to do would be to go back to Rory's, but I can't. I need my big brother. I need to talk to someone who's been through worse than this and made it to the other side. After I see Gray, I'll brave the reporters at home, pack a bag and Booboo, and head for Lake Geneva. I can hide out there until I decide what to do tomorrow and pretty much the rest of my life.

I pull at Rory's T-shirt. It says, "ANNUAL CREATURES AND FEATURES EXTRAVAGANZA 2004" on the front and "YEAR OF THE JAWA" on the back. What the hell is a Jawa? The shirt's too small, so "CREATURES AND FEATURES" is stretched across my chest and almost unreadable. The shorts she loaned me are jean cutoffs she wore in high school. She's outgrown them, but they're still too big for me, and I have to hike them up.

How does Rory buy clothes? She's small and delicate on top and normal-size on the bottom. Come to think of it, she's a better dresser than I'd thought. I'd never even noticed the disproportion.

I decide to take a back road to the camp in case reporters are staking out the main road. It takes a little longer, especially when I realize I've spent half an hour going the wrong way, but I finally recognize an abandoned barn and a small farmhouse. Of course, by then it's almost four and camp's probably already over, but I can't find my way home until I find a reference point.

But the farmhouse is apparently the best I'm going to get because about a half-mile past the farmhouse, my Z4 slows and won't respond when I hit the gas. I shift into neutral and it sort of coasts a bit farther, then sputters and stops. What the—?

I glance at the fuel gauge and want to bang my head on the steering wheel. I'm out of gas. I've been meaning to get some for two days, but every time I think of it, I get fired or am publicly humiliated again.

Okay, time to call in reinforcements. I reach in my red Fendi bag for my cell and pull out three credit cards, a tube of M·A·C's Coconutty lipstick, a piece of gum, a ten-dollar bill, a tube of NARS's Shanghai Express, Great Lash mascara, an emery board, a hairband, a paper clip, and a tape measure.

I pull open the glove compartment and paw through a ring of paint chips, Ralph Lauren sunglasses—oh! I've been looking for these—an old bottle of OPI Redipus Oedipus nail polish, a map of Cleveland—don't ask—and about a dozen condoms. I guess at some point I was feeling optimistic. No more. Because my cell phone is sitting under an empty pizza box in Rory's apartment. How could I be so stupid!

Okay, no big deal, I'll walk to the gas station, in the red-flowered flip-flops, and buy gas.

I glance around. Hmm. The odds of a gas station being close don't look favorable. I'm on a gravel road, surrounded by fields and cattle, and the last building I saw was the abandoned barn. Okay, no problem. I can wait until someone drives by and hitch a ride.

To tell the truth, I'm pretty proud of myself. I'm being so calm in the face of all these crises. All is not lost. Someone will drive by any moment.

One hour and four minutes later, I start walking. I'm still not panicking, but I'm starting to feel a little uneasy. In the hour I've been standing on the side of the road, next to my obviously incapacitated vehicle, only two cars have driven by, and neither stopped to help me. Do I look like a serial killer or something? I mean, come on. What are the chances that a woman holding a Fendi bag and standing next to a BMW Z4 convertible on the side of a farm road in Illinois is a serial killer? Like ninety-nine-thousand billion to one?

I take a deep breath, and clutch my friends tightly. Mitsy always says that diamonds are nice, but credit cards are a girl's new best friend. What can't a girl do with MasterCard and Miss Visa?

I don't remember passing any gas stations, so I decide to follow the road until I 1) reach a gas station, 2) reach the camp, or 3) am mauled by an angry cow who doesn't like me trespassing on her field.

An hour later, I'm hot, tired, limping, and pretty sure I'm going to die out here. I don't know if these fields are planted with corn, but I'm starting to imagine all kinds of *Children of the Corn* scenarios as the sun sinks lower. I am so screwed.

No one knows where I am, which in light of recent events should make me happy. The irony is that now I'm so lost, even I can't find me.

I limp to the top of another hill, promising God to send money to orphans or monks or anyone He wants if He'd just make a bottle of water appear. I'd drink tap water at this point. I'd drink blue Gatorade!

At the top of the hill, I stumble from surprise. There's no bottled water, but in the distance I see lights, and I hear music, singing . . . angels?

Garth Brooks. Well, if God's got friends in low places, then we're in Heaven. Otherwise, I think I've staggered upon the Bait Shop, where Gray, Dave, Cindy!, and I ate a few weeks ago.

I stroll—okay, limp—inside, wave the ten-year-old hostess away, and head straight for the bar on the deck. I distinctly remember seeing someone talking on a phone back there.

The place is more crowded than you'd expect for early evening, even on Saturday, so I have to wriggle through a few people to reach the bartender.

I lean both elbows on the bar and say, "I need water, and I need to use your phone." My voice is raspy, and all semblance of politeness eked away a couple of miles back with the sole of my right flip-flop.

"Sorry," the bartender says, barely glancing at me. "Phone's for staff only."

"I'm staff."

"Nice try."

I snort. After what I've been through, he thinks "nice try" is going to faze me? "Hey." I tap the shoulder of the guy on my left. "Do you want another beer?"

"Uh—okay."

"Bartender, get this guy another beer. There. I'm staff. Now give me the phone before I—"

A small metal object is thrust in front of my face. I squint and read *Nokia.* Nokia! A cell phone! All is right with the world.

I snatch the cell, turning to pledge undying devotion to the saint who's blessed me with this holy relic, then scream and drop the phone as if it were the key to an eternity spent burning in Hell.

Satan catches the phone before it hits the deck. He grins. "Yeah, I like to scream at this thing sometimes, too."

"You."

"Sucks, huh? You thought you were rid of me."

Dave. Why is Dave here? Oh, of course *Dave* is here. The question is why I'm here, and more important, *how* I got here. Dave holds the phone out to me again.

"Still need to make a call?"

I sink down on a bar stool next to him. "Oh, what's the point?" I put my head in my hands. "I'm tired of trying to hold it together." I put my forehead on the bar.

"Stu, a margarita for the lady and another beer for me."

I lift my head. "Just water, please. Three glasses to start."

"You're a cheap date."

"Ha-ha."

He frowns. "I didn't mean it that way. Sorry, I—"

I shake my head. "It's okay. Make fun of me. I'm at the wallowing-in-self-pity phase anyway." The waiter puts three glasses of water before me, and I down them like a frat boy at a keg party. I slam the last glass on the bar and say, "Another, Stu. Keep 'em coming, buddy." I feel like laughing, but I'm afraid if I start, I won't be able to stop.

"Are you okay?" Dave asks.

I give him a sidelong look. "Am I okay? Well, I guess that

depends on how you define 'okay.' Is humiliation on a national TV show okay?"

Dave shrugs. "It's not the end of the world."

"I see. How about getting fired from your job because Dai Hoshi, the billion-dollar global media conglomerate, will sue your ass for breach of contract if you aren't terminated immediately? Is that okay?"

"It's not good, but—"

"How about your phone ringing constantly and your house staked out by reporters who hope to buy their next car from the profits made by selling your story?"

"Red—"

"Or, oh, is it okay if you're pictured in the paper with a guy's hand up your skirt? Is that okay? Wait, is it okay if, on top of all that, your car runs out of gas and you have to walk for like two hours in Rory's clothes and cheap-ass flip-flops just to get to a"—I raise my voice—"hole in the wall, where they won't even let you use the phone! Is that *okay?*"

Dave looks at me for a long moment. "That pretty much sucks."

He says it with such a straight face and in such a sincere tone that I burst out laughing.

"Bartender, another water for the lady."

I smile at him. "Thanks."

"Want to talk about it?"

"Not really."

"Want a real drink?"

"Better not."

"Want to hang out and watch pudding wrestling?"

"What?"

He gestures to the area near where the band has taken up residence. "They're having pudding wrestling tonight. You know, women clawing at each other while sliding around in a tub of pudding. Can't ask for much more than that."

"No, I guess you can't."

We sit in silence for a while, me sipping my water, Dave swigging away at his beer. It's not an uncomfortable silence. Not that it's comfortable being with Dave. I'm hyperaware that he's beside me, that he's drinking a Sam Adams, that he's spun the cell phone on the bar eight times now. It's the silence of two people who don't know where they stand with each other and aren't sure if they want to try and puzzle it out again.

Finally, Dave says, "Who were you going to call?"

I shrug. "I don't know. Rory, I guess, but I've already imposed on her too much."

He glances down at the T-shirt, and I wonder if he notices the shoes and remembers them. Then he says, "I'll take you home." I nod again. We're silent, and I can feel the tension rising in him. He's trying to decide right now whether he should say anything or not. My head is telling my legs to start walking before he opens his mouth, but they're not listening.

"I saw the television premiere."

I stare at the ice in my glass.

"And the photo in the paper."

Three pieces of ice float at the bottom, shrinking in the water surrounding them.

"Your legs looked pretty hot in that skirt."

I jerk my head up. "What?"

"It was a short skirt. You've got good legs." He frowns. "Good everything, actually."

"Not good taste in men."

Dave ponders this. "Momentary lapse of reason? I mean, before the dickhead, you went out with me."

"That wasn't good taste. You made it impossible to say no."

He finishes his beer. "Yeah. I'm still trying to figure that one out."

"Thanks." Jesus, I can't win today.

Dave shrugs. "Sorry, but I put a hell of a lot of effort into getting you to go out with me, and you're about the furthest thing from what I want in a girlfriend."

"Again, thanks."

"Oh, and I'm your type?"

"Please."

"That's my point. And yet—" He pauses and I find myself holding my breath.

"And yet?"

He turns to face me, his honey-hazel eyes drinking me in. "And yet we're both sitting here."

"Hey! I know you!" A large woman wearing Daisy Duke shorts and a spandex halter top steps between Dave and me. She turns to the biker dude beside her. "Jim. That's the girl from the TV."

Jim narrows his eyes at me, and my heart thuds. They cannot possibly recognize me from one TV show. I was wearing my hair different. I was wearing clothes that fit.

"Hey, I think you've got the wrong—" Dave begins.

"Oh, yeah." Jim nods. "That's her. The girl who was in the paper, spreading her legs for the prince."

I jump off the bar stool. "Excuse me? Who the hell do you think you are?"

Dave grabs my elbow, but I jump back all on my own when the woman sticks her face in mine. "Who died and made you queen? Don't you talk to him like that. I'm gonna kick your ass."

"Okay, hold on," Dave says. "Why don't we just forget about this? I'll buy you a beer."

The woman puts her hands on her hips. "Who are you? Her pimp? I don't want your shitty beer."

"Dave, let's just go."

"Yeah, tuck tail and run," the woman sneers.

I shrug. What do I care what this woman thinks? I just want to put on my pajamas, take a bath, and sleep for a week. "Dave, let's go."

"Not so tough now, are you?" Jim taunts.

"She could beat the shit out of this piece of trailer trash." Dave flicks a finger at the woman. "Do it with style, too."

"Oh, fuck you!" the woman screams.

Jim's laughing.

"Dave," I whisper, "come on."

Dave's not listening, though. He takes a step toward the woman. "I think you owe my friend an apology."

She snorts. "I'd lick her feet first."

"I'd like to see that."

I grab Dave's arm and tug. "Dave, it's okay. Let's *go*."

"Yeah, and what happens if Tanya wins," Jim asks, and I don't like the glint in his eyes.

Dave considers, then says to Jim, "I don't know, what do you want?"

"I want to go home."

"Hold on a sec." Dave waves my protest away, eyes locked on Jim. A chuckling Jim.

"Okay, if the little princess here loses, she has to flash us."

"No nudity," the bartender says from behind us, and I realize the whole place is listening.

"Just the top," Jim argues with the bartender.

"No!" I yell.

"No nudity," the bartender says, shaking his head.

"Aw, come on," Dave argues.

I round on him. "Dave!"

"Oh, sorry. Knee-jerk reaction." He looks at Jim. "No can do."

"I think she should kiss my ass." Tanya thrusts forward an abundant hip. "Right here." She turns and points to one bulbous cheek.

"You're on," Dave says.

"No, you're not. I'm leaving." I take three steps before someone grabs my arm and yanks me back.

"The wrestling ring is this way," some guy I don't even know says.

Tanya is already halfway there, and Jim reaches for my arm.

"Don't even touch me."

"I got her," Dave says, and the next thing I know, Dave's got his arm around my waist and he's dragging me toward the pudding-filled wrestling ring.

"Dave, no! Stop!" I squirm and struggle until he has to lift me off the ground to keep me moving.

"Shh. We can't go back on the deal now."

"*We!* I didn't agree to this deal. If you care so much, *you* go fight her."

"You're not going to fight. Get a lock on her and hold her down for thirty seconds. Then she'll be kissing your feet. Here, better give me your shoes."

He removes both flip-flops, then hoists me up and over the ropes into the ring. Tanya's already waiting, ankle-deep in butterscotch pudding. As my own feet sink in, I make one last effort to escape, but come up against Dave blocking my way.

"Just calm down. You're going to be great. Pretend she's the dickhead."

I stop struggling against the ropes and consider this. All

day I've been so angry and ready to murder Nicolo. Maybe I would feel better if I smash Tanya's face into pudding. I glance over my shoulder. She's staring at me, hunched forward, teeth bared.

Fuck! No way! "Let me out," I tell Dave when he tries to block the ropes again.

"Can't. We made a bet. You've got to hold up your end."

"*You* made a bet!" I scream, frantic to escape the snorting bull behind me and the quagmire of pudding drawing me down. "You fight the gorilla back there."

There's the sound of a bell, and the bartender gives me a little wave from a corner of the ring. The red bell next to him is still vibrating. But before I have time to consider the bell and what it implies, Tanya heaves her bulk toward me. I scream and lean/trudge to the right just in time. She hits the ropes, and comes back for more.

14

I've Got It Bad and That Ain't Good

I sludge around the perimeter of the wrestling ring, moving as fast as the thick pudding allows. "Dave!" I cry when Tanya starts to come after me. "Dave, get me out of here."

"Fight, Red! Kill her!"

Okay, forget Dave. New plan. I reach Tanya's corner, and pause to look for another escape. Unfortunately, Jim is there, grinning up at me. I think I was doing better with Dave, especially when Jim reaches through the ropes and gives me a push.

I scream, falling back into the pool of pudding. A giant butterscotch wave fans out on either side of me. I struggle to my knees, shaking pudding off like a wet dog.

"Red, you okay?" Dave says, and I swear I hear a chuckle

in his tone. He is so dead. I turn to glare at him, and he yells, "Watch out. Duck!"

Tanya is coming for me, but I can't stand in time to avoid her. I'm saved only because she slips and flops into the pudding. Unfortunately the brownish-orange wave from Tanya's fall throws me off-balance, and I go down again, this time with a gurgle. I come up for air, gagging at the thought of nonhomogenized pudding in my mouth, but I don't have the time to contemplate the disease or food poisoning scenarios because Tanya's crawling straight for me. She tries to snatch my shirt, and I flop away.

Tanya grabs my ankle, but I kick back and slip out of her grasp. "Dave!"

"Hold her down!" Dave's voice rings out over the roar of the crowd, who are cheering and catcalling now because Tanya and I are covered with pudding. "Kick her ass, Red."

"You kick her ass! I want ou-owwww!"

Tanya grabs my shirt and hauls me back. I flail, then she flails, and we fall backward. I land on top of her, and when I get my breath back, I scramble up. She grabs my leg, and I try to wriggle out of her grasp, kicking her in the jaw.

She stares up at me, tears smarting in her eyes.

"Oh, my God! Are you okay?" I lean down and put a hand on her shoulder.

"What are you doing?" Dave yells. "Take her out."

"Shut up! She's hurt. I'm so sorry. Are you okay?"

Tanya's eyes narrow. "You bitch!" she yells and lunges for me. We go down in a splash of butterscotch yellow.

"I said I was sorry," I mumble before she grabs my hair and slams me facedown in the pudding again. Okay, that's it. Between layers of brownish-orange, I see red.

Tanya must die.

Mustering what must be superhuman strength, I push

Tanya off me and manage to pull free of the sinking morass. I suck in gallons of butterscotch-tasting air, then cough as pudding goes down my windpipe. But this time I ignore the discomfort and hunch over, looking for my foe. When I spot her, I give a little growl and lunge. Tanya's so surprised, she doesn't move fast enough, and I put her in a choke hold and dunk her head in pudding.

She struggles to get out, but Gray has taught me well. No one escapes this hold. From far away, I hear a voice calling my name, and then my arms are pried free of Tanya's neck and a towel is thrust into my hands, then another, and when I wipe away the caramel-colored goop, I look into Dave's smiling eyes. They're sort of a dark butterscotch color. "You won," he says. "Don't kill her."

"I'm going to kill you." I start swinging, and he jumps back.

"Hey, I said you won. Here"—he thrusts his beer in my face—"drink this."

I take it and down the rest of the bottle, grateful to taste something, anything but butterscotch. Even something as disgusting as beer.

Three or four guys are standing around us, mouths hanging open. Hopefully they're impressed with my beer-guzzling capability, not sickened by my pudding-covered exterior.

The majority of the Bait Shop's patrons did not witness my chugfest. They're still over by the ring, watching Tanya get back on her feet. Or maybe they're excited because her top's down around her waist. She doesn't seem to notice. They clear a path for her as she stomps over to me. She looks horrible, smeared with orangey-yellow slime, globs of it hanging from her nose and hair.

God, if I look half that bad, I'm killing myself. Wait. I'm killing Dave.

"Looks like you're going to have to kiss my feet," I say.

She sneers. "You kiss my ass first."

"That wasn't the deal."

"Screw the deal." Tanya pushes me back, and I prepare to smack her, but Dave grabs my arm. Finally, I say, "You want me to kiss your ass? Fine. Turn around."

Tanya smiles triumphantly, turns, and waggles her butt in my face. It's such a large target. Layers of flesh hang out on either side of her shorts' frayed hem, jiggling as she wiggles, butterscotch pudding dripping from the fat.

I give Dave a sidelong glance, then look pointedly in the direction of the restaurant—our exit. He follows my gaze and looks back, frowning. I give him a naughty smile, and the furrow between his brows deepens, he tenses, and then he shakes his head, mouthing, *No.* I give him a little wave, turn back to Tanya, and, planting my hands flat on her behind, send her sailing over a table, knocking two guys over and spilling a tray of beers.

Chaos erupts, most of the bar's patrons cursing me, but I don't wait for them to make good on their promises. Instead I scramble into a run, tipping a table and a pitcher of beer in the process. Dave grabs my hand as I pass him, and we fly through the door into the restaurant. Dave knocks into a waiter holding a tray of food, and the nachos and burgers topple over.

"Sorry!" I yell as we race up the stairs. I can hear Tanya and the rest of the people from the deck behind us, but I don't turn. Dave and I reach the entry hall, shove the door open, and leap into the parking lot. "Where are you?" I scream.

"There!" He points to the Hummer, near the back of the parking lot, and we run for it.

We separate as we near the tank, Dave heading for the

driver's side and me for the passenger's. Dave fumbles for his remote, and the alarm beeps. I reach the tank a second before he makes it around to his side, then I pull open the door and freeze.

Leather and new-car smell. Shit. I'm covered in pudding. I already ruined his Land Rover's interior after the Gatorade Incident. I can't ruin the tank, too.

Dave pulls open the door on his side, and yells, "Get in!"

"But your leather!" I hear the Bait Shop's door open, and I glance over my shoulder as Tanya and Jim burst through. They pause, scanning the lot for us.

"I don't give a shit. Get in!" Dave yells as he starts the Hummer.

"Wait." I grab Rory's T-shirt and haul it over my head. The underwear I borrowed is wet from pudding that seeped through, but I use the T-shirt to wipe off my arms, then throw it down. Tanya's seen us now, and she's running toward the Hummer.

"Get in!" Dave yells.

I pull Rory's shorts over my hips, not bothering to unbutton them, trying to wipe pudding from my legs as best I can. I toss the shorts on the gravel with the T-shirt, then climb onto the Hummer's running board. From the corner of my eye, I see Tanya slip on the gravel in the lot and go down about two yards away. That's all the motivation Dave needs, because he hits the gas as I'm still crawling in.

We peel out of the parking lot and, spurred by the adrenaline racing through my system, I lower my window, lean out, and scream, "You lost!" And then I do something slightly immature.

I moon them.

Dave turns the Hummer sharply, leaving the Bait Shop and the pudding wrestling friends and fans in our dust.

I duck back into the Hummer and glance at Dave. "Well, that was fun. What now?"

"Custard wrestling?"

"I was thinking mousse. It's smoother."

He looks at me, shakes his head, and we both burst out laughing. He's laughing so hard that he has to pull over, and it takes a few minutes to get it under control. Finally, between chuckles, Dave says, "I can't believe you pushed her."

"Why not?" I say. "She deserved it. *I won.*"

"You're a trip, Red. Remind me not to play Monopoly with you."

"I don't think board games are your main concern right now. What the hell was all that 'Kick her ass' and 'Take her out' shit?" I sock his shoulder. Hard.

"Ow."

"Ow? Ow is having your hair pulled out while your face is buried in pudding." I hit him again, but he catches my fist before I make contact and hauls me across the seat. He's not laughing now. In fact, he's got that same scary-serious look he had on his face in Rory's bedroom.

It's amazing to me that Dave is looking at me like this. But no matter how many times he sees me at my worst— dripping with blue Gatorade, drunk, covered in pudding—he always makes me feel beautiful, like he sees past the exterior and into the real me.

"You know my favorite part?" he asks, face close to mine, breath tickling my cheek.

I shake my head, feeling my insides wobble.

"When you did the striptease in the parking lot." He glances down, and I'm suddenly very aware that all I'm wearing are a blue cotton bra and Rory's bikinis with a picture of a chicken and the words "CHICKS RULE."

"It wasn't a striptease. I didn't want to ruin your leather."

"You can't imagine how much I appreciate that." He leans forward and, too late, I realize he's going to kiss me. I'm so surprised I don't even kiss him back.

He licks his lips. "You taste like butterscotch."

"But it's unhomogenized butterscotch. Who knows where it's been?"

"It's been on you," he says.

His hand cups my jaw, and seeing that look in his eyes again, I say, "Wait. I'm dirty."

"I like you dirty."

My skin heats, and my heartbeat kicks up a notch.

"Half the time I worry I'm going to mess your hair up." He leans back and assesses me. "Not too worried about that right now."

See what I mean? He likes *me,* not the mask I wear. *Me.*

Dave leans forward and kisses me, and I kiss him back. I've kissed Dave maybe ten times, but except that time at Rory's, I've never *really* kissed Dave. Kissing Dave always felt like joking around—fun, playful.

I don't want to play anymore. I'm giving up the role of princess, stuck-up bitch, and fashion maven. Well, maybe not the last one. But I'm sitting on the side of some farm road miles from Chicago, wearing the most unsexy underwear ever, covered with pudding, and Dave still wants to kiss me. This feels real. What did Gray say about me backing away whenever a guy gets too close to the real me? This time I'm not going to hide.

It's a risk, allowing myself to be so vulnerable. This week I was on national TV consorting with a particularly lewd vibrator, I lost my job over a sex scandal, and most recently I won a pudding wrestling match. I think I can do pretty much anything right now.

And so I let Dave kiss me, and when he starts to pull

back, I tug on his hair, pull him close, and kiss him with my whole heart and soul, like I've only ever kissed two other men, one when I was fifteen and one I thought I'd marry.

Dave tenses, sensing my shift. There's a moment of indecision on Dave's part, and I feel that empty chasm in my belly yawn with fear. Then his arms go around me, and he returns the kiss with equal passion. When I draw back, he stares up at me, and I'm the one who looks away first. So many questions in his eyes, and I don't know how to answer them right now.

Dave reaches for his shirt, pulls it off, and hands it to me. "Seems like I'm always giving you T-shirts to cover up with." His voice is ragged and low.

"That's your job," I say and pull the T-shirt over my head.

"What's yours?"

I run a finger lightly over his bare chest. "Taking them off."

He groans, and I smile before scooting back to my side of the tank. He gives me a long look, puts the tank in gear, and steers us back onto the road.

"If we find a gas station and you take me back to my car, I'll leave you in peace."

Dave slips a CD into the player, and "Santeria" by Sublime comes on. "Maybe I don't want to be left in peace."

I catch my breath. "But you're always saying that I'm high-maintenance."

"You listened."

"I always listen. Hey"—I point to the road—"there's a gas station."

"Yep," Dave says, but we don't slow.

"We're not going to the gas station?"

"By the time we get gas and find your car, it's going to be dark. We can come back tomorrow."

I nod. "Okay, that makes sense, but I left my house keys in the car. All I have are credit cards and—oh, no!—I don't even have those. They're in the pocket of Rory's shorts, back in the Bait Shop parking lot."

"You can call and cancel them at my place."

I close my mouth and sit very still. I've never been to Dave's place, and I can't think why he'd take me now unless he intended me to stay the night. And he's not having me stay the night as an act of charity.

He could take me to Rory's. I could also crash at Josh's or Gray's. But Dave's taking me home—to his home. I steal a glance at him, then look quickly away. He's an arm's length away, and that expanse of bronze bare chest felt really good under my fingers a moment ago. I turn the AC on, feeling a bit too warm all of a sudden.

I take a deep breath of Freon. "So, we're having a sleepover?" I say.

"Right."

"Will there be pizza and ice cream?"

He raises a brow.

"Rory and I always order pizza and get ice cream."

"This isn't that kind of sleepover."

This is it. Me and Dave. There's no question what's going to happen tonight. The question is what it means. And what I want it to mean. I look out the window, then back at Dave.

"A sleepover without pizza and ice cream sounds kind of serious, and I seem to remember a discussion about me being high-maintenance and you not being a good mechanic."

He glances at me, then back at the road. "I'm a quick learner," he says, and then, "You can fill out a service evaluation in the morning."

I snort. Arrogant man. "Maybe I'm not interested in your

services. Maybe you've done enough today, getting me involved in that butterscotch pudding fiasco."

Dave stops for a light, and I notice that we're getting close
to the city again. Thank God.

"Then we order pizza and pick up ice cream." But he
doesn't sound like he's too worried we'll be arguing over
toppings and the last slice. He sounds pretty damn sure of
himself, in fact.

Twenty minutes later we pull in front of a gorgeous three-
flat brick apartment building on West Waveland in Wrigley-
ville. It's like practically inside Wrigley Field.

"I've got the front unit on the middle floor," he says, "but
we all share the roof. Got a perfect view of left field."

As we climb out of the Hummer—me in Dave's T-shirt,
dried pudding, and nothing else—I say, "I didn't know this
area was so popular." It's a Saturday night, and the sidewalks
and sports bars are crowded with people, but it's a very different crowd from the trendy people out and about downtown and in Lincoln Park, my neighborhood.

"Yeah. I'm a walk away from Cubby Bears and Murphy's
Bleachers."

"Never been."

Dave slings an arm around my shoulder. "Not your scene,
Red. For starters, no pudding wrestling."

I scowl at him, and he fishes a key out and opens the door
to the building. Taking my hand, he leads me up a flight of
stairs, then unlocks the door to his apartment.

"This is nice," I say. "I didn't think they had cute buildings like this in Wrigleyville." What's more, I wouldn't think
Dave would live in one. But he is an ad exec, so it's not as
though he's living in poverty.

"They renovated this one a year or so ago."

That becomes increasingly obvious when Dave opens the

door. Right away I notice the hardwood floors, the granite countertops, and the adorable bay window. The decor is understated but tasteful—dark wood, dark fabrics, no clutter. The place could use a few personal touches, but it has tons of potential. I step inside, the hardwood floor cool against my bare feet.

Dave shuts the door and tosses his keys in a bowl with loose change and a couple of dollar bills.

"So, do I pass?" he asks with a smile.

I smile back. "I thought your evaluation came in the morning."

"I better get to work, then. What do you want for dinner?"

I take a moment to answer. If I say pizza and ice cream, then all bets are off. If I leave it up to him, anything or nothing might happen.

I pad to the bay window and look out. "Order whatever's easiest."

"Nuh-uh." He heads for the kitchen and flips on the light. "I'm cooking. Do you like pasta?"

I turn around. "I don't know. Are we talking Chef Boyardee or Vivo?"

Dave folds his arms over his chest. "This is that high-maintenance thing I was talking about."

"I'm just asking."

"Okay, this is how it's going to play. You go take a shower and get cleaned up, and I'll make dinner and pour drinks."

"Fine." I head toward the hall where I assume his bedroom is. "See how low-maintenance I am?"

"Right. When you get done, I'll pour you a glass of wine. Alcohol makes you more tolerable."

"How sweet. Ply me with wine, then take advantage of me."

"That's the idea." He waves down the dark hallway, presumably at the bedroom and bath. "Check in my closet. There might be some girls' clothes left."

I raise a brow.

"Not mine." He shakes his head. "Ex-girlfriend."

Hmm. I head back to the bedroom, switch on the light, and smile. He's got a king-size bed with gorgeous wrought-iron head- and footboards. There's also a very nice armoire in the corner, but I have a feeling it houses the TV, not his clothing. The bed is made, there aren't any clothes on the floor, and the place even looks dusted.

Is Dave gay?

I step into his large walk-in closet and blink in surprise. His clothes are hung neatly—pants on one side, shirts on the other, suits in the back. Since I'm not too excited about wearing his ex-girlfriend's clothes, or even trying to wrap my mind around the idea of Dave and an ex-girlfriend, I grab one of his T-shirts and a pair of boxers from a shelf, then head into the bathroom.

Again, I'm impressed. Bright lights, marble floors, really cute pewter towel rods and drawer pulls. And it's clean, too.

I take a long shower, washing my hair about seven times to get all the pudding out. Dave has some kind of shampoo/conditioner/hairspray all-in-one brand, which I'm sure is wreaking havoc on my hair. I wrap myself in a thick Egyptian cotton towel, and as I'm drying off, I yell, "Don't you have any body lotion?"

"Get real," he calls back.

"Leave-in conditioner?"

"Two words, Red. High-maintenance."

I laugh, though I do wish he had some lotion because my skin feels dry after all that rolling around in pudding. And

I've seen more split ends in my hair lately, so leave-in conditioner would be nice.

"Jesus Christ. Dave's right," I say to my reflection in the mirror. "I *am* high-maintenance."

I slip on Dave's T-shirt and boxers. As I pull the shirt over my head, I savor its scent. Mmm. Classic eau de Dave. I can't really describe it. The closest I can get is to say he smells like laundry detergent, soap, and all the things I adore—pine trees, vintage Valentino, French doors opening on a garden in bloom, Frank Sinatra, new cars, and Cole Porter songs.

I brush my hair and rub it with the towel, leaving the long curls to dry naturally. Too damaging to blow-dry it without any real conditioner. When I pad back to the kitchen, I see that Dave's put on a fresh T-shirt and gray athletic shorts. He's standing at the stove, stirring something in a pot, one eye on it and one watching the basketball game on the portable TV on the counter.

"Hey," I say.

"Hey." Without looking away from the game, he hands me a glass of red wine.

"What are you making?"

"Penne pasta in vodka sauce."

I frown and peer over his shoulder. Penne pasta is waiting to be added to a pot of boiling water, and the vodka sauce is simmering away. When I glance up at him, he's looking at my chest. "You're wearing my Cubs T-shirt."

"You're cooking. Like, really cooking."

He shrugs. "I'm Italian. My family owns a vineyard and a restaurant in Sonoma, so what do you expect? I pretty much grew up around food and wine."

I sip the wine. "It's good."

"One of our best years, a pinot noir from 1989. You don't want something too heavy with this."

The announcer yells, "That's another foul, and Chicago calls a time-out." Dave turns back to the TV, but I reach around him and flick it off.

"Hey!"

"We've had enough sports today."

"Is that possible?"

"Very possible. Got any good CDs?"

He points to a shelf. "Over there. Pick what you want."

I stroll over, frown at his collection of Bruce Springsteen, Pink Floyd, and John Mellencamp. Finally I stumble on a Sinatra CD and the soundtrack to *When Harry Met Sally*. I put it on, and Dave shakes his head.

"I *knew* you were going to pick that one. What's the deal with you and sixty years ago?"

I lean on the counter next to the stove as Dave adds the penne to the boiling water. "I like vintage—music, clothes, dancing."

"Why?"

"I don't know. I guess because my grandma used to watch old movies and play a lot of big band music. I grew up with it, danced to it. And I like everything couture. If I'm going to wear Gucci and Ferragamo, why not Chanel and Schiaparelli? They're the best. The originals."

He transfers the pot of pasta to the sink. "And look at you now. How the mighty have fallen."

"Dressing up is overrated," I say.

He laughs, and pulls two plates from a cupboard. "I agree. I liked your outfit in the car."

"Yeah, yeah," I say, taking the plates as he ladles vodka sauce on the pasta. The dining table is covered with papers and memos from Dougall Marketing, so we sit on the floor and eat off the coffee table. I can't remember the last time I ate a real meal like this. I can't remember a time when my life felt this genuine. Between the staged "reality" TV shows, and the unreal twist my life has taken in the past few days, I almost don't know who I am anymore. But with Dave, everything is easy. I don't have to be a princess. He likes the regular me.

"More?" he asks when I've cleaned my plate.

I shake my head. "I'm stuffed."

"No room for dessert?" He lifts my plate and carries the dishes into the kitchen.

"Hey, Dave," I say as I follow. "Let me do that. You cooked."

He turns on the faucet. "I'll do it. Just relax."

"But I feel so spoiled."

He grins. "And that's new?"

"Shut up." I hop onto the counter next to the sink and watch him rinse the plates and silverware. "You're very good at that."

"What are you good at?" He leans down to grab the dishwasher liquid from under the sink.

"Interior design. But I sort of lost my job."

He shrugs. "So, get another interior design job." He finishes with the soap and closes the dishwasher.

"Wish I'd thought of that, Einstein. Problem is that Interiors by M is the best in the area, and after all the glowing press about me lately, I doubt many firms are going to want to hire a designer fired by the best and involved in a public scandal."

Dave leans against the counter. "So? Start your own firm."

"I can't do that."

He raises a brow. "Why not?"

"I—I—" Hmm. I don't really know why not. Dave's waiting for my answer, and since I don't have one I decide to change the subject. "So, what's for dessert?"

"What do you want?"

I think for a moment and say, "A cappuccino and tira-misu."

Dave raises a brow.

"Hey, you ask an open question . . ." I say defensively.

"My mistake. I *might* have gelato."

"That's what I said. Gelato."

Dave pulls the freezer open. "I've got strawberry gelato. Sound good?"

I nod and he pulls out two spoons, then reaches above me. "Bend down. The bowls are in the cupboard behind your head."

I lean down, so that my face is inches from his. Dave's arms are on either side of me, his body between my legs, dangling from the counter. "Dave," I say.

Our eyes meet.

"I think I'm going to pass on the gelato."

All the Way

I slide my arms around Dave's neck and wrap my legs around his waist. "Will you be crushed if we skip dessert?"

"Yeah." His voice is low and husky, his eyes dark, dark gold.

I pull him closer and tilt my head, then run my lips over his jaw, pausing to kiss the hollow of his neck. He sucks in a breath, and I feel the thrill of heat and excitement sizzle down my spine.

I run my hands down his back, slide them under his T-shirt, and allow my fingers to caress bare skin on the return journey. I pull the T-shirt over his head, and before he can kiss me, I lean forward and press kiss after kiss to his chest. By now his hands have found their way under my shirt, and he's rubbing my back in slow circles.

He circles around to my ribs, then freezes when my hands dip to his abdomen, and I run a finger just inside the waistband of his shorts. He's hard, and I brush gently against the tip of his erection.

He groans, and I feel it all the way to my belly. I kiss his ear. "You like that?" I run my finger over him again, more deliberately, and his hands tighten on my waist. He splays his fingers as he does it, a reflexive gesture, and the tips of his thumbs brush the undersides of my breasts.

I'm not prepared for the jolt of pleasure that rocks through me at that intimate touch. I have to work to keep myself from giving into that rush of sensation, pressing hard against him, offering myself up.

I *really* want this man. I don't want some guy with a title and the ego to go with it. I want to feel like this all the time. I want Dave. And even worse, I want him to want me. *Really* want me, ache for me like I do for him. I want him as overwhelmed by these feelings as I am. I want him scared and excited, and on the verge of . . . of what?

I don't even know what I feel—triumph, wariness, horror. I mean, what am I doing here? All this feeling, this emotion, this control I'm giving him, it's terrifying. If I let him in, if I let him have the real me, then what? What if he doesn't want me in the end? What if the real me isn't likable?

His thumbs move slightly, heating my skin, and I can't stop the breath from catching in my throat. He hears my breathing hitch, and his hands slide up, cupping my breasts. I gasp, unable to stifle the sound, or keep my head from falling back, arching to give him more access.

I shudder, try to get a grip on the sensations, the emotions, but he won't stop kissing me. His tongue teases me, taking just enough that I want him even more. I can't breathe, I can't think, I can only feel. Then, just when everything starts to grow dim and fuzzy, he pulls away. Not much. Just enough that I can breathe again, get a grip on reality.

"Shit, this T-shirt is huge. Are you under here?" he mumbles, hand caught in the voluminous folds of his shirt covering me.

I don't help. I take a shaky breath, blink, then stare at him. His head is bent just so, his hair tousled and sun-streaked. My gaze travels lower, over his broad football-player shoulders, corded with muscle and sinew, tan arms around me.

He looks up, his hazel eyes so dark they're almost gold. I don't know what he sees when he looks at me, but his pupils enlarge, go black.

"Take it off," he says, allowing the bunched cotton to fall from his grip. He nods at the shirt, his eyes challenging.

I see the opening, the chance to snatch my veil back. Right now I'm so raw, so exposed. Given one moment, I can bury my real self again. Every instinct I possess tells me to go for it. Now is my chance. But will I ever get another? And what if my brother is right, and I'm stuck in a loop of trying to fix me when I'm not even broken?

His hands settle on my knees, slide warmly over my thighs. "Take it off. I want to see you."

And that statement affects me more than any other he could have made because in a minute it won't just be my body naked before him, but my soul. I'm so afraid, afraid of being vulnerable and rejected.

I grasp the hem of his shirt and tug it off in a shaky, awkward jerk. Teeth clenched, I stare at him in apprehension. He doesn't hesitate, reacting instantly, gripping my hips and pulling me roughly to the edge of the counter until I'm locked against his abdomen.

One hand wraps in my hair, pulls hard until my head is tilted back and my body bowed, then he brushes his lips over one breast. In contrast to the almost painful grip on my hair, his lips are soft, barely there. He does it again, this time with his tongue, and the moan I've been stifling breaks through.

He takes one nipple in his hot, wet mouth, and I arch harder against him. My legs grip his waist tighter, and my hands fly to his shoulders. Leaning forward, I cup his jaw and kiss him lightly, trying to tone things down, but Dave's not having it. He deepens the kiss until I'm right back where we left off. He gives me no quarter, is relentless, and demands the same from me. Slowly, I give in. I can't stop myself. I kiss him back just as deeply, just as thoroughly, and I fall into the chasm. I plummet down, down, spinning and whirling in a torrent of confusion laced with pleasure and need.

"Sure you don't want any gelato?" he murmurs, his voice a deep growl.

"I'm sure," I pant. "Unless you've got mint chocolate chip or"—He cups one breast, taking the nipple between thumb and forefinger. I gasp—"or Rocky—Road—or—oh, my God—oh, do that again."

I'm embarrassingly eager and fervent, breathing hard and pressing against him, dizzy with need. I try to slide off the counter, but Dave catches me halfway and lifts me back up.

"Not so fast."

"Isn't that my line?"

"Not tonight."

I shiver. He grips the waistband of my boxers and tugs them down. I wriggle out of the shorts, eyeing the height of the counter. Dave's tall, but not that tall.

"This isn't going to work," I say. "The—oh!"

He runs a finger up the inside of my thigh, and I squirm.

"What's not going to work?" he asks, leaning forward to kiss my abdomen.

"Um, mmm." I close my eyes, and when I open them, he's looking up at me. Oh, God. He's got to think I'm an idiot. How can he stand there, that half-smile on his lips, looking so completely cool and unflustered?

"The—the—" I gesture to the surface I'm sitting on.

"Counter?"

I nod. "It's too high."

"It's perfect."

"No, but—ummm . . ."

He tilts my hips back and kisses my belly, making a slow, wet trail downward.

What seems like hours later, I have to agree that the height was perfect. I'm sprawled naked on the counter, Dave stroking my calf leisurely. I keep thinking I should sit up, but I'm too limp and heavy.

"How are you ever going to use these counters again?" I murmur.

He gives me an uncomprehending look.

"I mean, like, to slice tomatoes?"

"You're worried my cooking might be affected?" He grins. Ugh! I hate him, so lucid while I'm barely coherent. It should be the other way around.

He wraps his arms around me, pulls me up. "Maybe it's time we went to bed."

I freeze. More? More! Of course, more. He's still aroused. "The bedroom?" I let him take me into his arms. "Please." I wiggle forward and slide down.

Dave doesn't move, so it's skin-on-skin, and my heart starts pounding again. My feet touch the floor, my body pressed tightly against Dave's. "Mmm . . . warm," I say, putting my arms around his neck and pulling him down for a kiss.

After a moment, Dave pulls away. "Before we do this, before we go in there, I've got one request."

I roll my eyes. "I know, I know. Oral sex."

He grins. "That would be nice, too, but what I want is you."

"What do you mean?" As soon as I ask the question, my legs begin to quiver and my stomach clenches.

"I want you." I stare at him, and he reaches up to cup my face. "It's all or nothing with me, Allison. I've tried it other ways, and it doesn't work for me. I want to be with you—not the rich girl, not the interior decorator, not Miss Designer Label."

I shake my head again. "That *is* me."

"No. You jealous of me kissing Cindy"—he puts a finger over my lips, stifling my protest—"you apologizing to Pudding Girl for kicking her when she's about to take you down, you doing a striptease so you won't ruin my upholstery—*that's* you."

"No, those are me on a bad day." I bite his finger lightly.

"Maybe your bad days aren't really so bad. Look how this one turned out."

Hmm. I'd like to argue with that, but as usual, I've ended up having more fun wrestling and chugging beer with Dave than I ever do at society parties, fashion shows, even shopping. Well, maybe not shopping.

Dave runs a hand over my hair and kisses me softly. There's a tenderness in his touch that I've never felt before, and I sort of forget about shopping. I forget about everything but me and Dave.

I come awake slowly, feeling the slow caress of Dave's fingers up and down my arm. I open my eyes, and he's propped on one elbow, watching me.

I give him a cat smile. "Ready for more?"

"No." He gives me a warning look. "And I mean it this time. You're going to kill me."

I snuggle into him. "There are worse ways to die."

"Yeah, but I need to live because I intend to enjoy you again later."

I laugh, roll on my back, and pull the sheet under my arms. "So, can I ask you a question?"

He raises his brows skeptically. "It's not enough you've got my body, now you want my mind, too?"

"Right. For some reason I get the feeling that *I'm* the one with the emotional intimacy issues."

He doesn't argue, even though I want him to. I want him to say, "Get out of here. *You?*" But it wouldn't be true. I'm obviously way more comfortable with the physical.

And tonight the physical wasn't even so comfortable. Not that it wasn't awesome. Dave and I connected. It felt like our first time and the hundredth time all at once. But it wasn't like any other time for me—any other but one.

My first time. That first time was missionary position, and the thing I most remember is the feeling of powerlessness— the sensation of stifling weight and my insides being ripped apart. I hadn't wanted to stop. I'd just wanted to slow down, to understand what was happening, to let the pain dissipate into something tolerable.

But I'd had no control.

I've never let that happen again. I've had sex lots of ways, but the only acceptable positions are those where I'm on top or equal to the guy. I don't do missionary. I mean, the guy might roll me over for a moment, but it doesn't last long.

With Dave I didn't realize I was under him until the end, when he rolled off me and pulled me into his arms. That whole time I never thought about being pinned under him, being powerless. I mean, there were other things on my mind, but that's never stopped me from freaking out before.

Now, waking up with him beside me, I feel vulnerable, and I need to expose a chink in his armor, to even the score.

I narrow my eyes at him, searching. "Okay, so you never talk about ex-girlfriends."

"You don't talk about ex-boyfriends."

"That's because you can read about him in the paper. Now, don't interrupt. My turn for questions."

He spreads his hands apologetically.

"Also, I don't have any of my ex's clothes in my closet. When did you break up?"

He rubs his temple. "You really want to get into this?"

"Yes." I pull his hand down and rub my cheek against it, then reach up and smooth the line between his brows.

"Okay, but this has got to go two ways."

"Fine." I swallow, knowing he was going to say that. Maybe wanting him to say it?

"Fine? Red, I've known you more than three months and you've never yet answered a personal question."

I stretch. "I'm more amenable after an orgasm or two."

"Then you should be downright submissive by now."

"Are you going to answer the question?"

He leans his shoulders against the headboard, and I pause to admire his flat stomach and the way the sheet rides low on his hips before looking up at him.

"We broke up six months ago. She was using me to get a ring out of the guy she really wanted. He's in the military. I knew about him, but I thought it was over." His jaw is tense, but his voice is cold and unemotional. I can feel my eyes widen. Dave is always so easygoing, so relaxed.

I sit up, facing him, legs pulled under my chin. "So, she thought if she made her boyfriend jealous, he'd propose?"

He nods.

"Did it work?"

"I don't know. I think he was seeing someone else, too, so maybe they deserve each other."

We're both silent for a few moments. The street outside is quiet now; the bars have closed and everyone's gone home. There's only the distant sound of traffic and the ever-present Chicago wind.

"Did you love her?" I say without thinking. *Way* too personal there. "Oh! Never mind. I can't believe I just said that."

He gives me a puzzled look. "Why? It's not a secret or anything. Yeah, I loved her—at least I thought I did."

"So, is that why you didn't want to sleep with me?"

"You're never going to forgive me for that rejection, are you?"

"Like I'm really upset."

"Uh-huh." He looks toward the ceiling, as if appealing to some divine power for patience. "Okay, my turn. Have you ever been in love?"

I stiffen. "You don't pull any punches, do you?"

"I'll take that as a no."

I look down, tracing the blue and gray pattern on the sheets with my finger, wincing at my chipped polish.

"But you must have had serious boyfriends."

I nod. "Yeah, and that's why I couldn't stay with any of them. I didn't love them." I glance up at Dave. "I tried really hard, and I thought maybe I could be happy without love, but I wasn't."

Dave takes my hand and twines his fingers in mine. I tighten my hold on him and whisper, "I don't know if I *can* fall in love." When I look at him, his face is open and nonjudgmental. I can go on or I can leave it at that. He's not going to pry; he's not going to judge me; he's not going to coo and offer me pity.

"My brother got in some trouble when he was a kid. Stole a car at seventeen, arrested for heroin possession at nineteen."

"How old were you?"

I should stop now. I shouldn't tell him this. But I can't get it out of my head. It's eating me up, and I have to let it go or it's going to take over. And if Dave hears this and he still wants me, then maybe this is someone I can really trust. Maybe Dave and I have a future.

I hear myself say, "We're four years apart, so I was fifteen. My parents were really busy—parties every night, galas, benefits—and they didn't pay that much attention to what we did. Gray started hanging out with these junkies, you know? They'd be in his room all night shooting heroin."

"You didn't tell your parents?"

"I don't think I really knew what was going on, but even if I had, I wouldn't have said anything. I had a crush on one of the guys Dave hung around with. Chris. He was older, you know, and I thought he was really cool. I wanted him to like me."

Dave's hand grips mine harder. "You don't have to tell me this," he says quietly. "You don't owe me full disclosure."

Exactly what I'd been thinking. I swallow. "I want to," I whisper and take his other hand in mine. "I want you to know me, and I don't want anything between us. You don't believe me, but I really like you." The words are incredibly hard to say, and I'm trembling inside as I squeeze them out. "If I act kind of aloof, I think it's because I don't want to get hurt." I meet his eyes and hold his gaze. "You could hurt me, Dave."

He nods and squeezes my hand. No platitudes, no promises that he won't. We both know that's not how real life works. Life is hazardous. I've never achieved anything worthwhile without first risking everything, and if I want this to work, I have to take the risk.

"Chris hurt me. I don't know, maybe it was my fault"—I hold up a hand—"and don't give me that bullshit about how I was too young and wasn't to blame. I wanted him to notice me. I was a cheerleader, and I went around in my little cheerleader outfits."

He shakes his head. "Ruthless."

"I know. If the guys were out by the pool, I'd decide my tan needed work and put on a skimpy bathing suit."

"Did your brother see any of this?"

"Yeah. But he was so strung out. I think he said something to Chris one time about me being jailbait, but that didn't stop him—us."

"You were a virgin?"

"Yeah, and believe it or not, there was a time I didn't have a lot of experience. I mean, I guess I knew what he wanted, but I didn't really get it. Sex was something to make him like me, but when we finally got to that point, I was scared."

"He raped you?" Dave's grip on my hands hasn't tightened, but his voice is hard, angry.

"No. I didn't say no. I didn't know how to, maybe. He fucked me and he was gone. He got what he wanted and moved on, I guess. I was freaked out, crying and afraid I might be pregnant, and Gray finally forced me to tell him what was wrong, and I think he went after Chris. I don't know exactly what happened, but I think they were kicking each other's asses, and the police showed up and Gray had heroin on him and went to jail."

"Fuck," Dave whispers.

"I know. And all these years Gray's blamed himself for not watching out for me, and I blame myself for him going out that day. If I hadn't told him what happened, he wouldn't have been arrested."

"You don't know that."

"I ruined his life, Dave. You don't know how hard it's been for him to get past his record."

"Hey"—Dave pulls me to him, hugging me against his warm, bare chest—"Gray made his own choices. He had the heroin on him and he went after that guy. You're not responsible for that. You were a kid, and you were in over your head."

"I knew what I was doing," I murmur into the hollow between his shoulder and neck. I close my eyes, feeling very tired suddenly. "I always know what I'm doing."

"Yeah? What are you doing right now?"

"Sleeping."

"In my bed. Naked. With me."

I smile. "Yep." I pull his mouth down to mine. "See, I know what I'm doing."

Night and Day

Sex seems different in the morning. What was really hot the dark night before feels kind of awkward when you wake up next to the guy in bright sunlight. Another bit of advice: Don't stay the night. A lot less uncomfortable that way.

Not that I follow my own advice in this case. I don't have anywhere to go anyway. But I guess Dave does because when I wake up, he's not beside me. His side of the bed is cool, and I don't hear him moving around. Immediately my stomach clenches. Is this it? Now that Dave's seen the real me—warts and all—he's not interested?

I get up and pad into the living room. His clothes are gone, and mine—technically also his, but the ones I was wearing last night—are slung over a chair. I stare at the T-shirt and boxers. It's hard to believe that a week or so ago, I was a wildly successful interior designer, drove a BMW, wore Versace and Gaultier, and dated European royalty.

Look at me now. I'm jobless, my car is in a cornfield some-where in northern Illinois, I'm naked, and my commoner boyfriend—if he *is* even my boyfriend—has taken off. I walk into the kitchen. And he didn't even make coffee before he left.

Guess there's nothing to do but get dressed and make it myself. Then I'll call Rory to come pick me up. I turn to leave the kitchen but can't stop myself from glancing at the counter next to the sink. The dish soap is knocked over, the sponge is still sopping wet and in the sink, and the cutting board is on the floor.

I bite my thumb, warmth oozing through me at the mem-ories. I'm still standing there, staring at the counter, when the door opens and Dave walks in. In one hand, he's got a tray with two cups of coffee, and in the other a paper bag.

He stops when he sees me and smiles. "This is nice."

"I was about to get dressed. Where were you?"

"Went to get breakfast, but I don't think I'm hungry any-more." He sets the bags on the kitchen table and pulls me into his arms. Suddenly all my fears and worries—my job, my car—are gone.

Back in bed, Dave tells me that before he picked up break-fast, he filled a canister with gas for my car.

I set my bagel on his chest. "So food, shelter, fuel . . . did you pick up anything for me to wear?"

He grins. "Sorry, Fashion Girl. The mall isn't open this early on Sunday."

"Oh, my God." I sit bolt upright. "Where's your phone? Can I use it?"

"Yeah." He hands me a cordless phone. "What's wrong?"

I shake my head. "The pictures with Nicolo came out yes-terday morning, and I haven't talked to my parents or Gray yet. Even Rory doesn't know what happened to me after

I left her place. I better call them before they stick my picture on the back of a milk carton."

"I'd buy that milk." He kisses my forehead. "Go ahead. I'll take a shower, then we can go get your car."

I dial Rory first. I don't have to explain as much with her, and chances are, my parents have called her looking for me.

Hunter answers. "Dave⸮"

Fudge. Caller ID. Forgot about that. "No, it's Allison. Is Rory there⸮"

"Yeah. Why are you calling from Dave's⸮"

I wish I could bury my head in the pillows. I hadn't really considered whether I wanted this thing with Dave to go public, but I guess the decision's been made for me. "Hunter, it's kind of a long story."

He's silent. I hear the water in Dave's bathroom start and the sound of him brushing his teeth. Come on, Hunter. I know you're not Einstein, but you can figure this one out. Finally, Hunter takes a sharp breath on the other line. "*Oh.* Holy shit! Um, okay, here's Rory."

"Allison⸮ What's wrong⸮ Are you okay⸮"

"I'm fine."

"Then why is Hunter acting like C-3PO on crack⸮"

I sigh. "I'm at Dave's."

"Are you serious⸮ Wait. Are you at Dave's or *at* Dave's⸮"

I roll my eyes. "I'm *at* Dave's."

"So you're *at* Dave's or at Dave's⸮"

"Rory, we had sex, okay⸮"

"Aagh! I can't believe it! Is this some kind of Jedi mind trick—no, you wouldn't do that. Was it good⸮ No, wait. I don't want to know that about Dave. Okay, how about, did you do it more than once⸮"

"Rory, have my parents called you⸮ I left my cell on your

kitchen table, and I forgot to call when I got to Dave's last night."

"Yeah, I bet you did. Actually, your mom did call yesterday evening. She didn't sound worried, but she never sounds worried."

I close my eyes. It's when Mitsy least sounds worried that she's the most frantic.

"But she was spelling a lot."

Bad news. "What did you tell her?"

"That you stayed here Friday night and went out to hang with Gray yesterday. Did you find him?"

"No. I had a . . . transportation problem. Then there was the butterscotch pudding—never mind, I hope they didn't call in the SWAT team yet."

"SWAT doesn't deal with missing persons. They—"

"Okay, Rory, I have to go." I hear the shower turn on in Dave's bathroom.

"But wait! I want to know how you ended up at Dave's. I want details. Pudding? Come on!"

"Later."

I hang up and dial the number for my parents. My dad answers on the second ring. "Holloway residence. This is Donald."

"Daddy, it's me."

"Allison! Where the hell are you? Your mother has been calling all over, looking for you."

"I'm fine. I left my cell at Rory's and I haven't been home because there's a flock of reporters outside my place. Look, can I ask a favor?"

"Go ahead." That's my dad's business voice. He sounds like that whenever he's thinking he might get the losing end of some stock buyout or something.

"Can I hole up at the lake house for a week or so؟ Just until my profile goes down a bit؟"

"Sure, but what about your job؟"

I bite my lip. "Um, well, Daddy, I'm sort of looking for a new job."

There's a long pause. "Do you want me to call Baxter؟"

Baxter is my dad's attorney.

"I don't know yet. It's kind of my fault. I—I violated my contract." Silence. "See, when I signed the contract for the *Kamikaze Makeover!* show, there was a stipulation that none of the contestants could fraternize with the producers. I sort of fraternized."

"Nicolo؟"

"Uh-huh. And Dai Hoshi found out and threatened to sue if Miranda didn't terminate my employment."

"Why the hell would you violate your contract؟ Oh, hold on. I need a drink. Here's your mother."

The shower is still going, and Dave's singing some Green Day song.

"Allison؟" My mother comes on the phone. "What's your father T-A-L-K-I-N-G about؟ Do you know what I'm going through right now؟ Lucinda Chippenhall is trying to get me kicked out of the Junior League. *Me!* She says my family is a disgrace. What did you do to her؟"

I explain my whole story to her, feeling pretty much like I did when I was thirteen and threw a party while they were out of town. It started out with a few friends, but then some of the high school guys came and brought beer and pretty much trashed the house.

"But I don't understand why you don't simply ask the P-R-I-N-C-E to talk to Dai Hoshi and work this whole thing out."

"Mom, did you *see* the paper and the cable news shows yesterday morning? I'm not talking to Nicolo."

She huffs. "Oh, now's a fine time not to talk to him, after he's had his hand up your skirt. And for God's sake, Allison. It's not as though you're a virgin. If you'll have sex with our pool guy when you're home from college, you'd think a prince would be a step up."

I hear my dad say something in the background, and my mom says, "Donald, just stay out of it. We did it your way with Grayson, and look how it turned out. Now we do it my way."

Great. Mitsy's way. This ought to be fun.

"Look, Mom, I have to go."

"Why do you refuse to go out with nice men?" She sounds exasperated. "Look at Tad! Look at Bryce. Now look at Nicolo. If you're going to sleep with someone, why can't you sleep with someone E-L-I-G-I-B-L-E?"

I grit my teeth and stare at the ceiling, wishing she'd shut up and stay out of my life for once. "Mom, now isn't such a good time for me. I had a rough day yesterday and—"

"Where are you? Why does the caller ID say 'Tivoli David'? Who's Tivoli David?"

"Dave. He's a—friend."

"Oh, for Pete's sake, Allison! It's been twenty-four hours and you're already sleeping with some other guy? Who is he this time? A trash collector?"

Okay, I'm seriously about to lose it. In the calmest tone I can manage, I say, "No, he's an ad exec and a friend of Rory's."

She sighs. "Honey, you know I love Rory, but her friends are not exactly the kind you want to associate with. How much do ad execs make? Who are his parents? If Lucinda Chippenhall hears about this—"

"Mom! Screw her and the Junior League and all of it! I'm not going to marry Dave. I just needed a place to stay, and he offered. I have to go now."

"So now you're *living* with this guy?"

"No, I'm not living with him. Dad said I could crash at the lake house. There's nothing going on with Dave, okay? He's a nonentity, so put him out of your mind. Now, can I go?"

"I hope you mean that because I don't want to see you make a mistake. I mean, marry this guy, and where would you be?"

"Got it, Mom. He can't afford me, okay? I'm hanging up."

I know for a fact I make more money than Dave. In April, Rory was helping Hunter with his taxes, and I saw his W-3 or whatever that thing is called. Hunter makes about the same as Rory, but that's still less than I make—made. Hunter's been at Dougall longer than Dave, so it stands to reason Dave makes less than Hunter, which is even more less than I make—made (do not tell Rory I said "more less" because she'll go off on the impossibility of something being both more and less, but we know better).

I get a weird tingly sensation on the back of my neck, and I have a sinking feeling Dave is behind me. I listen for the shower, but it's silent now. Oh, God, don't let him have been there the whole time.

"*You* can't afford you, Allison," my mom says. "What are you going to do about your job? Who's going to hire you now that you've been featured in pornographic TV shows and pictures?"

"Mom, are you supposed to be helping? Because I'm not feeling better here. Look, I'm going to the lake house, and I'll call you from there. You know I'll be okay for a while even without a job. Good-bye."

She sighs heavily. "Hold on, here's your father."

"Allison, don't dip too deeply into your trust fund. That money needs to last. You might want it for something important."

Have I mentioned my trust fund? It's one reason I'm not quaking with fear over being jobless. I'm no Paris Hilton; still my trust fund is probably the equivalent of five years of Dave's salary.

"Dad, I have to go."

"I want you to do something for me when you're at the lake house," my dad tells me. "I ordered some flags, and they'll be arriving later this week. Would you accept delivery and put them up?"

Not the flags again. What is it with this small flag complex?

"If you can't get the flags up, have the delivery guy do it. Offer him a hundred bucks or something."

"But don't sleep with him!" my mother yells in the background. Why couldn't I be an orphan?

I hear a rustling in the closet behind me, and coward that I am, I still don't turn around. "Accept delivery on monster flags and put said big-ass flags up. Got it, Dad. Anything else you want me to do to make sure the neighbors know they're vastly inferior to you and your manly flags?"

"Smartass," he says, but he's laughing. "Call us when you get settled. Love you, darlin'."

"I love you, too."

I hang up and slowly turn to look at Dave. He's standing, shoulder jammed against the bedroom door, and his face tells me everything.

He heard.

"Ready?" he says.

Okay, I'm lying in his bed, naked under this sheet and I have yet to shower, brush my teeth, or even stick my hair in a ponytail. Forget the fact that I have no clothes and we'll need to make a stop at Neiman's for some makeup. "Do I look ready?"

He shrugs. "Hurry up. It's time to go."

I frown at him. "Dave, I know you probably heard that, but I didn't mean—"

He looks away. "If you want a ride to your car, I'm leaving in five minutes. Otherwise, find some other nonentity to take you."

17

Shout and Feel It

Fudge. Fudgesicle! I wrap the sheet around me and follow Dave into the living room. "Dave, I'm sorry. I didn't mean all that stuff. You know how moms are. She was going on and on, and I wanted her to shut up."

He turns when he reaches the kitchen table. Behind him, I can see the cutting board, still laying on the floor amid the rest of the disorder from last night.

"And telling her I'm a nonentity shuts her up?"

"Yes."

His eyes narrow.

"No! I mean, I sort of have a track record with losers—you know, the UPS guy, the gardener—and she gets freaked out."

"So I'm on a level with the UPS guy?"

"Stop, okay? Don't deliberately misunderstand."

"You said I couldn't afford you."

I press a hand to my forehead.

"Who the hell do you think you are? You think because you've got more money than I do, you can treat me like shit?"

I reach a hand out, willing him to take it. "You know it's not like that."

He shakes his head. "All I know is you're back to the same old shit. You wanted a quick fuck with a nonentity, you got it. You can go back to your prince now."

I stare at him. "How can you say that? After last night, after what I told you—"

"After last night, what? Nothing's different. I thought you'd changed, but you're the same old princess."

"What am I supposed to do? Tell my parents who you really are?"

"And who am I really? Who am I to you?"

"Dave, you know who you are. You know I care about you." You're the only person who's seen the real me. But I don't say it.

"Then why not tell your parents? I'm good enough to sleep with, but not good enough to take home to Mom and Dad?"

I bite my lip. Dave's right. I'm not being fair to him. How can we start a relationship if I want to keep it hidden? But even if I'm ready to be real with Dave, I just can't be that vulnerable to the world. Dave's asking too much.

And so, like Gray always says I do, I hide.

I throw on the boxers and Cubs T-shirt from the kitchen chair, grab the phone, and dial information and then a cab company.

Dave's watching me silently, and I can't talk now or I'll

cry. I rush into Dave's bathroom, splash water on my face, put toothpaste on a finger and rub it over my teeth, and then use my fingers to comb my hair into some semblance of order.

When I step out, Dave's standing in the hall. I look up at him. "I'm sorry," I say, "for everything."

I open the door and slam it shut behind me, and then I wait on the sidewalk outside the building until the cab pulls up. Dave doesn't come down, and I don't look up.

About five hours later I finally make it to Lake Geneva. I took the cab to Josh's, and he and Carlos helped me evade the reporters to get into my town house for clothes, toiletries, and Booboo Kitty. Then they took me to my abandoned car. I'm so lucky to have friends like Josh and Rory, but right now it's just nice to be alone. And since no one else is here, I've decided to sleep in my parents' room. The bed and closets are bigger, and their bathroom is attached.

I tend to overpack, so I have to move some of my dad's clothes into the closet in my room to fit all my stuff. I'm just about done with the transfer when my cell rings and I pick it up off the bed before Booboo bats it onto the floor. Now that she's had her can of cat food and a bowl of dry food, she's sated and sleepy and doesn't want to be disturbed.

"Hello?"

"Hey, it's me."

"Hi, Rory. Thanks for bringing my cell to Josh's this morning."

"No problem, but I'm calling on behalf of your mother."

I sit on the bed. "What does that mean?"

"Mitsy called, and she told you to tell me that she told me—wait, she told me to tell you—oh, blast it! Hold on."

I hear shuffling and the rustle of paper.

"Okay, here it is. Do not take any calls from Lucinda

Chippen-something until the vote is over. There's soup and cereal in the pantry, the keys to the boathouse are by the door, and, oh"—she pauses—"don't sleep with the flag delivery guy."

I heave a sigh. "And she couldn't tell me this herself because . . . ¿"

"She's not talking to you."

I shake my head. "Fine. Well, you tell her that whenever she's ready to stop being mad at me for things I have no control over, then she knows where to find me."

"Do I have to¿" Rory asks. "I'm sort of scared to say that to your mom."

"Call Grayson and tell him to tell her."

"Oh, that's another thing. She's not talking to him, either."

"Why not¿"

"I think he committed the sin of defending you."

"Okay, I'll call him and smooth things over. Sorry you're all involved in this now."

"Oh, it's okay. It's way more fun than my family. You know, over there it's all peace, love, and the rest of that Bantha fodder."

The next morning Rory calls from work to check in. She's got another message from Mitsy, something about how I should try to act more mature.

Me act more mature.

In the morning sunshine, my feet propped on the deck railing, legs stretched in the sun, I'm thinking that if it gives me a reprieve from my mother's whining, maybe immaturity has its perks.

I make coffee, make breakfast, take a walk, paint my nails OPI's Don't Wine . . . You Can Do It, play with Boo-boo, call my cousin Cassie and a few friends of mine who live on the lake, Josh, Rory, Grayson, and then I get really desperate and call Carlos and even Rory's freaky sister Stormy. Finally, I glance at my watch. Ten-thirty. That's it? Will this day ever end?

I wander around the house, listening to Cab Calloway's "Are You Hep to the Jive?" Mitsy had the house redecorated about five years ago, but it could use a little touch-up.

I sit down to make a list, singing along with Cab. Then I pull on clothes and shoes, and dance out of the house.

A week and a half later, the house looks awesome. New drapes in the kitchen, a feng shui furniture arrangement in the living room, new spreads in my room and the guest room, a new shade of paint in the half bath, and a brighter wallpaper border in my parents' bathroom. I've spent more than my monthly salary, but I made it through three long, drawn-out days.

In celebration of my decorating triumph, I squeeze into a bikini from my high school days. It's faded and snug, but I'm only going to lay out on the dock, so no one will see anyway.

I slather on sunscreen and am sticking my Yucatán If U Want painted toes into flip-flops when Rory calls.

"What's up?" I say.

"Your mother is talking to you again."

"Oh, great. Did she tell you to call and tell me that?"

Rory sighs. "Yeah. Are you talking to her? I'm supposed to call and report back."

I slide the patio door open and step outside. "Yes, tell her that if she calls, I'll talk." What else can I do? My mother is never going to change, and the Junior League politics will always mean more to her than they should, but that's my mom. And she's the only one I have.

"What are you up to?" Rory says. "Did you finish the decorating?"

"Yep. Now I'm going to lay out on the dock."

"Okay, I officially hate you. I'm up to my ears in spread-sheets."

"Well, drive up and visit." I head down to the dock where I've already got my lawn chair and blanket ready.

"Can't. I have to work."

"Okay, well, why don't you ask Hunter if he wants to come for the Fourth? Maybe I'll invite Gray or Josh and we can have a party."

"Sounds good. But how are *you* doing? Are you okay up there all by yourself? I feel like you're in exile. And you still haven't told me what happened with Dave."

I lay on the lounge chair and I throw an arm over my eyes and think how to explain everything I've been pondering the past week and a half. Decorating was a distraction from boredom, but it's also a really good thing to do when you need to think. For some reason, painting and wallpapering frees my mind to consider whatever might be bothering me. Finally, I say, "Rory, you know how you're always saying that I never mess up and I'm so confident—"

"And perfect and beautiful and stylish."

"Yeah, all that. Do you really think that? Do you think I don't have any problems?"

"No, I know you have problems." She pauses. "You're just better at hiding them than other people."

"That's what I mean. I hide the real me behind designer clothes, too much makeup. I don't let people see the real me."

"Is that what you think or what Dave says?"

"Both, I guess. You know, working on *Kamikaze Makeover!* made me think. All those shows that play at real life aren't real life at all. They're as scripted and choreographed as any sitcom."

"You're just now figuring that out?"

"No, but I think what really got me is how the producers create the reality they want the audience to perceive. That's what I've been doing in life."

"Maybe it's a defense mechanism. You've had some rough things happen to you. Can't Dave understand that?"

"I told him about Chris and my first time."

"Then he has to understand."

"He does, Rory, but it was me who hurt him. As much as he understands me—has always understood me—it hurts when you diss someone to your parents."

"Oh, Allie. Do you want me to call him?"

"No, this is my problem. I'll deal with it. I guess I just have to decide if I'm going to go on being a perfect facade or if I'm ready to show the world the real me."

"You'll make the right decision. Right now, wish me luck, I have to go call your mother."

"Better you than me."

But I've barely had time to put a CD in my portable player when my cell rings again.

"Allison? What have you done to my H-O-U-S-E? Rory tells me you've been redecorating."

"Just some paint and wallpaper border, Mom. It looks good."

"Wallpaper? Where?"

I turn onto my stomach and adjust the phone until I'm comfortable. "Hey, Mom, you know I love you, right?"

That surprises her, and she sputters for a moment before saying, "Allison Lynn Holloway, what did you do to my house?

"Nothing, Mom. I just love you."

"Oh, good," she says, clearly uncomfortable with the new me. "Have you found another job, yet?"

"I will, Mom, but I have to wait until my profile is lower.

The second *Kamikaze Makeover!* aired last Saturday and Gray said the reporters started calling again. The last one airs on the Fourth. I was thinking about sending out some résumés after that."

"The Fourth! Allison, that's a week away!"

Okay, there's being real with Mom, and there's being a glutton for punishment. "Hey, Mom, can I call you back? I'm kind of busy here." Tanning can take a lot out of a girl.

"Wait. Before you hang up, I wanted to tell you that I forgive you for what you put me through with Lucinda Chippenhall. I won the vote, and I won't be kicked out of Junior League."

"Great, Mom. I'm thrilled. Love you. Bye."

I close my eyes and try to remember times when my mother was sweet and loving—like when I was sick or needed a new outfit.

My mind wanders back over events in my life, and eventually it wanders to Dave. I glance at my cell screen and see that it's 11:30 A.M. Dave's probably heading out to lunch now. Maybe he's meeting Hunter. Maybe he's taking a new girl out. A twenty-two-year old advertising chick who likes beer and basketball, and won't tell her mother that Dave's a nonentity.

Fudge. I roll onto my back. I hate that between moving furniture, wallpapering, and jiving, I keep thinking about Dave. Worse, I hate the way things ended between us. I even hate that he hates me. I need something to take my mind off him. Mitsy's right. I need a job.

But right now the idea of working for another Miranda isn't all that appealing. Look how much I got done here, by myself. I've got way more potential than I thought. Miranda was holding me back.

I open my eyes. Maybe I should think about starting my

own business? Dave said it could be done. People with far less potential than I have start their own businesses all the time. And I've got added advantages. I've got style, connections, and, most important, capital—my trust fund. It would probably be too easy. I've already amassed a client base and maybe I could steal Josh away from Miranda. I could ask Rory to do my financial stuff and Hunter to do the advertising, Josh and I could decorate the office, my dad could probably tell me where the best office real estate is.

And the best part is I could make sure my firm gives something back to the community. We could go into Englewood and paint houses or make over a community center. And not set it on fire this time.

I could really do this. But what would I call the firm? Maybe Mitsy can think of something . . .

A shadow falls over me.

"Miss, do you live here?"

The sun in my eyes, I squint up at the tall figure of a man looming over me.

"Yes. Why?"

"I'm delivering your flags."

A Chicken Ain't
Nothing but a Bird

I sit up and pull the towel around me. "Oh, great. I've been expecting you."

Without the light in my eyes, the delivery guy's face becomes clearer. He's an older black man I've seen around many times.

"I need you to sign for these." He holds out a clipboard and leans the long cardboard box against the lounge chair.

I take the board and sign. "Hey, can I ask you a favor?"

He narrows his eyes. "You can ask."

"Would you mind helping me mount those flags? My dad is really anxious to get them flying. I'll pay you."

He stares at me, then glances back at the house, and back at me. He scratches his salt-and-pepper hair thoughtfully. "When you ask if I'll help you, does that really mean you're going to help?"

"Yeah. I mean, I'll hand you the tools and get you a glass of water."

He frowns.

"I mean beer. And money."

"All right." He heaves a sigh. "Let's go."

We walk up to the deck, and I leave him unwrapping the box to search for cash and a beer. The beer is easy, but when I count my cash, I've only got eighty-seven fifty-two. And one of the pennies is Canadian, so he might not accept that.

"Here's your beer," I say, strolling out on the deck. "Bad news on the money front. I've only got eighty-seven dollars and fifty-one cents. Fifty-two if you count the Canadian penny."

"Just give me the beer, and we'll call it even."

"I don't mind paying you."

"I know." He pulls out the first flag and unfurls it. It's the Massachusetts state flag.

"My dad's family is from Boston," I say.

He nods and starts on the next one. "Like I said, you keep your money. You go buy yourself one of them pretty dresses like you used to wear when you were a little girl." He gives the ugly black cover-up I've pulled on a disapproving look.

"You knew me back then?"

He shrugs. " 'Bout as much as you knew me, but I seen you around. Always wearing that princess outfit." He chuckles. "You were a handful."

The next flag unfurls, and it's white with a huge cocktail glass on it. We both frown at it. He looks up at me.

"Hey, my dad ordered these. I'm just accepting delivery."

"Whatever you say." He starts on the next flag.

"So when did you see me in my princess dress?"

"Oh, often enough. I remember you when you was—oh, let's see—probably four years old. Your ma was dragging you along the sidewalk downtown and you were sucking your thumb and frowning at her, stumbling over a pile of pink skirts, a lopsided crown on your head. Pretty soon your ma looks down at you and sees that thumb in your mouth."

"Uh-oh," I say. I don't remember the time he's talking about, but I remember the Thumb Wars.

"Uh-oh is right. Your ma says, 'Get that thumb out of your mouth. Little girls don't suck their thumbs.' You looked up at her with those big green eyes and you says, 'I'm not a little girl. I'm a princess, and princesses do what they want.'"

I wince. "It's a miracle I'm still alive."

"It's a miracle you turned out to be a decent person. Least it looks that way so far."

He unfurls the third flag, and it's got a lighthouse with the words *The Holloways* around it.

"I'm Jebidiah, by the way. But you can call me Jeb."

"Okay, Jeb, what do you need to get these things flying?"

He rattles off a list of items, and ten minutes later I hand him a hammer, a screwdriver, and measuring tape, then watch him go to work. After a while he says, "So, now I've got my own kids. All three in college, but the littlest girl always reminded me of you. She used to dress up like a princess, too."

I sip my Diet Coke and nod, thinking about the little girl at the first house we made over for the show. "I bet she was adorable."

He leans over to shove a flagpole into the bracket he's attached. "She was. But she was always comparing herself to the other girls, and what she had was never good enough. So one day when she was about twelve, I sat her down, and know what I told her? I said Sheila, I've lived here a long time, seen a lot of princesses, heard about even more from my daddy and granddaddy. Those girls, they look happy on the outside, but inside they's dead. I told her that being rich or famous ain't gonna make you happy if you aren't happy with who you are in here first." He taps his chest.

It's as if someone's just turned on the light in my brain. You have to be happy with who you are inside. You have to stop trying to make yourself perfect, and just be you.

"Me, I prefer a simple life," Jeb says. "I may not have much, but I'm happy. And I'm healthy." He slips another flag in its mount. "I can still do an honest day's work." He steps back and gestures to the three new flags.

"Looking good," I say. "Where's the fourth one?"

He frowns and checks the box. "This is it."

"Let me see the invoice."

He hands it over and I scan it. "The last one is back-ordered. Damn. I hope it gets here before my dad comes up. He's got a thing about these flags."

Jeb drains the beer and hands it to me. "Looks like I'll be seeing you again. Thank you for the beer and the conversation. You have a good afternoon."

"I will. And Jeb, thanks for telling me about your daughter."

Jeb waves and heads back to his truck, and I sit sown on the deck. Just who do I want to be? And who am I inside?

That's easy. A sister, a daughter, a designer.

With a nod, I go inside to clean up. After a shower and a nap, I'm ready for business. I find an old passbook Rory and I used to write each other notes in school, turn to an empty page, and start scribbling ideas for my new business.

That doesn't take long, since I don't have many ideas, so I sketch an office layout and decorate it on paper. Then I decide to check out what I need to start my own business, and by the time I log off the Internet and shut my laptop, it's almost nine at night.

I've filled the passbook and a few napkins with all my notes, but I don't feel like I've learned anything. I don't even know where to start. I frown. Maybe I should go to the library tomorrow and see if the librarian can help.

I stand and stretch, then hop off my parents' bed and walk onto the balcony. The lake is quiet and dark, and there's a smattering of stars above. Just for fun, I twirl around.

Then I glance at my cell phone. It's lying on the nightstand, right where I left it, right where it's been the last two hundred times I looked at it. I am such a chicken. I'm such a chicken I'm growing feathers.

All night I've been thinking about calling Dave, but I'm too much of a coward. That doesn't stop me from thinking about him, especially now that I'm putting his business idea into practice.

Screw it. Before I can talk myself out of it, I grab the cell and walk back onto the balcony. Curling up in the lounge chair, I scroll through the numbers until I find Dave's. I stare at it.

In my head I hear, Bock-bock-bock-bock-*bock!* Stupid chicken!

I hit Call and try to remember to breathe.

"Yeah?" It's Dave, and he sounds sort of distracted.

Bock-bock.

"Dave? Hi, it's Allison."

No response. Complete silence. Except for the chicken: Bock-bock-bock-bock-bock.

"Um, don't hang up on me, okay?"

"Okay."

That's two words out of him, and one of them was an agreement not to hang up, so that's good, right? Bock-*bock!*

"So, I'm at my parents' lake house, and I was thinking about you."

No response. Bad sign. I stare at the dark water of the lake. "I was thinking about what you said about me starting my own business."

"Yeah."

I roll my eyes. He's not making this easy. "I'm going to do it. I've been working on it pretty much all day, and it's not just going to be a regular firm. We'll do community service projects, too."

"Uh-huh. Why are you telling me?"

I shrug, hugging my shoulders tightly as the breeze comes in over the water. B-b-b-bock! "I needed a reason to call." As soon as the words are out, I squeeze my eyes shut and wait for him to cut my head off. Now's his chance to lay me on the chopping block, pluck me, and fry me in cutting remarks. He can take revenge for all the times I hurt him.

"You don't need a reason," he says after three heartbeats. "You can always call."

I bite my lip. "Thanks. Dave, I'm sorry about what happened. I didn't mean for you to overhear. I wasn't even thinking when I said it. I didn't mean it."

"Yes, you did."

I don't argue. The evidence is sort of against me.

"You don't think I'm good enough for you," he continues when I don't protest, "and no matter how often you tell yourself otherwise, you can't get past it."

"No," I say forcefully. "I've just got this idea of who I should be with, but I don't care about that anymore. It's a fantasy. You're not."

"You say that now, but we've been through this before. Let's not—"

"*No.* Don't tell me it's over. I like you, Dave. Really. Like maybe I might even—" *Love you,* I think, but I still can't say it. My throat closes up, and I have to take a shaky breath before I can go on. "If it's over, then make it be because I'm not your type or something, not because I fucked up. Not when I'm trying to make up for that."

There's a long silence. I mean, *long.* I'm afraid Dave might have put the phone down and walked away, it's so long. The chicken threatens to start bocking again, but I push it down. I'm trembling all over because the words, though unsaid, hang in the air between us. I could really fall in love with him. But what he said is true, too, and I could screw this up all over again.

Finally Dave takes in a breath. "Okay."

Okay? What does that mean? "Okay, what?"

"Okay, you're still my type."

The trembling eases a bit, and I'm able to breathe. "Rory and Hunter are coming for the Fourth. Will you come, too?"

"I'll think about it. Look, I have to go. I'll talk to you later."

And that's the end of that. I lean back in the chair and stare at the lights in the houses on the other side of the lake. I don't feel worse, but I don't exactly feel better, either.

By the Friday before the big weekend, I've read every library book I could get on starting your own business, made a rough business plan, filled out some loan applications online, and asked my dad to fax me a list of available properties.

I've also had my dad contact Baxter about a possible lawsuit against Nicolo. Why should I be the only one who suffers because we fraternized? It takes two to fraternize. Not to mention, after some of the comments the photographer made on TV, I might have a good case against Nicolo for defamation.

Baxter's working on it.

I spent the morning on the phone with Josh, trying to convince him to give up his lucrative, safe job at Interiors by M to come be my partner in my shaky new venture. I don't mention that 50 percent of small businesses fail in the first year, and 95 percent fail in the first five. Josh can do the research himself if he wants those statistics.

They don't matter because we're not going to fail.

I can't fail. I've never worked so hard in my life. My hair hasn't been washed in two days, my nails aren't painted, and I haven't touched my makeup bag. I glance down at my clothes. I think I wore these yesterday.

After lunch I take the books I have on marketing onto the deck and start reading. I'm trying to understand market segmentation when I hear someone come up behind me. The last flag is supposed to be delivered today, so I turn, expecting Jeb.

"Hey, Jeb. Want a—" My voice dies as Dave climbs the steps to the deck.

He's wearing black jeans, a tight black T-shirt, and dark sunglasses. His hair is tousled and almost gold in the sunlight.

"Hi." He leans a box on the rail.

I stare, openmouthed. "Hi."

"Am I still invited for the weekend? You don't look like you're expecting me."

I brush my hair out of my face and straighten my tank top. "Um, everyone is coming tomorrow. Work."

"So I have you all to myself." He glances around, not

looking in the least like he's going to explain why *he's* not at work. "Who's Jeb?"

"The delivery guy."

"Oh, yeah. Here's your delivery then. I signed for it." If he thinks it at all strange that I haven't moved or strung more than five words together, he doesn't act like it.

"Thanks. It's a flag for my dad."

Dave glances at the flags behind him. "He doesn't have enough?"

I swallow and force myself to stand, wishing I'd worn something more attractive than this paint-stained tank top and gym shorts. "He's got this thing about one-upping the Boyds." I point across the water, then step closer so I can see the Boyds' house, too. "They've got six flags, so my dad's got to have seven. It's like flag envy or something." I stare at the Boyds' flags, flapping in the breeze, and shake my head.

When I look over at Dave, he's looking at me. He reaches out and I tense. "Relax," he says, taking an errant curl between his fingers. "I'm not going to bite." He looks down at my hair and then at my face and then at my clothes. "You look"—he pauses to consider—"natural."

We're standing very close, and I can smell that soap and Frank Sinatra scent of his. I take a shaky breath.

"I've been redecorating and working on my business plan. I would have cleaned up—"

He drops the curl. "Why? I like you better this way."

"Guys always say that," I say, rolling my eyes. "Then you marry the girl and complain that she let herself go. Fudging typical."

He's grinning. "Now this is the Red I know. When I first walked up, I thought you were going to have a seizure."

I frown at being so transparent. "I was just surprised to see you. When I didn't hear from you, I thought—"

"You weren't my type?"

I nod and step back, nervous again at the way he's read my mind. "Something like that."

Dave catches my wrist before I can step out of reach. Our eyes meet, and he gives me a long, assessing look. He doesn't tug at me or grip my arm. He just holds me still and very slowly brings me to him.

When I'm pressed against his chest, my emotions a mixture of fear and desire, he murmurs, "You're still my type, Red. You'll always be my type." He brings my captured wrist to his lips and kisses my palm. I shiver, and he smiles. "Maybe I shouldn't say always. I guess if you run me over or something, then all bets are off, but right now you're very much to my taste."

"Toad," I mutter, pulling away, but he hauls me back and slides his arms around me.

My heart pounds with excitement, and I can't catch my breath. This is what I wanted. This is what I've missed. I can't resist wrapping my arms around his neck and melting against him. I like the way being held by him feels—a contrast between the pleasure of connecting with his body and the pain of having all my senses on edge.

"So if I'm your type," I say, "does that mean you forgive me?"

"Don't push it, Red." But he leans down and brushes my lips with his. "I missed you," he confesses. "And I thought about you, what you told me that night at my house. But I wanted you to call me. I've always chased you, and you make it so hard sometimes. I wanted you to show me you were willing to work at this, too. Then you called."

"So all I had to do was call?"

"Not so fast. You're still on probation." He kisses me again, then pulls back and looks over my head at the house and the grounds. Swinging me around, he then surveys the lake. "Not too shabby."

"I'm glad you approve."

"I don't know. You still need one more flag."

He releases me and we—okay, *he*—hangs the last flag. It's green and white and says, "19TH HOLE."

Once we get the flag up and I take a digital photo to e-mail to Dad, I'm hoping Dave will pull me into his arms again.

He doesn't. Instead, he takes a seat at the table on the deck and pulls a file folder out of a briefcase I didn't notice before.

"What's this?" I say, taking the folder and sitting next to him.

"Few things I pulled together for you."

I open the file and flip through the pages. "This looks like a marketing plan." I smile. "I was just working on that."

He lifts the marketing books on the table in front of us. "How's it going?"

"Um, not too great." I study a chart Dave's included in the folder. He reaches over and turns it right-side-up. "Oh, thanks. I read to the part on market segregation and—"

"Segmentation."

I glance up. "Yeah, whatever, and then got confused and had to go back. Oh, my God!" I pull a paper out. "You did one of the zip code thingys for me. I was reading about that PRIZM thing right before you got here."

Dave lifts the passbook. "Are these your notes?"

"Some of them. There's more on those napkins."

"Who's Cody Anderson?"

"Huh?" I peer over his shoulder. "Oh, those aren't my business notes. That's an old passbook Rory and I used to write in. My notes are in the back." I try to flip the pages, but he seems more interested in the junior high exchanges.

"You really had a thing for this Andrew Ridgeley, huh?"

"Rory called dibs on George Michael."

Dave frowns at me, uncomprehending.

"Wham! You know, 'Wake Me Up Before You Go-Go'?"

He groans and flips to the business scribblings. A moment later he says, "Red, I think you better take a look at some of those financial books again."

"Why?"

He points to a page. "Because DG does not stand for Dolce & Gabbana. It's the stock market abbreviation for Dollar General Corporation."

I frown and scan my notes. "Oh, that makes more sense. I'm kind of new to the stock market thing. But no worries. Rory said she'd help with that part. I need you to help me come up with a great marketing and advertising plan. I want to make everyone in Chicago sit up and take notice."

At midnight, I tell Dave that I refuse to listen to one more thing about SBAs, SBICs, CDCs, or LowDocs. And if he even thinks about mentioning EWCP, I'm going to hit him.

I trudge upstairs alone, shower, brush my teeth, and fall naked into my parents' bed. Dave's all the way downstairs in the guest bedroom, not that we discussed the sleeping arrangements. He put his duffel bag in there, and I didn't ask.

When Rory and Hunter get here, they can have Gray's room. Unless Josh and Carlos come. In that case, I'll take my room, give Rory and Hunter the master bedroom, and Josh and Carlos can take Gray's room.

My head is pounding and my eyes are burning, but I can't fall asleep. It's freaking me out that Dave is here.

And, as usual, I don't know where we stand. I mean, he said he forgave me. But he's down there, so maybe he meant it when he said I was still on probation. Or maybe I place too much importance on sex. He can forgive me, even if we're not having sex. Right?

I snort and flip over. That is so not how guys work.

I stand. In my rush to get here, I neglected to pack any pajamas, so I pull on my mom's white silk robe and step onto the balcony. Dave and I moved inside after the sunset, so I haven't been outside all evening. It's surprisingly mild for July. I lean my elbows on the rail, and as the breeze ruffles my hair, I close my eyes.

The house feels different with Dave in it. When Nicolo was here, I felt young again, like I'd stepped back into my princess dream. But were those really my dreams, or just fantasies I've been too stupid to let go of?

Dave isn't my fantasy, but when I'm with him my heart races and my breath catches, and he makes me feel alive. I'm all grown up when I'm with him. I can't play princess, and I don't always get my way, and it's actually kind of nice.

Jeb's right. Being a princess ain't all it's cracked up to be.

I open my eyes and stare out at the lake, like I have a thousand times on a thousand nights like this one. Still no bad-boy pirate prince coming to rescue me. A flash of movement catches my eye, and I focus on the edge of the dock. Dave's standing there, between the wooden planks and the grass, looking up at me. A moment later, he's gone.

When he steps onto the balcony, I don't move. I let him wrap his arms around me and rest his chin on the top of my head. We stare at the dark water and the stars, breathing together.

"When I was little, I used to come up here and keep watch."

"What were you looking for?" His voice is a deep rumble vibrating through me.

"A pirate ship."

He chuckles. "Do pirates frequent Wisconsin lakes?"

"This one did. He wasn't just a pirate, either. He was a pirate *prince*." I feel Dave stiffen slightly, and I turn to face him. "I was thinking about that fantasy tonight. Then I looked out and saw you." I stop, not sure I really want to say this.

"Then you saw me," Dave prompts.

"I saw you, and I thought"—I swallow, lower my voice—"maybe all this time I was just waiting for you. Maybe I never really wanted a prince after all."

He leans down and kisses me, his lips brushing softly against mine. The tingle of pleasure flows all the way to my toes. When he pulls back, he rests his forehead against mine. "I'll help you with the marketing plan, I'll hang up your crazy flags, I'll even play the pirate. But I draw the line at wearing an eye patch."

I nod. "A guy's got to have limits."

"Exactly."

"And I don't really care about the eye patch." I kiss him lightly. "As long as you have a sword."

It Had to Be You

I wake Saturday morning with a pirate in my bed. A naked pirate who's looking at me as though he's thirsty, and I'm the rum punch.

"Oh, no. Not more pillaging."

"I thought you liked the pillaging part," he murmurs, kissing my ear, then running a hand up my bare back.

"I like every part."

We make love, the slow, leisurely morning kind of lovemaking, then just lie in bed and watch the lake come alive.

After a while I turn to him. "How is this going to work? You know, once we get back to Chicago?"

He brushes the hair back from my forehead. "You're going to start a business and force me to go to galas and soirees, and I'm going to take you to basketball games and dingy bars, and when you get too high-maintenance, I'm going to throw you in a vat of pudding."

"Promises, promises. Come on. Get up. Rory and Hunter will be here pretty soon."

A half-hour later, I'm regretting dragging Dave out of bed. I ask him one question about business, and he gets all huffy.

"Okay, Dave, forget it. I have a marketing plan anyway."

He runs a hand through his hair. He's in the kitchen making waffles and fresh orange juice. "Giving away a day at the spa is not a marketing plan," he says through clenched teeth. "It's a gimmick."

I pull two plates from the cupboard and set them down with a *thump*. "If it gets people to choose my firm over someone else's, it's a marketing plan."

"No. It's temporary, and it's a gimmick." He checks the waffles. "You need a brand, something that'll last." He glances at me. "Something that reflects you—sophisticated, elegant, classy."

I beam at him. "Really? You think so?"

He mumbles something, but I kiss him before he can get too grouchy. I take down some glasses and say, "I'm not even wearing makeup."

There's a clatter at the stove behind me. "Yes, you are. You spent like ten minutes in the bathroom this morning putting on makeup so you wouldn't look like you were wearing makeup."

"Okay, but I'm not wearing nail polish."

Outside a horn sounds, and I stand on tiptoes to look through the front window. "Rory!"

Dave grabs my shoulder before I can race to the door. He pulls me close and murmurs in my ear, "We'll finish this conversation later. Maybe naked you won't drive me so crazy."

I give him a lingering kiss, then smile up at him. "Oh, you

know you like it. You'd be bored without me to test your sanity."

Rory knocks on the door and tramps in. As soon as she sees me in Dave's arms, she squeals and yells, "You made up! Now we can be friends-in-law."

"What the hell is that?" Hunter says, coming in behind her with their suitcases. Wide-eyed, he looks around. "This place is huge. Do you have a Jet Ski?"

Rory and I exchange a look and change the subject. Josh and Carlos show up next, then Grayson. He's brought supplies for s'mores and reminds me right away that I promised to throw him off the dock.

Saturday afternoon we all laze around. The boys attempt to barbecue while Rory, Josh, and I gossip. Then Gray decides to take us out on the boat, and I go with him to the boathouse for extra life jackets.

We're halfway down the path when Gray says, "So you and Dave, huh?"

I smile at him. "Me and Dave." I stop and grasp his arm. "I really like him, Gray. I mean, I'm scared, but I'm excited. Am I just being stupid?"

Gray gives me a look like you're-my-little-sister-you're-always-stupid, but says, "He's crazy about you."

My eyes widen. "He told you that?"

Gray glares at me. "I can tell, Allie. Don't mess this one up."

We start walking again, the dead pine needles crunching under our feet. "It wasn't your fault, you know," I say. "That thing with Chris. I've never blamed you." He doesn't look at me, but I peek at him and see his jaw is tight. "I'm just sorry that you went to jail because of me. Because you went after him."

"What?" Gray stops, turns to face me. "I went to jail because I was a junkie and was stupid enough to carry heroin around with me. That had nothing to do with you."

"Yeah, but if you hadn't been fighting with Chris—"

"Then I would have done something worse. Have you been blaming yourself for that?"

I shrug, and he grabs me and pulls me in for a hug. I seem to be evoking this response a lot lately.

I hug him back, a tight bear hug, and say, "I love you, Gray."

"Back at you, brat."

"Hey, have I told you about my friend Natalie?"

The boat ride is fun, and by the time we get home it's dark. Gray's promised Mitsy he'd bring a book on the dangers of liposuction to my aunt, so he heads over there. Rory and Hunter settle in for the *Star Trek* marathon on TV and Josh recruits Carlos to help him brainstorm names for our new business.

Dave and I go skinny-dipping.

Sunday afternoon we make s'mores, and Gray teases me until I try to throw him off the deck. No surprise, I end up going in instead.

I'm just finishing drying my hair after showering when Josh taps on the bathroom door and pushes it open.

"What's up?" I say.

"Rory told me the last episode of *Kamikaze Makeover!* is tonight."

I meet his eyes in the mirror. "You're kidding."

He shakes his head. "Want to watch? It's not every day you get to see three Japanese guys win a million dollars."

I set the blow-dryer on the counter. "It should have been us. It was my fault we got disqualified."

"Sweetie, who cares? I'm a celebrity!"

We settle in front of the TV, Rory and Hunter on the couch, Dave and I snuggled into the big armchair, and Carlos, Josh, and Grayson lying on the floor.

It's pretty weird to watch myself on TV, especially considering all that was going on during the filming. I thought I was going to be a princess. I thought everything was perfect.

Then Nicolo comes on-screen, and everyone looks at me. Dave squeezes me around the waist. "You haven't seen this part?"

"No. I think this is where they announce the winners. That's obviously not us."

Nicolo begins to explain his role in the competition and how hard it was to choose the winners and how excited he is to be part of such a great project. He looks happy, and he probably is. Of course, he doesn't know that when he steps offstage they'll be a subpoena waiting for him.

Payback time, Nicolo.

Nicolo announces the winners and hands over three huge checks for a million dollars.

Josh sighs. "That could have been us."

I nod, still staring at the screen. At the smiling Prince Nicolo Bourbon-Parma. That could have been us.

"You okay?" Rory asks.

I look at Dave. I'm sorry I lost the money, but I'm not sorry Nicolo's out of my life. Prince Charming, he's not. Once you clear away the title, the connections, and the money, you're left with an ego and a pretty face. No substance. An illusion.

"I am now." And I take Dave's hand in mine.

Later that night, Dave and I are on the balcony. He sprawled, pirate-style, on the lounge chair. The lights a out, and the balcony's in shadow. I'm feeling my way do℣ his chest with my lips, giving him teeny, tiny kisses so t' the journey takes a long, long time.

Dave grips the arm of the chair, and says through gritted teeth, "I'm going to have to file a complaint with the Pillaging Committee. This is torture."

I nip his skin and he sucks in air.

I smile up at him, then give an exaggerated frown so he can see it in the dark. "Now, look what you did. I'll have to start all over again."

"Sweet Mary, mother of God. If you so much as—" The words end in a strangled groan as I flick my tongue over his belly button and move lower.

"Dave! Hey, you up there?" It's Hunter. I don't look, but it sounds like he's out on the dock.

I kiss lower, and Dave takes a shaky breath.

"Dave?" Hunter yells again.

"What?" Dave growls.

"You were a Boy Scout. Come down here and build us a fire. Rory wants marshmallows, and Gray went into town."

I flick the button of Dave's jeans open and slide the zipper down. Dave groans again.

"Dave? Did you hear me?"

"Fuck," he mutters. Then, "Ask Josh to do it."

"Hello! Are you listening to yourself?"

I slide a hand inside his jeans, and he curses again. "Hunt, away."

will. First get down here and start a fire."

ick, fuck, fuck." Dave scrambles up, and I sit back, ing him with an innocent smile. He fumbles with the on his jeans, pulls the T-shirt over the bulge, and takes in his hands. "Do not move. Stay right there. I'll be vo minutes."

e storms through the French doors, then sticks his ain. "Two minutes."

and close my eyes. Leave it to Dave to be a Boy

Scout, and consequently the only one of us who can get a fire started. But talented as Dave is, I don't think he'll have the fire going in less than two minutes. He's more pirate than Boy Scout.

"Allie?" Rory peeks her head out. "Can I come out?"

I sit up. "Yeah. Grab that chair. We can watch the guys play caveman. Me fire, you none."

Rory giggles and settles next to me. "You seem happy."

"I'd be happier if your boyfriend didn't call my pirate away in the middle of foreplay."

"Yuck, okay?" Rory shakes her head, and we listen to the guys arguing over fire-starting techniques below. Dave sounds unusually grumpy.

I turn my head to look at Rory. "Remember when we used to come up here and play princess?"

She laughs. "Yeah. I wanted to grow up and be Princess Leia."

"Do you still want to be a princess?"

She stares out at the water, considers. "No. It's a lot of work fighting the Empire. Who's got time for that with a career, friends, boyfriends . . . ?"

"Yeah," I say quietly.

"What about you?" Rory asks after a moment. "Do you still want to be Princess Allison?"

A tongue of blue fire leaps up from the pit on the side of the yard, and Dave and Hunter jump back, cursing. Rory and I roll our eyes.

"I don't want to be Princess Allison anymore." I stare at the fire, then the lake and beyond—at all the mansions, the Porsches, and the yachts, bobbing in the ghostly dark of the water. "I think I'll just try being me."

Want More?

Turn the page to enter
Avon's Little Black Book—

the dish, the scoop and the
cherry on top from

SHANE BOLKS

If My Life Was a Reality TV Show, It'd Be *Survivor*— "Outwit, Outlast, Outwrite"

4:46 A.M.

The alarm clock beside my bed screeches. I beat it into submission.

5:01 A.M.

I stumble into my office, hands outstretched until I feel the chair in front of my computer. As I slide into it, my toe squishes into something soft and wet. I pry my eyes open. Cat hairball. Again.

5:09 A.M.

Hairball removed from toe and carpet, I open my personal e-mail, hoping my editor has gotten back to me about fabulous new proposal I e-mailed last night at 11:37 P.M. No reply. I check my watch. It's 6:10 A.M. in New York. What are they doing up there? Send a follow-up e-mail to ask if my editor ever plans to read fabulous new proposal or whether she's just going to sit on it indefinitely.

5:18 A.M.

Open business e-mail account, where I know there will be dozens of gushing fan letters waiting for me.

From: Grwzbig	Subject: Enlarge your penis!
From: Hornebyz	Subject: Hot babes
From: Buckher	Subject: Group sexxx
From: Mom	Subject: Please call
From: Bookfan	Subject: Good, Bad, Ugly Book

I delete all except the last as Spam, and open what I expect will be an embarrassingly flattering e-mail.

From: Bookfan@ . . .
Sent: Thursday, 11:58 P.M.
To: shane@shanebolks.com
Subject: Good, Bad, Ugly Book

Dear Ms. Bolks,

I read your book *The Good, the Bad, and the Ugly Men I've Dated.* I wouldn't have normally bought it, but I liked the title. Ms. Bolks, I don't know if you realize this, but your book doesn't make any sense. What is a Han Solo? A Princess Leia? A Wookiee?

I never saw the movie *Star Wars,* and I don't want to. Are all of your books going to be this confusing? I didn't get this one.

Sincerely,
Bookfan

I check the time and decide I have a few minutes to respond.

From: shane@shanebolks.com
Sent: Friday, 5:23 A.M.
To: Bookfan@ . . .
Subject: My wonderful book

Dear Bookfan,

Thank you so much for writing to Ms. Bolks. We are sorry to send this automatic response, but Ms. Bolks is much too busy and receives far too many letters and e-mails to respond to each personally. She thanks you for the voluble praise about her book. She is blushing from delight and embarrassment.

Sincerely,
Management

5:46 A.M.

I had better write a few pages on my current work in progress. It's only a matter of time before editor calls with effusive praise for fabulous new proposal, and all that flattery could take a chunk out of my writing time.

Open current w.i.p., sumptuous historical romance. It's due in a week, but no worries.

I scroll to the last page, thirteen. Hmm. I thought I'd done a bit more than this. No matter. I'll just slave away all day and catch up in no time. I reread the last line.

"When Brad walked into the room, she caught her breath. Her heart sped up, and her bosoms heaved."

Brad doesn't sound like a very historical name. Perhaps I should change it to Russell or Orlando or Ben?

And doesn't *bosoms* seem like an overused word? A search reveals I've used it seven times in thirteen pages. I'm going to have to pull out the thesaurus.

Breast, bust, chest . . . substitute *bust* and then try to think of the next line.

5:49 A.M.

Fingers poised over the keyboard, waiting for inspiration.

5:50 A.M.

Still waiting. Fingers getting tired.

5:51 A.M.

Ah-ha! Got something!
The . . .

5:51 A.M.

Damn! False alarm.

5:52 A.M.

I check e-mail again to see if editor has responded.
Nothing.

Back to w.i.p. Realize forgot period on last sentence. Add
punctuation. Now we're making progress.

6:03 A.M.

Decide to read Squawk Radio, my favorite blog.

6:30 A.M.

Fiancé awake and wanders into office. Asks why I'm
staring into space instead of writing. I tell him I'm imagining I
am one of the Squawk Radio ladies and channeling my inner
bestsellerdom.

Fiancé asks when I'm leaving for my workshop. Check
watch.

6:33 A.M.

Shit!

6:34 A.M.

Race to the bathroom to shower and dress. Wish desperately I'd thought to review workshop notes more last night, but
fabulous new proposal took all my attention. Now I'll have to
wing parts of workshop titled "How I Got Here: Tips from a
Multipublished Author."

6:38 A.M.

Where am I exactly? If I don't finish sumptuous historical
romance and editor does not like fabulous new proposal, will
have to retitle workshop "How I Was There: Tips from a Has-
Been."

6:47 A.M.

Who am I to give workshops? Know nothing! And having very bad hair day. Should really stay home because I'll probably be laughed out of workshop anyway.

6:59 A.M.

Last check of e-mail. Still no word from my editor. It's eight o'clock in New York. What are they doing up there? No time to fire off another e-mail, so kiss fiancé good-bye, jump in the car, and race to my workshop.

7:18 A.M.

Sitting in Houston traffic.

7:34 A.M.

Sitting in Houston traffic.

7:56 A.M.

I know! I don't have to talk about me in the workshop. I'll talk about Nora Roberts. Everyone always wants to hear about her.

7:57 A.M.

Realize I don't actually know Nora Roberts.

8:30 A.M.

Arrive at the conference. Discover workshop is actually a panel. Yay! Less time to make a fool of myself. I'm so relieved there's a panel discussion. Maybe one of the other speakers knows Nora Roberts.

9:03 A.M.

Just began talking. One audience member already asleep.

9:20 A.M.

First question. Where does inspiration come from? Stall for time.

10:37 A.M.

I've successfully deflected all other audience questions and distracted the attendees once by asking a particularly garrulous member about her plot. She went into great depth, and by then the audience had forgotten the question.

11:12 A.M.

Is this ever going to be over?

11:23 A.M.

I wonder what's for lunch.

11:30 A.M.

Jump up because my cell phone is ringing. Assure the audience it must be my editor and I absolutely *must* take her call.

It's my mother. She asks why I haven't called her, especially after she sent an e-mail.

My spam filter is going berserk lately, I tell her, and it probably caught her message.

She asks if I remember the lunch meeting scheduled with wedding planner at reception site downtown. Tell her of course I do. I am, after all, a responsible bride-to-be.

11:36 A.M.

Shit!

11:43 A.M.

Sitting in Houston traffic.

11:50 A.M.

Sitting in Houston traffic, furiously texting apology message to workshop coordinator. Explain that my editor loved my new proposal and needed me to fly to New York right away. Hint that Nora Roberts wants to meet me.

12:08 P.M.

Breeze into wedding coordinator meeting. Right away I'm bombarded with questions about eight different shades of lavender tulle and asked to choose the hue I want. Realize I do not care which shade is on the backs of chairs. Am I a bad bride-to-be? Attempt to deflect question, but wedding coordinator isn't interested in my close personal relationship with Nora Roberts.

12:15 P.M.

Should not be given license to marry. Am obviously not worthy of bride status. Close eyes and randomly choose a shade of lavender.

12:31 P.M.

Now there are five bouquets of purplish flowers to look at. Do I like lilacs, irises, orchids, hyacinths, or dahlias best?

Point to irises and say, "lilacs." Am terrible, terrible bride.

12:33 P.M.

Call fiancé to tell him we cannot get married, am bad bride-to-be. He tells me if I cancel the wedding, I will have to give beautiful engagement ring back.

12:34 P.M.

Decide am very good bride-to-be, just have deficiencies in flower and tulle departments. Vow to work on these.

12:36 P.M.

Fiancé reminds me to pick up gifts for the birthday parties we're attending tonight. Loudly tell him that one of the parties is for his good friend, and hadn't he better buy his own friend his present. Fiancé reminds me that I got out of sex last week by promising to buy the present for him. Damn.

1:03 P.M.

Stuck in Houston traffic.

1:24 P.M.

Run in to Wal-Mart and pick up video about potty training. Have heard friends with kids rave about video.

1:35 P.M.

Dash in to liquor store. Buy bottles of vanilla vodka and Diet Coke.

1:45 P.M.

Stuck in Houston traffic. Agent calls. Has read fabulous new proposal (finally someone has!) and is not sure how to pitch it. It seems my suggestion of the *Divine Secrets of the Ya-Ya Sisterhood* meets *Pet Sematary* isn't working for him. Wants to know what my identity as a writer is.

Think for a moment and come up with nothing. Complain question is too hard, and what's his job anyway if not to figure out my identity. He keeps badgering and then mysteriously I lose reception on cell phone.

1:50 P.M.

Voice message from agent. I have to get back to him with answers about identity. Accidentally delete message.

2:03 P.M.

Walk into my house and search for wrapping paper for party gifts. Mother calls and wants to know how we can cut wedding costs. Can we trim the guest list? Who is this Nora Roberts I've invited, anyway?

Finally she decides I should design and print the invitations on my computer. Agree, though have no idea how to accomplish this on six-year-old computer with only Windows 98.

Call publicist and give her new invitation assignment. She warns it'll cost about $100 an hour. No problem. My mom is paying for the wedding.

2:43 P.M.

Check business e-mail again. No fan letters so fire off

message to my website designer, asking if my e-mail server is down.

Check personal e-mail. Finally! A message from my editor . . .

2:56 P.M.

Am in depths of despair. Writing career is over. Proposal was not high-concept enough.

2:57 P.M.

Lie on bed trying to think of a twist for new proposal.

3:00 P.M.

Can think of nothing. Total blank. Am now entering has-been land.

3:05 P.M.

Still lying on bed. Still thinking.

3:07 P.M.

Turn on TV. I'm missing *Dr. Phil*!

4:02 P.M.

Want to watch *Oprah*, but an author's work is never done. Go to office and make to-do list.

1) Figure out identity.
2) Think of high-concept twist.
3) Finish historical romance.

5:00 P.M.

Exhausted from the long day of work I put in, ask fiancé for back rub. Fiancé refuses. Too busy making dinner. It's pasta, or so he says.

6:30 P.M.

Arrive at birthday party—critique partner's daughter is turning one. Sing songs. Play games. Must leave early for other party, so make a big production of leaving special gift with CP's teetotaling grandparents.

7:10 P.M.

Arrive at fiancé's friend's thirtieth birthday party. Hand over gift. Receive funny look when it's a potty training video. Oops.

8:20 P.M.

Stuck in room with three mothers. Conversation centers around color of babies' poop. Cannot escape or fiancé will find me and yell about gift mix-up.

8:23 P.M.

Still listening to poop discussion. Try very had to seem interested. When time comes, do not want label of bad mother-to-be.

8:33 P.M.

Poop discussion continues. Eyes glaze over and feel sort of nauseous. Try desperately to pay attention. Do not want to be voted off Poop Island.

8:35 P.M.

Jump at chance for another vodka-based beverage when asked. Resign self to being bad mother. Cannot even discuss poop for thirty minutes without drinking.

8:48 P.M.

Am asked my opinion on diapers, specifically, which is better for soft, green presolid food poop as opposed to harder postsolid food poop. All mothers turn to stare, awaiting my answer. Mumble something about biodegradable diapers—saving the environment and all that—and am banished from the circle.

9:10 P.M.

Am forced to join new tribe: the bitter divorced and cynical singles. We make fun of the mothers, and I start to enjoy myself until the criticism turns to engaged couples. Try to hide my ring, but too late.

10:01 P.M.

My flame has been extinguished and am now without tribe. Only friend is vodka. Half-empty bottle of vodka in hand, stumble into friend's office and decide to e-mail editor new fabulous proposal. Something with a vampire. And a were-wolf. Editors love that stuff.

11:46 P.M.

Fiancé carries me inside house and forces water and aspirin down my throat. Assures me will be good mother when time comes, but am no longer allowed to pick out friends' birthday gifts.

11:50 P.M.

Get up to brush teeth and slip in something soft and wet. Cat hairball. Again.

SHANE BOLKS is the author of *The Good, the Bad, and the Ugly Men I've Dated* and a former public school teacher in Houston, Texas. She also writes historical romances under the pen name Shana Galen. Shane writes full-time, which requires daily trips to the mall because shopping is the only activity that really allows her to think (that's her story and she's sticking to it). Check out the latest news, excerpts, and contests at www.shanebolks.com.